AN *Abbey* RETURNED

Copyright © 2023 Robert MacGuffie

All rights reserved.
ISBN: 9798390034514

No part of this book may be reproduced or used in any manner without written permission of the copyright owner except for the use of quotations in a book review.

This is a work of fiction. Names, characters, places and incidents either are the products of the author's imagination or are used fictitiously. Any resemblance to persons, living or dead, events, or locales is entirely coincidental.

AN *Abbey* RETURNED

Robert MacGuffie

ALSO BY ROBERT MACGUFFIE

Chinook's Farewell
Chinook's Spirit
Chinook's Mother Lode

For my sister, Linda Marie

ACKNOWLEDGEMENT

The author wishes to express his appreciation to Sally Vallongo and Molly Schiever for editing the manuscript. Thanks go to Doug Miller for his continued support of my writing endeavors.

CHAPTER 1

Dr. Guillermo Gerona pulled his emerald-green vintage Cadillac into the parking lot of Sycamore Hospital for the Criminally Insane. He leaned back in his seat, closed his eyes, and listened to the last refrains of Omara Portuondo's soulful rendition of "Solamente Una Vez." This song, long his favorite, always returned him to the days of his youth in Camagüey, Cuba.

For a moment, in his mind's eye at least, the sturdy hardwoods of southern Indiana were replaced with swaying palm trees and rustling sugar cane fields. Gerona turned off the engine and made his way to a helipad, and an aerial tour of the historic institution, a landmark with a dark and troubled reputation.

At the urging of an old colleague, he had left a lucrative psychiatric practice in Cleveland to join the staff as superintendent. Today was his first day in the powerful yet risky position. Instead of pondering the professional pitfalls that might lie ahead, he was distracted. As he walked along the well-trimmed pathway, the muscular, tanned, graying physician with a debonair pencil mustache turned his memory to the past, recalling his early days in Cuba.

Born into rural poverty, he aspired to a more meaningful life in the big city. As a teenager, he left the hard labor with little pay in the sugar cane fields behind and took a bus to Havana. There he found jai alai, the fast and lethal game that he immediately took to. Later, as a professional jai alai player, he found more opportunities came his way, including medical school. After completing training and residency, he opened a dermatology practice in the capital city.

Gerona's rumination ended abruptly as he reached the helipad. He climbed into the small helicopter and buckled up. The pilot, whose name tag read "Donovan," looked up from his flight instruments and offered his hand. "Billy Donovan at your service. Welcome aboard, sir."

Gerona shook Donovan's hand and said, smiling broadly, "Guillermo Gerona at your service, Billy Donovan. I'm really looking forward to my first flight in a helicopter."

Turning back to his controls, the pilot started the rotors spinning, then pulled back on the collective pitch control. "The hospital ground covers about 700 acres," said Donovan. "We'll make a circle around the grounds first, then I'll fly over the hospital as close to the ground as I can, so you can get a more detailed view."

Donovan's words fell on deaf ears as Gerona tried with all his might to suppress a chuckle. The diminutive young man at the controls reminded him of Mickey Rooney playing the role of a helicopter pilot Mike Forney, rescuing downed pilots in the 1957 movie, *The Bridges at Toko-Ri*.

Finally under control, he mumbled, "That's fine."

Tipping the helicopter a bit to the right, Donovan remarked, "Directly below us is the patient's cemetery. There are over 500 patients buried there. They were destitute, had no family, and there was no other place to bury their remains."

Gerona felt a rage building inside as he looked down at the small white crosses in precise rows, each one marking a grave. Why so many deaths? Since accepting this position, he'd learn of some of the horrific documented abuses by staff and inmates, in this august building. There had to be a better way than this, he told himself.

"Now we're over the prison farm. It's still in operation today, although it's not as extensive as it once was. At one time, the farm provided food for all the other state institutions in Indiana. As you can see, there are only a few cattle and swine left today."

"Did the inmates work on the farm?"

"They did at the beginning but too many escaped, so instead they had to hire people from the outside."

""That's too bad; work can be therapeutic if it's used properly in treatment," Gerona said, still trying to shake the images of the rows of graves from his mind.

"'The building to your right is where they made furniture," Donovan said, pointing out a large red building that looked like a barn. "They made superb furniture out of oak. They still use the rockers on the wards and most of the desks, tables, and other furniture for the hospital were made there. After they stopped making furniture, they made tin cups and license plates in that building for a short period."

Gerona's mind was flooded with so many thoughts, an information overload. He would sort them out later over his first cigar of the day. "What's that large building below?"

"That's the maintenance building. There we service all the equipment used at the institution including the trucks, cars, and buses. The building nearby is the boiler room. All buildings are heated by steam heat and the main boiler is there. Now we'll swing over the hospital."

Gerona stretched his neck to look down, studying a series of flat black roofs topping a massive assembly of buildings. Connected, they formed a large rectangle. The buildings enclosed a courtyard the size of two football fields.

An Abbey Returned

Near each corner of the structure, the buildings were extended outward in a design that looked, from above, like crosses. Suddenly Gerona bolted forward in his seat and, with a startled look on his face, blurted out, "From up here, I would think I was looking down on a monastery, not a maximum-security prison hospital!"

"Funny you should say that," Donovan commented. "The building was built between 1906 and 1914 by an order of Trappist monks, from Germany ... Bavaria, I think. It was the largest poured concrete structure in the country at the time, with fourteen-inch walls and steel-reinforcements right down to the bedrock. There are catacombs beneath the main floor. The monks named the building, The Abbey of Saint Alexander of Jerusalem."

"He's the saint the Romans threw in the lion den. The beasts refused to harm him," Gerona chimed in, demonstrating his staunch Catholic upbringing.

"For reasons unknown, the monks did not inhabit the building. They did not try to sell it, but simply abandoned it," Donovan said, shaking his head.

"That's strange," Gerona said, thinking that it might've had something to do with the outbreak of the First World War in 1914.

"It sat vacant until the state took it over in 1915. They decided its structure was perfect to house those found guilty of crimes while insane or who were otherwise too dangerous for other state psychiatric institutions." The pilot lowered the helicopter onto the landing pad.

"Thanks Mickey, I mean Billy," Gerona said with a smile. "That was an excellent tour. I'd like to talk to you more about the hospital some time. You're very knowledgeable." He stepped down from the helicopter.

At the imposing main entrance to his new workplace, Gerona handed his briefcase to a burly security guard who opened it, glanced inside, and quickly returned it. "This is the key to every lock in the institution," the guard said, handing Gerona a large brass key.

He pushed a button under his desk and the steel door swung open. Gerona entered the institution, his senses on high alert. As he walked down the concrete floors of the narrow hallway lined with highly polished, unmarked steel doors, the metal taps on the heels of his expensive Italian shoes made a loud clicking sound.

When Gerona reached the door that had "Superintendent" painted in large black letters, he paused and reflected on the recent events that had brought him to this place. He'd traded a profitable and comfortable psychiatric practice in Cleveland for what his best friend Rafael Fuentes, referred to as a "ticket on the Titanic."

Over Cuba Libres and cigars, Fuentes, a prominent Cleveland politician who was instrumental in Gerona's gaining U.S. citizenship, had exclaimed, "Are you crazy, Guillermo? Why would you give up the best practice in the Cleveland to take over a snake pit? That place is a chamber of horrors. You can't reform it. They'll eventually have to shut it down and they'll blame you. If you take the job, you've committed professional suicide."

The trigger for all this had been the call months ago from Graciela Cevallos. A fellow Cuban immigrant, she'd been a brilliant student in psychology. Gerona first met her when she showed up for her residency, under his supervision at the Cleveland Veterans Administration Hospital.

Despite having had little contact with her since the residency, Gerona had tracked her and knew that she had a brilliant career in private practice, and was now the Commissioner of Mental Health for the state of Indiana.

With little preamble, Graciela said, "I'm offering you the most paramount challenge of your career. It's a crucial mission and will be extremely arduous."

"A crucial mission, you say. Just what would that be?"

"Taking over a contentious hospital for the criminally insane that has been in crisis for years." She paused for several moments, then said with emotion, "You're the only person who could take on this task."

With that being said, Gerona declared, "You've got your man."

Remembering Fuentes' prediction made the new superintendent smile sardonically. He may have indeed bought a ticket on the Titanic. But that was not the worst thing in the world. He knew that his private practice would always be there, that he could return if things did not work out.

It was the challenge that got him. He'd been challenged before, often, and had met each one head-on. Each time, he not only won but prospered as well.

In his youth, Gerona had been told that he'd never be a jai alai player. They said that he simply did not have enough athletic ability to play the very difficult game. Instead, he fooled them and became one of the best players in Cuba.

As a young student he'd been advised by well-meaning teachers that he was dense and should limit his goals to cutting sugar cane or working as a fisherman. Instead, he graduated from medical school. He even had a specialty: dermatology.

Then seeing his prospects for a medical career limited in the Socialist country, he moved his sights further away. As if on a dare, he left his homeland and immigrated to the land of opportunity for all—the United States. It was a huge risk; involving defecting and then sneaking into what he hoped would become his new home.

Entering illegally, he worked his way out of danger and built a life as a respected physician, teacher, and successful businessman. He was proud of being a prominent community leader, affectingly known as El Cubano. But now, he again had pushed himself beyond his comfort zone, taken on a big risk, and was preparing to start over in a new and uncertain setting.

"When he entered his office, he was greeted by a guarded smile from Donna Bascom, his secretary.

"Good morning, Dr. Gerona. I hope you had a good tour. Can I get you a cup of coffee?"

"No thank you, Ms. Bascom." Gerona replied, surprised by the friendly welcome since others had described this matronly employee as the Iron Maiden, a stern woman who rarely smiled.

Deciding to make his mark right away, he said, "I do appreciate your kind offer, but I've brought my own espresso machine. Besides, fetching me coffee is not in your job specifications. So far, you've been a professional secretary. But, as of today, you are now an administrative assistant. You have far more important duties than delivering coffee."

"Thank God," Ms. Bascom said, her smile broadening as she rolled her eyes. "The last administrators made me wait on them like they were children. What's more, they never assigned me any significant work."

"Well, you'll find that won't be the case with me. I want you to be my eyes and ears. Everything I ask you to do will be significant. In fact, the first thing I want you to do is to get me the resumes of all the professional personnel in the institution. I want to review them with you, since you have been around here for a long time, and have had plenty of time for observation. I also want you to prepare a personal written evaluation of the hospital during your tenure."

"Yes, Dr. Gerona," Ms. Bascom said, with another smile. I'll get on that immediately."

Next, Gerona entered his private office. Breathing a deep sigh of relief, he pulled out the desk chair, sat down tentatively, then slowly

An Abbey Returned

leaned back and put his feet on the desktop. Comfortable now, he reached in his coat pocket and pulled out a leather cigar case.

Deep-toned and well-worn, the case was an heirloom. It had been handmade for his grandfather by the best leather craftsman in Camagüey. He had passed it on to Gerona's father. Now, it belonged to Gerona—his prize possession. He kept it filled with four hand-rolled, unwrapped Davidoff cigars.

In Gerona's opinion, they were the finest cigars ever made in Cuba. Fortunately, Gerona had a friend who sailed the Great Lakes and would keep him supplied. Davidoff's, illegal in the US, had to be smuggled in from Canada.

Gerona loved the feel of the cigar case. In private, he'd rub it affectionately along the black stubble on his cheek. Today, he took a Davidoff from the case, snipped the end with his cigar cutter, put it in his mouth, and rolled it around with his tongue to get it moist. From the same pocket, Gerona pulled out a butane lighter, clicked it to light the tobacco, and drew in a slow delicious breath.

Next, he pulled the Indianapolis Star from his briefcase. Opening the paper, he began skimming the headlines. Suddenly his head snapped for forward, and he began reading aloud. "The Jacobs School of Music at Indiana University announces that Kenzie Fairfax Gainer, internationally renowned cellist, will be an artist-in-residence at the university this coming year."

Gerona could not believe his eyes. This meant that Mitch Gainer, Kenzie's husband and manager, would be with her. He dropped the paper and reached for the telephone to buzz Mrs. Bascom.

"How far is Indiana University from here?"

"It's about fifty miles," Ms. Bascom replied.

"Thank you."

Gerona hung up the telephone and returned to his cigar. He leaned back in his chair and blew a large smoke ring in the air. As he watched the smoke disappear, he thought a windfall may have just come his way. With some luck, he might just be able to recruit Mitch to help him reform the hospital.

He and Mitch had collaborated before, at the VA Hospital in Cleveland, when Mitch served an internship under his direction. They had effectively engineered an end to the use of shock treatment (ECT). Later, they had joined in a psychiatric practice in the lakefront city. He strongly suspected that Mitch would not be content to watch his wife play the cello at the university. He'd be looking for something else to do. Maybe, just maybe, he could entice him to the hospital.

At the same time Gerona was viewing Sycamore Hospital from the sky above, Chalmers Sprute, the only legitimate tycoon in Indiana and perhaps the Midwest, entered Yvette's, an upscale restaurant known for its fabulous brunch, followed by his two assistants. The restaurant was by reservation only. People sometimes waited weeks to savor their Eggs Benedict, the specialty of the house.

The hostess silently led the three men to a special booth, with a red velvet curtain to assure privacy. Sprute slid in one side, coming to rest directly in the middle, with his massive arms spread across the table.

The two assistants sat stiffly on the other side, spacing themselves so that one was seated directly across from the boss's right shoulder and other from the left. They sat in silence until the curtain opened and a waitress deposited a tray with steaming Turkish Sand Coffee, a hand-rolled cigar and cutter, and a butane lighter and ash tray.

Sprute, a man in his middle fifties who had amassed a fortune in real estate, the stock market, mining, and gambling enterprises, reached out with a meaty paw and grasped a small coffee cup between his index finger and thumb. Titling his head back, he threw the coffee down like it was a shot of bourbon. He then reached with his other hand and downed another cup of the steaming brew. The two bright-eyed and bushy-tailed blond assistants in their late twenties blew gently on their cups to cool the hot liquid.

"For Christ sake! Put the coffee back on the tray. Maybe the waitress can bring you a nipple next time," Sprute exclaimed, reaching for the last cup. After downing the coffee, he slammed the cup down on the tray, and pulled a huge cigar from his shirt pocket.

In no time at all, the room was filled with thick cigar smoke. One assistant's eyes began to water and he reached for his handkerchief. The other assistant began coughing, dropping his fork to cover his mouth.

Sprute leaned back in his chair, eyes on the ceiling, and puffed away. When the hot amber ash at the end of the cigar nearly reached Sprute's finger tips, he dropped it in the ash tray.

"Today we embark of what will be a highly profitable venture," Sprute announced in a piercing steely voice which immediately brought the two assistants to attention. "I have a contract for the sale of Sycamore Hospital, with the caveat that this must be executed on the quiet. In a few words, I'll give you all the background information you need to know.

"The hospital is controversial and has a long history of patient abuse. The state wants to close it. Unfortunately, there is a faction of people, mainly in the mental health community, who oppose closure. They've worked out an agreement to hire a new superintendent to transform the hospital to an efficient treatment facility. If this does not occur, the hospital will then be closed.

"However, the state has the absolute freedom to sell the hospital anytime it desires, regardless of whether or not the superintendent reforms the hospital. The state has made a decision to sell.

"But there is one potential problem. When they agreed to hire a new superintendent, they allowed the mental health commissioner, Graciela Cevallos, to select the person. She has recruited Guillermo Gerona, who is recognized as one of the top clinicians in the country. He just may be the one person who could reform the place. If he does, or comes anywhere close, it will raise havoc with the sale. Thus, it's important to arrange a sale as soon as possible—a cash sale with immediate occupancy. So now is the time for each of you to get your asses in gear and find potential buyers! You can pick up your Eggs Benedict from the waitress on your way out. Remember, keep things on the quiet."

CHAPTER 2

Mitch and Kenzie Gainer returned their rental car in Indianapolis and immediately took a cab to the nearest Audi dealership where they purchased two brand-new Audi 100 sedans: an agate brown, four-door for Mitch and a rally green, two-door for Kenzie.

The young, freckle-faced salesman accepted Mitch's check for payment with wobbly hands. He was bursting with excitement and appeared completely awestruck by Kenzie.

"Ms. Gainer, Ms. Gainer," he stammered, "Could I please have your autograph? My wife would be delighted. She's a fan of yours and has some of your recordings."

"It would be my pleasure," she said with a smile, signing "Kenzie Fairfax Gainer" on a piece of letterhead stationery lying on the desk.

"If you have any problems with the cars, or have any questions, call me at any time," the salesman said. He held the autograph in front of his eyes.

"How far is Bloomington from here?" Mitch asked with a touch of impatience.

"What? What?" the salesman muttered, still staring at the autograph. Suddenly he shook his head as if just waking from a dream. "It's about 50 miles. Just stay on IN 37-S all the way. It'll take you about an hour."

"Thanks, my good friend. It's been a pleasure doing business with you," Mitch said as they left. The two new cars were parked side by side.

"See you in Bloomington. Just follow me, or maybe I should follow you. You're the superstar." Mitch got in his car. Kenzie smiled and thumbed her nose at her husband, her long auburn hair swirling as she tucked herself into her new ride.

The first thing Mitch did when he got behind the wheel was find a classical radio station. To his delight, he heard a resonant male voice announce, "Now we will hear Mozart's Symphony No. 41 in C major, K.551, 'the Jupiter,' performed by the Cleveland Orchestra, conducted by George Szell."

Mozart had long been Mitch's favorite composer. It was his habit to listen to Mozart when he got up in the morning and before he rested his head on his pillow at night. Mozart's music gave him the same feeling he had when he received the bread and wine in communion—inner peace.

If he was feeling down, Mozart's music lifted him up. If he was feeling anxious, it calmed him. His worries disappeared when he listened to Mozart, as did his anger and fears. He particularly enjoyed listening to Mozart when he was driving. The music provided an environment where, for reasons he did not clearly understand, he could reflect on quandaries and gain insights.

When Mitch drove by the Soldiers and Sailors Monument, he remembered that Kurt Vonnegut wrote about the war monuments here in his novels. He smiled when he thought of Kilgore Trout, his favorite of all Vonnegut's people, and realized he may have a friend in Indiana after all.

As soon as Mitch left the metropolitan area and headed into the neat and orderly Indiana farm land, he immediately settled into Mozart and his thoughts. He could see himself walking up the gangplank, arm and arm with Kenzie, as they boarded a cargo ship in Hamburg, Germany, en route to Halifax, Nova Scotia. The twelve days they spent at sea were absolute delights, filled with reading, fine food, good conversations with the captain and deck hands, and complete freedom from all the demands of the outside world.

In Halifax, Mitch sat in the same pew in St. Paul's Church where, many eventful years before, he had noticed Kenzie, cello and bow in hand, for the first time. He stood by the altar where he and Kenzie became man and wife not long after.

The highlight for Mitch was walking into Brogan's Bog, the Irish pub, and having Jonathan Brogan, much older and grayer but still vital, welcome him again, much the same as he did years ago. It was there that Mitch found a refuge when as a youth, he fled his Idaho Nugget Valley home and came to Canada. Through some twists and turns seemingly guided by fate, he'd wound up on Canada's eastern shore.

After his and Kenzie's paths merged, they built a rich life of learning, music, adventure, and love. Mitch quickly realized the depth and breadth of Kenzie's musical gifts and her joy in sharing them with a public who never tired of watching her bend over her instrument, drawing forth the heart of every beautiful piece she performed.

On his own quest, Mitch had delved deeply into studies of mind and behavior. More than anything else, it was his aspiration to help people change their behavior, increase their happiness, and overcome their problems.

As if in a game of tag played by two, they had followed their individual muses, finding ways to entwine their personal pursuits within a larger life together. Settling in Ohio, they both prospered professionally. Mitch earned a doctorate in psychology. While he built a practice in psychology, specializing in post-traumatic stress disorders, Kenzie won a chair in the prestigious Cleveland Orchestra.

It was in the Cuyahoga County metropolis that Mitch expanded his friendship with Guillermo Gerona, initially as an intern at the VA hospital, and later when Guillermo joined his own practice as a partner. They had built a relationship based on mutual respect and a taste for adventure.

During this gratifying period, Mitch was able to confront and make peace with issues from his turbulent childhood. Being an only child in an alcoholic family filled with constant conflict and anxiety had left a mark on him. His boyhood mentor, a clever and wise gambler named Chinook Swindle, had protected him and rescued him from the many pitfalls that had come his way. When Chinook died, he left Mitch some sacred and valuable land near an Indian reservation in Nugget Valley. But he also left him with a dilemma. On the land was Chinook's Mother Lode, the tribal casino that despite its great potential, was being brought down by mismanagement and crime.

Mitch suddenly was aware that the flat farm land had morphed into rolling hills and thick wooded areas. He suspected that Bloomington might be located in a more scenic and appealing place than he first assumed. Neither dramatic like Nugget Valley nor flat like most of Ohio, the rustic scenes passing by promised a landscape that would surprise and please with each season.

Then, as if bidden, Mitch's mind drifted back a decade or so when, with Gerona's support, he took a sabbatical from their practice and moved to Nugget Valley to take on the mammoth challenge of freeing Chinook's Mother Lode from the death grip of crooked managers.

Facing many obstacles and great peril, Mitch and Kenzie, as a team, helped rescue the casino from the jaws of a malicious drug cartel and established effective tribal leadership . This being done, they celebrated, jumped in a limousine, and drove away from Chinook's Mother Lode.

This marked the beginning of what Mitch referred to as "a first class, luxury, five-year tour of major foreign cities." From concert hall to concert hall, Mitch and Kenzie had lived a vagabond life, mainly in Europe and occasionally in Asia. While Kenzie performed to ovations and rave reviews, Mitch served as her manager. Although efficient in that role, Mitch did not view it as job.

"Being Kenzie's manager is the easiest job in the world. There is simply no work to it. The promoters call you. You negotiate terms, accept large sums from them, and follow Kenzie to magnificent cities," Mitch said. "You enjoy all the perks that come your way for being married to one of the finest cellists in the world."

Kenzie settled in behind the wheel of her new Audi. She looked over the instruments on the dashboard before starting the engine. It was exhilarating to turn the key and feel the engine respond. After all the hours spent in the passenger seat, while Mitch drove from Halifax to Indianapolis, she was excited to be in the driver seat.

As she pulled out into the traffic, she thought that Mitch's comments about her following him to Bloomington, then saying that maybe he should follow her since she was the superstar, may have been a "Freudian slip."

At face value, it was banter. Still, Kenzie knew it was more than that. She suspected, and had from the beginning, that when Mitch agreed to be involved full-time to her return to the concert stage, it was something he was doing for her, not what he would have chosen for himself. To let him know that it was not all about her and that they were really a team, she let Nathan Gardner, her excellent long-term manager, go. Although Mitch had no specific qualifications for the job, she had no doubt that he could handle it. He did, viewing the job as a challenge, and working hard to learn the delicate world of planning and negotiation. As it turned out, Kenzie reflected, Mitch had become much more efficient than Nathan had been.

Yet as time passed, Kenzie sensed restlessness in her husband. Although he would not admit it or perhaps even be aware of it, it was there.

Early in their marriage, she'd learned that Mitch was an adventurer by nature. He liked and needed new challenges. He'd abruptly left a prosperous and secure psychiatric practice in Cleveland, where he was gaining the reputation as an expert in the treatment of post-traumatic stress disorders, to take over a lodge and casino in Nugget Valley.

But after five years of touring, Kenzie thought a "time out" would be good for them and accepted the residency offer from Indiana University, with one of the country's most prestigious music programs. It would be a good break from the pressures of the touring and would give time them for relaxation and reflection.

When she followed Mitch into Bloomington, she noticed that he'd missed the road sign that pointed the way to the campus and made a wrong turn. She followed the sign, turned, and was waiting for Mitch at the main entrance of Indiana University when he arrived ten minutes later.

CHAPTER 3

Gerona spent the first weeks of his administration getting a feel for the hospital. His priority was to familiarize himself with the buildings and grounds, and meet each staff member. He made it clear that his door was always open and he was available to any concerns they may have.

One of Gerona's greatest strengths was his ability to observe. He believed that he could learn more by watching than by asking questions. When he met staff for the first time, rather than ask questions, he preferred to make a comment, something he suspected he thought the person could relate to. "That is a beautiful picture you have on your desk." Or, "this really seems to be a pleasant room to work in."

Although he had been repeatedly told by many that he was charismatic, he never quite believed it. He viewed himself as very ordinary human being who had become successful because of hard work, good fortune, and the help of other people. His body language was inviting, beginning with a broad smile. Gerona's natural warmth and genuine friendship radiated in his expression.

From the very first day, Gerona liked many things about Sycamore. He found the physical setting beyond his expectations. The main building, although built in 1914, was in great shape structurally. He was impressed with the cleanness of all the buildings, even the boiler room and maintenance areas. Inmate cells were not cramped and appeared to be as comfortable as any small space with only basic furnishing could be. The day rooms had nice oak furniture including comfortable rocking chairs. The commercial kitchen was restaurant quality. All the floors throughout the institution were waxed and highly polished.

It was inside the small hospital located on the upper level that he was most impressed. The surgery room was as sterile and well-equipped as any he had seen before, far superior to anything he'd witnessed in the VA hospital.

Even the setting was impressive. Eastern white pine, sycamore, red maple, and soaring tulip trees populated the grounds. The courtyard was landscaped with flower beds and well-groomed bushes. Gerona thought that the courtyard more suited to a resort hotel than a maximum security institution. He wondered if the area was more for show than worker and inmate inspiration. He made a mental note to find out.

His initial impressions of the employees were mixed. Those who worked in what he considered the support areas, such as maintenance, groundskeeping, and mechanics, were open, confident, and proud of their work.

The professional staff who worked with the inmates were another story. The social service personnel—social workers and psychologists—seemed distant from the inmates. Gerona got the impression that they were not spending their time on the wards where the inmates who needed their expertise lived. Rather they were huddled together in their offices doing paper work.

The nurses presented Gerona with neat, well-organized paperwork, outlining the nursing tasks that they had completed.

But their charts were missing what Gerona perceived to be "human information" about the inmates.

Gerona did not expect the correctional officers to be responsive. After all, they had been indicted by a grand jury for patient brutality. Some even had been charged with criminal offenses. They were castigated by the press, and the hospital had been publicly referred to as a "chamber of horrors."

During his introductory tour of the wards, Gerona asked no questions. The day hall was filled with inmates sitting quietly in rocking chairs watching television. How odd, it struck him—none of the inmates actually rocked in the big, comfortable chairs. Not one inmate bothered to look at him as he walked through the ward. The sense of defeat was strong.

When Gerona returned to his office and reflected on what he had seen, he thought for the first time that he may have bitten off more than he could chew. He knew that reform would be difficult. He originally believed that he would have at least a fifty-percent chance of achieving it. His brief tenure had already taught him that his chances for success would be far less than expected. For a moment, he wondered if he would have accepted the job if he'd known what Sycamore had really become.

As he pondered this, the telephone rang. He knew it would be Ms. Bascom, reporting for their review of her report on the state of the operation. The administrative assistant marched into Gerona's office without a word, stood at attention, report in hand, directly in front of his deck.

"Let's sit on the sofa; it will be more comfortable," Gerona said, pointing to the leather sofa facing his desk. Ms. Bascom appeared to be mesmerized by a vividly colored portrait of a boxer in fighting stance that hung on the wall over the sofa.

An Abbey Returned

"That's a portrait of Kid Gavilan, known as 'The Cuban Hawk,'" Gerona said. "He was the welterweight champion of the world in the 1950s. He came from my home town and was a patient of mine when I was practicing dermatology in Havana. It was painted by Cundo Bermudez, who is one of Cuba's greatest painters."

Ms. Bascom said nothing, handed her report to Gerona, and sat stiffly with her hands folded in her lap on one corner of the sofa. Gerona thumbed through the document quickly.

"I can tell at first glance that you have prepared a thorough and well written report."

"How can you say that? You haven't read it yet," Ms. Bascom snapped, turning from the painting and focusing directly on Gerona's face.

"That's an excellent comment, Ms. Bascom," Gerona said noticing that her eyes were as steely as Gavilan's. "That was not a cavalier remark. I meant exactly what I said. You see, Ms. Bascom, after years of practice, with the exception of fiction, I have learned to comprehend what I read by paragraphs and not sentences. I can tell early on whether a document is well-written written and meaningful. In your report, I found paragraphs composed of concise, declarative sentences. Your economical use of words indicates that you know exactly what you want to communicate and you present it in an unambiguous fashion. This is precisely what I'm looking for in a report."

The stern look on Ms. Bascom's softened and she turned her eyes back to the portrait. "You know there is a certain beauty and elegance in that battered face."

"You have good eyes, Ms. Bascom, and can see beyond the flattened nose, the puffy eyebrows, the scars and dents on the cheeks. Bermundez, in his genius, brought forth the true man who was a champion, a warrior beloved by all of Cuba. You notice that Gavilan is not in the typical boxer's stance with his knees bent and his gloves held high directly in front of his face. His right hand is in the typical position but his left hand is held low with his arm open next to his hip. This is the position for his famous 'bolo punch.' It was the same motion that he used to cut sugar cane with a machete when he was a child. There is nothing that speaks more of Cuba than Kid Gavilan's bolo punch."

"I think I'll like working for you, Dr. Gerona," Ms. Bascom said, folding her hands on her lap.

"I'll like working with you as well, Ms. Bascom. We'll make a good team, I'm sure." Gerona thought that the ice between the two of them might be thawing a bit.

"Tonight I'll review your report in detail but now I want to you react to my observations of the hospital."

"I'll be glad to," Ms. Bascom said softly.

"I learned more about the institution that I expected from my helicopter tour and walk through the building. One thing is perfectly clear to me—there are many changes that need to be made if the hospital is going to survive. If things remain the same, the state will close us down," Gerona said, pausing to look up at Kid Gavilan.

"You're right," Ms. Bascom said, nodding.

"We simply cannot change everything at once. My mind is flooded with things that should be changed immediately. The key will be to come up with a list of priorities and focus on them one at a time as we move up the list. The question is which changes to implement first. Although no one has said anything to me, I sense that we will face some time restrictions. The more time passes without observable changes, the more the politicians will move to close it. They do not want any more public outcries about the treatment in this facility."

"I agree completely, Dr. Gerona," Ms. Bascom said, shifting a little closer to the doctor on the sofa.

"Frankly, Ms. Bascom, this challenge is too colossal for you and me to face alone. We need a right-hand man on our team. I have someone in mind, and if we are lucky we just may get him."

Ms. Bascom shifted back to her original position on the sofa. "Are you thinking about finding someone from the inside or the outside?"

"From the outside, definitely. You're our eyes and ears on the inside, but we need someone from outside who will bring a fresh view. What do you think?"

Ms. Bascom twitched a bit, then replied, "Strange as it seems, that's a difficult question for me to consider. I've never had a boss ask me that before."

"Don't think of me as a boss. I'm just a team member with a different role than you. That's all."

"Would you consider people who are not working at Sycamore but are working at other state institutions or people who have political connections to be insiders or outsiders?"

"That's a very astute question, Ms. Bascom. I would consider both to be insiders who would likely bring a biased view. That's the last thing we need on our team. What we want is someone who would have a more objective—and, as I previously said—a fresher view. We won't make any positive changes unless we're innovative. If we're not, it will just be the same old thing, over and over again, with the same results."

Ms. Bascom looked up at portrait, focusing on the Cuban boxer. "I think, Dr Gerona, that you're taking an excellent step in the right direction to saving this place."

"Well, thank you, Ms. Bascom," Gerona said, as he stood up. On his way to his desk, he patted Ms. Bascom on the shoulder.

"I'm going to jot a few things down as we chat to come up an outline of how we will proceed to make this institution a treatment facility and not a warehouse of unfortunate human beings. Tell me, Ms. Bascom, what you see as our first priority."

"The first thing that I suggest is that you immediately contact Lynsford Laggins, the head of security," she replied. "Any changes you make will have to involve him. Unfortunately he's the real power around here. Everything does go through him."

"How did that come to be?"

"I'd rather not answer. It would much better if you found that out by yourself. You'll learn more that way."

"You're right," Gerona said, nodding his head. "That will be our first priority. I have the feeling if I do not get him onboard with we are trying to do, they'll be no need for other priorities."

"You're right." Ms. Bascom moved to a chair in front of the desk. Let's change gears. I'll briefly give you some of my impressions of the institution. I've been very impressed with the physical environment around here. The setting is excellent and is all you can ask for in a treatment facility. I particularly like the spaciousness and the cleanliness of the place. The grounds are outstanding but I did not see any evidence of their being used by the inmates."

"You have to remember that this is a prison and there are concerns for safety," Ms. Bascom replied. "In the old days the grounds were used by the inmates but the institution was plagued with escapes. So they put an end to it by making the grounds off limits."

Gerona was mulling this over. This is more like a prison and not a hospital. He liked that she called things the way they were.

"I agree that security is an issue, but I think we could explore ways of maintaining security and still make use of some of the resources that will be useful in treatment. That would not be a top priority, but something to explore."

Ms. Bascom started to speak but thought better of it and closed her mouth. After a few moments of silence, she asked, "What are your impressions of the people working here?"

Gerona was visualizing patients walking in the spectacular courtyard. He made a mental note that he would make that happen.

"I was very impressed with the staff working in maintenance and the like. They seem to be doing an excellent job, and I was pleased that they seemed to enjoy their work and take pride in it."

"There are a lot of Mennonites and Amish around here," Ms. Bascom said. "They have a strong work ethic and are strong and upright people."

"We're very fortunate to have them. I don't see any changes that are needed there. But the professional staff is another story. I sensed apathy among them, as if they were just going through the motions. Only the nurses seemed focus on their tasks. But even there, I sense patients are only viewed as cases, not as people, with the exception of the nurses who seemed to be very focused on the nursing tasks.

"I could see that the security people were very efficient in guarding the inmates and maintaining order. However, they, too, seemed to have little of what I would call human interactions with the inmates.

"They were very restrained, which I expected because of what has happened here. I knew I would not get much of a read on how they how they really feel about their jobs, or how they function. That will take time," Gerona concluded.

"That's a bleak assessment of the professional staff, but I'm afraid it's accurate," Ms. Bascom said somberly.

"Has it been that way for a long time?"

"Unfortunately, yes. It got much worse when we had a riot about ten years ago. The security people took over the institution and it's been that way ever since.

"The social workers come and go. Mostly, they're young kids fresh out of school. They leave once they find out that this really is a prison and not a treatment facility. The ones who stay either transfer to security or just ride it out until they can retire without doing any more than they have to."

"The hospital seemed to be operating well." Gerona said. "I spoke with the doctor-on-call and the place was spotless."

"Yes, the hospital provides good emergency care. The patients are transferred immediately to a local hospital for anything serious or require longer care."

"I didn't see any psychiatrists during my tour," Gerona mentioned, thinking of the incompetent psychiatrists he encountered when he worked at the VA hospital. They were only interested in using Electroconvulsive Therapy (ECT). He doubted that he would find any better quality staff working here. "I understand that they don't work full-time."

"We have a contract with a group who sends them around when need them. They're usually on grounds a couple of days a week. You did not see John Musgrave, our chaplain. He's been on vacation. You should make a point to make contact with him next week when he returns. He's the bright star there."

"I'll make a point of that, Ms. Bascom, for sure. If he's as bright a star as you say, I'll be well pleased," Gerona said, with a warm smile.

Ms. Bascom's face flushed and she stiffened in her chair.

"That's enough for today," said her new boss. "We've covered a lot and I think we're the same page. That's good. I want to get touch with a former colleague of mine. He has just arrived in Bloomington and I would appreciate it if you would find out how I can contact him. You might first try the music department at Indiana University. His wife, Kenzie, will be an artist-in-residence there."

"You mean Kenzie Fairfax Gainer, the cellist, is his wife?' Ms. Bascom exclaimed.

Gerona felt good that he had finally said something that excited Ms. Bascom. He decided that she was really not "the iron maiden" she was purported to be.

"Oh, by the way, Ms. Bascom, there's one more thing I'd like to discuss with you before you leave."

"Certainly," Ms. Bascom replied curtly, returning to her seat.

"As you know, there has been much scuttlebutt about patient abuse and mistreatment at Sycamore Hospital over the years. You've been here a long time and have seen many things. Could you tell me what is fact and what's fiction?" Guillermo asked, tilting back in his chair, resting on the arms, and folding his hands beneath his chin.

"Yes, I've been here a long time, beginning as an attendant the day after I graduated from high school. I intended to work at the hospital for about a year, so I could finish my stenographer-training program and obtain a job as a court reporter. After a few months, the superintendent needed a new secretary. I got the job and have been here ever since. You'll be the sixth superintendent I have served."

"Did you finish your stenographer training?"

"Yes, I did," Ms. Bascom replied with zest. "I was even offered a job as a court reporter in Fort Wayne which I declined. I'd found my home at Sycamore Hospital where I've received adequate compensation, great benefits, and have been well treated overall. In addition I can also moonlight to earn extra money by working with local attorneys and at times, the court. I did that many times as a single mom when I was putting my kids through college."

Ms. Bascom paused and took a long look at Guillermo's prized portrait of Kid Gavilan. "I see so much in that battered face," she murmured, turning her head as if she were speaking to someone behind her.

"As far as abuse is concerned," she continued, looking Guillermo directly in the eyes, "there is only one incident of abuse I personally witnessed. It occurred in the day hall during my last days on the ward. We were sitting at a table, taking a break, when one of our most difficult patients began arguing with an older female attendant. She was sitting across from her, drinking a cup of steaming hot coffee in one of those heavy tin cups they made at the hospital.

"The patient stood up and began screaming obscenities and spat at the attendant. She leaped up, struck the patient in the mouth, splitting her lip, and spilling hot coffee down her neck. Blood flew everywhere, some landing on my cheek. It looked like a massacre. Security rushed in and took her and the attendant from the ward. I never saw either one again or heard anything about the incident."

Guillermo winced when he heard the gruesome tale. His mind had turned to the days of his youth when he was walking barefoot in a ditch near a field. There a group of men on a chain gang were bundling cut stocks of sugar cane, placing them in piles so they could be collected later by trucks. Suddenly, a guard on horseback turned on one of the prisoners with a bullwhip, thrashing him on his face, bare back, and shoulders.

After receiving several mighty blows that cut him to ribbons, the muscular prisoner was able to latch on to the end of the whip with one hand. Then he secured a grip with both hands and pulled the guard from the horse. As he tumbled down, the guard reached for a machete and thrust the blade into the side of the prisoner's neck, bringing forth a gush of blood that splattered him as he hit the ground and rolled on top of the fatally wounded man.

When Guillermo saw the blood jet from the prisoner's body, he let out a wail, closed his eyes, bent over, and placed his hands on his wobbly knees to steady them. He knew that that he had to get the hell away from there. With the sounds of screaming men ringing in his ears, he staggered down the ditch like a drunken sailor. When the screaming sound faded, he opened his eyes and broke into a full sprint toward his home.

Bursting into his home, Guillermo rushed to the bathroom to wash away the uncleanness that overwhelmed him. As he stood in front of the sink, he glanced at the mirror on the wall and shuddered when he noticed a bloodstain on his cheek. Afraid to touch it, either with his hand or the towel, he washed around it, hoping that it would eventually fade away. But what he did not know was what the blood brought with it would not fade away, leaving him with a lifetime of disturbing nightmares of the brutal event and a profound aversion of any form of physical violence among human beings.

When Ms. Bascom saw the horrified look on her new boss's face, she wondered if she had been too graphic in her account. In particular, she wished she didn't use the word "massacre" in her tale.

Speaking in a much softer voice, Ms. Bascom continued with her story. "One day I was taking some patient files to the nurse when two guards were dragging a patient whose nose was splattered all over his face. His lips were also cut and he was bleeding profusely. 'That son of a bitch slugged me and broke my nose for no reason,' the man screamed at one of the guards, a hardnosed hillbilly called Stomper."

"I suppose he was called Stomper for obvious reasons," Guillermo said, shaking his head.

"That was his reputation. All Stomper did was smile at the nurse and tell her that the patient slipped and fell down the concrete stairwell. When I noticed that the knuckles on one of

Stomper's hands were red and scraped, I suspected that there was abuse but I couldn't confirm it."

"I can see why you would suspect abuse but you're correct, you can't confirm what you did not witness," Guillermo said, blowing on his hot cup of espresso coffee before taking a sip.

"Innuendo! Innuendo! "Innuendo!" Ms. Bascom exclaimed, her face flushed and her fingers drumming on the desk. "It was so despairing when I was working on the wards. There was constant chatter about such and such taking sexual liberties with patients or even raping them, pushing their faces into scalding bowls of water, gagging them to suppress speech, and physically beating and torturing patients in sadistic ways. Some rumors were even worse: Women patients dying from botched abortions and shock treatment used as punishment."

Ms. Bascom paused, took a deep breath and, speaking with quivering lips, said, "I don't like talking about or even thinking about my time on the wards. It was a very unhealthy place to be and I had to block it from my mind. But sometimes, it all comes back in terrifying dreams that leave me shaken and badly frightened."

Guillermo reached over and patted Ms. Bascom's hand. "I know," he said softly. "People's cruelty to each other is incomprehensible. The best I can do is seeing it as pure evil."

"Well that all changed for me when I went up front," Ms. Bascom declared.

"Up front?"

"Sycamore Hospital is divided into two distinct sections, "Ms. Bascom explained. "The back is where all the patients, the hospital, the wards, and the medical units are. The front section includes the superintendent, all administrators and their support staffs, and other personnel who run the hospital.

"There's only minimal personal interaction between the front and the back; most communication is done by memo and, occasionally by telephone. The only exception is Captain Laggins, the head of the correction officers, who does not hesitate to interact personally with staff. But he's fairly new, having come to the hospital shortly after the patient abuse charges were made."

"That's unfortunate," Guillermo remarked, "a hospital has to function as a team with each individual member working toward a specific mission to be successful."

Ms. Bascom nodded. "When I think about the work environment since I left the back, I get stuck on the word 'impersonal.' There's a code of secrecy that prevails and we don't share much about the work we do particularly when it involves patients. This makes for a formal atmosphere where people do their jobs, mostly paper work, efficiently, without fanfare. It may be said that the job setting is sterile but not unpleasant. Best of all, unlike the wards, there is no gossip mill or innuendos made about patients of staff.

""Patient treatment, either good or bad, is addressed. The only way we know that patient abuse is being questioned is when a staff member from the attorney general's or the governor's office appears accompanied by a stenographer for a private meeting with the superintendent. We are not privy to the outcome of such a meeting."

"I think I get the picture, Ms. Bascom," Guillermo interjected after glancing at his watch and learning that it was long past closing time. "Thank you for your comments. They've been most instructive."

CHAPTER 4

Mitch Gainer had just finished a round of golf at the university course, located a few blocks from where he and Kenzie were staying. Playing golf nearly every day for the past month and a half they'd been on campus was becoming a habit. It was his way of staying out of Kenzie's hair and giving her the space she needed to make this university experience a meaningful one. This would be her only artist-in-residence and she wanted to get everything out of it that she could.

Mitch was pleased that this was exactly what she was doing. Her days were filled from sunrise to sundown with tutoring, giving lectures, meeting with faculty, and most of all dealing, with the media. In constant demand for interviews, she never turned down a request.

Best of all, she would be reunited with Tullamore Dew, the Irish folk band that she was playing with when she first met Mitch in Halifax. Despite her already jammed schedule, she would play the fiddle for a short medley when the group performed on campus.

Leaving the golf course, Mitch strolled along the sidewalk toward their newest home. He felt out of kilter; things were not quite right with him. By the time he reached the sidewalk leading to the front door of the Tudor-style Indiana limestone house, he knew exactly what was wrong.

He was bored!

The phone was ringing as he opened the door. Receiver to his ear, he immediately recognized the deep voice, the Latino inflection. "Guillermo, it's good to hear your voice again. It's been a while."

"Too long, Mitch. The last time we spoke you were boarding a freighter for Europe."

"That's right. It's been well over five years ago. How did you know I was at Indiana University?"

"How can I not know? It's the biggest news in the state of Indiana, "Guillermo said with no discernible sarcasm. "Kenzie's face and name have been plastered all over the Indianapolis newspapers. Even though you're not mentioned in the stories, I knew you wouldn't let her out of your sight. I called the university and got your telephone number."

Mitch could hear Guillermo inhaling; he visualized his friend drawing on a big Cuban cigar, leaning back in his chair with his feet on his desk.

"You wouldn't be smoking a cigar, would you?"

"How did you know that?"

"Because I'm psychic and can smell the damn smoke over the telephone line! And, by the way, why are you reading Indianapolis newspapers in Cleveland? You're strictly a Plain Dealer man."

"Because I'm not in Cleveland. I'm here in Indianapolis. They tell me it's not far from where you are in Bloomington.

"Good! How long will you be here? We need to get together before you leave."

"I'm going to be here to a while, Mitch. I've taken on a new job."

"What!"

"I'm now the superintendent at Sycamore Hospital for the Criminally Insane."

Mitch stared at the receiver, struggling to comprehend what he had just heard. "What about the practice in Cleveland? Did you give that up? You must be going through male menopause to take a position in a bureaucracy, particularly as a hospital administrator."

"You may right, Mitch. I've been having hot flashes lately," Guillermo said with a chuckle.

Mitch heard him take another deep breath. He sensed that Guillermo had something up his sleeve. "OK, El Cubano, you didn't call me to make idle chit chat. What's on your mind?"

"You're absolutely right."

After a few moments of silence, Gerona began to speak, this time in a much softer tone. "It comes down to this, Mitch. I've taken on a colossal challenge, and have realized that I can't meet it with the resources available. I need help—the best I can get and that's you. Would you join me as a partner in this challenge? Simple as that."

Guillermo's words stunned him. Mitch dropped the receiver in his lap and put his hand over the mouthpiece. Not knowing what he would say, Mitch slowly picked up the receiver and began to speak.

"A challenge you say. Explain that to me."

"Sycamore Hospital is the last of its kind in the country," Gerona began. "It's been fraught with patient abuse and atrocities. I've been hired as a last ditch effort to reform the place. If I'm unsuccessful, the state will not hesitate to close the facility.

"I took this challenge because I felt that I needed it. Besides, there is nothing more satisfying to me than making something better. It provided an opportunity to use all my skill and knowledge that I have gained over the years. It would be my grand finale. Then, I can move to Miami or the islands, and enjoy the lifestyle I did when I was a youth in Cuba."

"And now you've concluded the grand finale could well turn out to be a grand fiasco?"

"It will be for sure if I don't get some help, and you're the only resource I know who can offer a chance to reform the place. It would be a true joint venture. I'm not imposing on our friendship; it's your expertise I need. Look what we did as a team to get electroshock out of the VA. Look how you reformed that Indian casino on the reservation.

"You're a natural reformer, Mitch."

Gerona paused. Mitch could hear him take a deep breath before he continued.

"If I know you, Mitch, you'll get restless. You'll be looking for something to do while Kenzie completes her residency. You know that they'll keep her busy. Left to your own resources, you'll not find campus life all that stimulating. Well, I can save you. I can give you something very stimulating to do right now. I guarantee it will make your experience in Indiana much more interesting."

Mitch laughed aloud and said, "You know me like a book, Guillermo. Yes, I'm interested in a challenge. I haven't really been tested since I left the reservation. I loved being in Europe and bring involved in the world of music, but it wasn't as exciting as being on the reservation. I didn't feel that I was accomplishing as much managing Kenzie's career as I did managing the casino."

"You've always had high-achievement needs," said Gerona, "and I know you had a lot to do with Kenzie's career blossoming the way it did when you took over."

"That may be true but what I really offered was the opportunity to be with her and support her emotionally. She plays better music when I'm around. It's as simple as that. So you see, her success has nothing to do with any managerial skills I have, or things that I did. The truth is that Kenzie's career manages itself. She's a superstar."

"That's plain to me, Mitch. If you join me, Kenzie will have to be your number-one priority, and mine as well, since we'll be working together. We'll have to work everything out with her in mind."

"That's what I have always liked about you, Guillermo. You're very bright and perceptive. How would you suggest that we work it out?"

"We'll have to be flexible. The hospital is less than an hour from Bloomington and you could drive back and forth. You will also have use of a house on the reservation—that's what they call our hospital grounds—at your disposal. You can stay over if you want. You can put in as many hours as you want, in any way you want. The important thing is that I have access to your mind. We have telephones, the mail, and courier services."

"I want to come to hospital as soon as can."

"Come whenever you want to," said his new partner.

After two quick Red Stripes and a long hot shower, Mitch put on a recording of Mahler's Third Symphony and stretched out on the sofa reading *Breakfast of Champions*. After a few pages, he drifted off. He found himself trapped in long narrow hallway, searching for a door that would lead him to Kenzie. But the hallway was endless and there were no doors, only plain white walls. He began running faster and faster but seemed to be on a treadmill, not going anywhere. Suddenly there she was, looking down on him.

"Mitch are you OK? You were really thrashing around. I thought you were going to fall off the sofa," Kenzie said, in a concerned voice.

Mitch leapt up from the sofa, went to the fridge, and opened a beer. "It's just another one of those damn fear-of-abandonment dreams," he grumbled.

"I'm sorry," Kenzie said, placing her hand gently his shoulder. "I know they're terrible."

"No they're not terrible. They're just frustrating. It's like being in a Kafka novel. I'm always going around in circles, searching for someone I can't reach," Mitch said, feeling sheepish.

Kenzie started to respond but hesitated, and then changed the subject. "This had been a long day. Why don't we have a glass of wine first and then go to bed and read."

"Sounds good. It's a nice evening. Why don't we go out on the patio? I'll get a bottle of wine. Have you eaten? Do you want some food?"

"Not really," Kenzie said, opening the door to the patio. "They had some food brought in after we finished our recording, and frankly, I'm stuffed."

They stretched out on the lounge chairs, sipping wine as they watched the sun set. The silence was broken when Mitch announced, "This back lawn is gorgeous. The gardener has really done a fine job. Look how thick and green the grass is. I love the smell of lilacs, and the dogwood tree is beautiful, one of the best I've ever seen."

"The lilac bushes and the flowers, particularly the azaleas and peonies, remind me of my grandmother's backyard. People used to come from miles around see it. She had tiers of flowers and there was never a time when some were not in bloom, except in the winter.

"Tell me about your day. How did the session go?"

"It was great," Kenzie said enthusiastically. "It's not often that I get the chance to play Mozart with a chamber ensemble. I was surprised that the students played as well as they did. They're all very talented."

"If I remember right, you played with the Academy of St. Martin in the Fields in Amsterdam," Mitch commented. "Are the students of the same caliber as those musicians?"

"Well no, Mitch," Kenzie replied, looking startled. "No, they're not at that level, but they are not that far below. They're just as much fun to play with and they don't make mistakes. For me, that's the main thing. I can't tolerate playing with musicians who make mistakes."

"You're just a damn perfectionist," Mitch said, laughing.

"Well I am with music, that's for sure."

"What else did you do? You worked about fourteen hours today."

"I spent most of the day with students, going over musical scores, and critiquing their compositions. Oh," she uttered, then took a sip of wine and, with a serious tone continued. "Over lunch, I listened to the faculty discussing Sycamore Hospital.

"They spoke of years and years of horrible patient brutality that resulted in criminal charges against staff. Finally, the public demanded that the place be closed. I almost left the table because I could not stand to listen to what they were actually doing to patients. It was so twisted and perverted, it almost made me sick," she exclaimed, her voice rising.

After several moments of silence, Kenzie went on. "Apparently the politicians did not close the hospital, in spite of the public demands, and have brought in a new administrator to make changes. The faculty passed around and signed a petition protesting this move. They are demanding that the hospital be closed. If what they say is true, it certain should be. I would have signed the petition if I could, but I'm not an Indiana resident."

Mitch felt his stomach tighten and a shiver go down his back. The new administrator was Guillermo and he was going to help his friend reform the place!

He suddenly felt a strong need to get away to clear his thoughts. "I'll be right back," he stammered as he got up from the chair. "I need to get a beer."

Kenzie, puzzled, watched her husband hurry from the patio.

After taking a beer from the refrigerator, Mitch sat down at the kitchen table and rubbed the cold bottle on his hot forehead.

What in the hell am I going to do? I have to tell her and tell her now. But what am I going to tell her? Do I tell her that I'm going to join Guillermo at the hospital that she scorns so much? If I do that it will that ruin her residency? She has looked forward to it so much. I will not ruin her work here. I will not cause her any grief. I will be honest with her and tell her what I need to do.

Mitch put the beer back in the refrigerator and returned to the patio. He kissed Kenzie on the cheek and, after a slight hesitation, began.

"I got a call today from Guillermo Gerona today. He's here in Indiana."

"What's he doing here?"

I must come out with it, right now. "You know the hospital that you just told me about," Mitch said, in a calm, clear voice. "Well, Guillermo is the new administrator and he's invited me to join him and help him reform the place while we're here in Indiana."

"What, this is unbelievable! I get it now! This is why you have been acting so strangely tonight. You didn't want to tell me that you're going to run off again, like you ran off to the Indian reservation. Only this time you're running off to a hospital for the criminally insane." With that, Kenzie left the room.

Mitch followed her into the bedroom. She was standing in front of the dresser, staring into the mirror. He threw his arms around her and held her tight. "I'm not running off anywhere. My place is here with you. You're my home and my family. This just happened today. I haven't made any decision as to what I want to do."

"Yes, you have, Mitch," Kenzie said calmly. "I know you far better than you know yourself. You're an adventurer and an opportunity for one has come your way. You cannot turn it down.

"I won't stand in your way. I love you for who you are and will stand by you, just like you stood by me when I went on tour abroad. I would not have made it without you. But I knew it was not easy for you to set your own career aside to do it."

Mitch felt his eyes water and had never felt more love for Kenzie than he felt at this moment.

"Let's go back out on the patio and have a glass of wine. I'll explain things to you. But, before I tell you about my working with Guillermo, I need to tell you that I did not set my career aside to go on tour with you in Europe," Mitch said, taking a sip of wine. "In the first place, I have never thought about having a career. I just go where life takes me. If I have a career it's with you."

"That's sweet of you to say," Kenzie said. "But there is more to it than that."

"Maybe, but to me a career is too narrow, too limiting. I don't think in those terms. When we left the reservation and went on tour, I was not setting a career aside. I was advancing it.

"Besides my work on the reservation was through. Don't forget, you helped me fulfill my promise to Chinook. You helped return the sacred land that he willed to me to the Indians. Going on tour with you to Europe was adventure—a very different one. I was glad that the opportunity came my way."

"I know you loved being in Europe," said Kenzie. "Those were very happy years for us. But I also know that being my manager was not really your thing, even though you were extremely good at it. I knew that you were doing it for me, because I wanted you to, not because that's what you would have chosen to do."

"You're right about that but it doesn't mean that I didn't enjoy it. It was another opportunity that came my way. Remember, you took leave from your performing schedule and came to the Wild West to help me fulfill Chinook's promise."

"Yes, I'm glad that I did. It was a magnificent experience for me. Tell me about the hospital," Kenzie said, rather abruptly.

Mitch could tell by Kenzie's demeanor that she had softened about the new venture with Guillermo.

"You're right as usual. I am going to help Guillermo. It's something that's come my way and I feel compelled to do it. It started with a simple telephone call. It was great to hear Guillermo's voice again. I was floored when he told me about the huge risk he had taken.

"I couldn't understand why he would do it. He's probably the most respected doctor in Cleveland and that's saying a lot. He's a legend in the Cuban community—known as El Cubano. Why would he leave all that to come to Indiana to try and restore a hospital, in crisis, with a terrible reputation?"

"I guess he's an adventurer like you, Mitch," Kenzie said, pouring another glass of wine.

"Maybe, but it's more than that. He has strong feelings about patient abuse and treatment in a mental-health setting. Remember I met him during my internship at the VA hospital. There he was, he was, a Cuban dermatologist who couldn't practice his specialty. Working as a physician at the VA was the best job he could find in the states. He proved to be the best therapist I have ever been around. While I was at the VA, he took me under his wing. Even though it was through ways some might question, he and I put an end to ECT."

"Yes, wiring the machines so the doctor gets the shock instead of the patient was not exactly kosher," agreed Kenzie, shaking her head. "Actually, it was unethical. You're both lucky you didn't get into big trouble."

"You're right," said Mitch, nodding. "I know it was a dicey ploy but I'd do it again. ECT does terrible things to people and should be eliminated everywhere." He reached for the wine bottle, pulling his hand back at the last moment.

"You know we did stop it. They took the damn machines out of the hospital and shut the program down. Unfortunately that's the last time we worked closely together. He went to Canada, then later, helped me out as a part-time consultant when I opened my practice in Cleveland. When I went to the reservation, he joined my practice, took it over, and ran it.

"When he called me this week, he told me that restoring the hospital would be very difficult. He doesn't think he can do it on his own. He said this was going to be his last challenge before he returns to the Caribbean or Miami, and he wants to give it his best shot. He insisted he needs me to work with him."

"And just how are you going to do that?"

"The first thing he said to me was that everything had to be worked out with you. He knows about your residency. He understands you are my priority. He said he would appreciate any time or effort I can provide, but your work in Bloomington is the priority.

"I won't have to spend that much time at the hospital. We can do a lot by telephone and in writing. The hospital is in Indianapolis and I can drive back and forth. If I need to stay over, there's housing. Mainly, he knows whatever we set up will first take into account your needs.

"You're calling the shots, Kenzie. This is your time and we'll make the most of it. If I don't like the place and the conditions, I won't take it. If I can see it's going to interfere with your residency, then I won't take it either. If you decide that this is a hairbrained scheme and you don't want me to do it, say so, and that will be the end of it."

Kenzie got up from the lounge chair and kissed Mitch on the cheek. Looking down at him fondly, she said, "Go. Go follow Guillermo. He needs you. And, it will be good for you."

CHAPTER 5

It had long been customary for Kenzie to play a piece of Mitch's favorite music for him each day. Today, it was Procol Harum's "A Whiter Shade of Pale," on her fiddle.

Then the doorbell rang.

"I'll get it," Kenzie said, setting instrument aside. She returned with a package and handed it to Mitch. "It's for you. A man from the hospital delivered it."

Mitch opened the package and began thumbing through a stack of newspaper clippings.

"This is some material Guillermo wanted me to see before I meet with him at the hospital tomorrow," he said, focusing intently on the clippings.

Suddenly he exclaimed, "This is unbelievable. They're reports on what was happening to inmates at the hospital." He held one of the papers for Kenzie to inspect.

"Here's one referring to the hospital as a 'Chamber of Horrors'."

"Another refers to it as a 'House of Shame'."

Mitch could feel the anger boiling in him, his voice rising as he read the headlines and handed the clippings, one by one, to Kenzie.

"Inmates are kept silent, amid fear, brutality and suffering. Kin finds inmate weak, bruised and toothless."

"Inmate reports swastika hung in cell. "
"Aide forced homosexual acts, inmates' statements say."
"No autopsies ordered in 26 hangings at hospital."
"Abuse killed 2 inmates, aide says."
"Man's 17-month legal battle frees wife from hospital."
"Social worker says hospital ignored beating reports."
"A former attendant reports she delivered an inmate's full-term baby at the hospital without a doctor present and under inhumane conditions."
"Ex-inmate says he saw murder at the hospital."
"Criminal indictments were issued to 37 employees and 15 ex-employees including torture, aggravated assault and sodomy."

Mitch handed the last document to Kenzie and began to tremble.

"I need to take a walk," he said, his lips shaking. As he was leaving the room, he turned to Kenzie. "When you're finishing looking at the clippings, burn them in the fireplace. I don't ever want to see them again."

Oblivious to his surroundings, Mitch trudged down the sidewalk, lost in his thoughts. *What have I myself gotten into? I can't go there! It's a hell hole, a snake pit! It's no better than a concentration camp run by the Nazis during the war. But I've already given Guillermo my word that I would join him. I can't break my word.*

Suddenly a car horn honked, bringing Mitch back to awareness. He was wandering in the middle of the street. He raced back to the sidewalk and ran back to his house.

Mitch was panting when he burst into the house. He headed straight for the telephone. He picked up the receiver, took a piece of paper from his pants pocket, checked the number, and began to dial. "I'm calling Guillermo right now to let him know that I'm not going to work with him."

Kenzie was sitting on the sofa reading. She calmly got up, walked over to him, and placed her hand on the mouthpiece. She firmly pushed the off button.

"Don't make an impulsive decision right now," she said. "You're upset. Wait until you've calmed down and thought things over. Then make a decision."

Mitch pushed her hand away and began to dial again. Then, receiver to his ear, he abruptly hung up the phone, walked over to the sofa, and sat down, holding his head in his hands. Kenzie put her arms around him and whispered in his ear, "Let's go to bed and read."

Mitch had barely opened *Breakfast of Champions* before falling fast asleep. When he opened his eyes again, his nightstand clock said 5:30 a.m. He reached for his flashlight, silently got out of bed, collected his clothes, and tiptoed from the room.

To his great surprise, he felt refreshed and energized. He had slept through the night without waking or dreaming. This just did not happen to him. Deciding to skip breakfast, he wrote Kenzie a brief note, telling her that he was joining Guillermo. He grabbed a paper cup of high fiber cereal, a bottle of Perrier water, and headed for the hospital.

When Mitch started the car engine, he began reflecting on the emotional roller coaster ride he had been on yesterday. My God, I was off my head. I felt bored, dispirited, ecstatic, manic, furious, and panicky—all in the same day. Suddenly, he smiled and said aloud, "I sure as hell feel good now."

He turned the radio on and found a station paying tribute to the Stanley Brothers, the legendary bluegrass musicians. This was a windfall for Mitch; he loved bluegrass, especially gospel. When he heard the ringing sounds of "I Am a Man of Constant Sorrow," it took him back to his days in Nugget Valley when he would sit around a campfire with miners from the south, drinking beer, and listening to them play bluegrass. He set the car's cruise control and settled in for what would be a very pleasant drive to the hospital.

For a moment, Mitch thought he was at the wrong place when he pulled in. Before was a large red-brick compound that resembled an old country estate that he had seen in England.

This can't be the hospital! The state would never have anything so elegant, not for the criminally insane. But when he looked up and saw a tower at the end of the building, and a guard surveying him intensely, he knew he was at the right place. He had found Sycamore.

Mitch parked the car and hurried toward the main entrance. Just as he reached to open the door, it opened. There was Guillermo, grinning from ear to ear. The two men shook hands. Guillermo placed his hand on Mitch's shoulder and led him to the helicopter pad.

"It's good to see you again, Mitch. I've arranged a helicopter tour for you."

"It's good to see you too, Guillermo. This is quite a place. It's hard to believe this is a prison. The grounds are immaculate; the building is almost palatial, far more impressive than any building on Indiana University's campus," Mitch said, as he climbed in the helicopter.

"I'm not going with you on the tour. I want you to take it all in by yourself. When you finish, security will take you to my office and we'll have some espresso and settle in."

After the tour Mitch found Guillermo in his office, leaning back in his chair with his feet on the desk, his nose buried in a newspaper. Glancing around the room, Mitch focused on the portrait of Kid Gavilan.

"I see you brought the 'Cuban Hawk' with you. He sure brightens this dismal place. I've never asked you this. Did you ever see him fight?"

Gerona looked up from the paper and removed his reading glasses. "Yes, I saw him fight many times in Havana, at the Palacio de Deportes in the 1940s," he said, smiling broadly.

"My father took me to my first fight in 1945, when Gavilan won the Cuban lightweight title. I remember that he knocked out Jose Pedroso. The last time I saw him fight was 1954 in Chicago, when he lost a fifteen-round decision to Bobo Olsen for the middleweight championship of the world."

Gerona got up from his desk and straightened the boxer's portrait. "You know, he is the only hero I've ever had. He was from my home town Camagüey. His real name is Geraldo Gonzales.

"He got his boxing name from a grocery store in Camagüey his manager owned—El Gavilan—which means 'the hawk.' He fought with a dancing, zig-zag style, always moving forward with speed. He had lightening reflexes and the heart of a tiger. He was known for his bolo punch—he threw with the same motion he used to whack sugar cane with a bolo knife when he was kid in Cuba."

Gerona returned to his desk, and in a reflective manner said sadly, "Unfortunately the Kid fell on tough times after he left boxing. His money was gone, so he returned to Cuba and his farm. He became a Jehovah's Witnesses preacher, but ran afoul of the government. He was banished and is living in Miami, mostly on the streets. He had a stroke, too. It's too damn bad! He deserves much better."

"I'm sorry to hear that," Mitch said sympathetically. "He was also one of my favorite fighters and I remember him being tougher than hell, Unfortunately he took a lot of punches. Did he suffer brain damage?"

"I haven't heard that. They say his mind is sharp. Still, I'm sure the punches may have something to do with his ill health."

After a period of silence, with both men looking at the portrait of the Cuban boxer, Gerona spoke. "I sent you the newspaper clippings to give you some idea of what you're getting into. I don't want you to have any illusions about what we face here."

"Yes, I admit, they were disconcerting," Mitch said, wiping his forehead as if he were erasing the vivid images of the newspaper articles from his mind. "I knew that Sycamore Hospital would not be a country club, but I did not visualize the extreme cruelty that apparently was taking place here. If true, it's unbelievable. It's the first time I've seen a hospital referred to as a 'chamber of horrors.'"

"Unfortunately, that's a well-earned title," Gerona said, looking up at the ceiling. After pausing for a few minutes, he cleared his voice and continued.

"I've been on the phone all morning with Graciela Cevallos, the commissioner of mental health. She's an old friend. I supervised her internship at the VA shortly after you graduated."

"I think I remember the name," Mitch interjected. "If memory serves me, I had her in a practicum class. She's a very attractive Cuban woman who always had a broad smile on her face."

"You remember well," Gerona said, with a smile. "She's hard to forget. She's the one who hired me. On day, out of the blue, she called. Hell, I had no contact with her in years. Anyway, she told about Sycamore and ask me if I would take it over—a last-chance effort to save it. The state wants to close it because the patient abuse has been going on for years. Still, she lobbied successfully for one last chance to reform the place. Before I knew it, she talked me into accepting the job."

"Ha! Ha! That last comment is pure bullshit, and you, my good friend, know it," said Mitch, jumping in. "No one ever talks you into doing anything you don't want to do. Like you told me when you first called me, you took the job because you wanted one last challenge. Has something changed? Are you getting cold feet?"

"Yes something has changed, and no, I'm not getting cold feet," Gerona said firmly. "Graciela told me today she thinks she was set up. She now believes the state is going to close the place, regardless of whether we establish a good treatment program or not. She thinks that they are just buying time until they can make other arrangements for the patients. They're using me and, according to her, my reputation, as way of giving the impression that they are interested in reforming Sycamore Hospital."

"Like the Indians on the reservation always say, you can't trust the government. Unfortunately, I think they're right," Mitch commented, shaking his head.

"I'm not stupid, Mitch. I knew exactly what I was getting into. I know that with anything political, anything bureaucratic, people say one thing and do another.

"However, I don't. I took this job to reform the place and that's what I'll do, in whatever time they give me. I feel bad for Graciela because she's very upset, and threatening to leave her job because of it. I also do not want to disturb your and Kenzie's time in Indiana with a venture that's not going to be successful."

"Don't worry about me," Mitch said firmly. "It's not the outcome that brings me here. It's the chance to be on the firing lines again, with the only mentor I've had besides Chinook. This isn't a ticket on the Titanic. It's a challenge for me and I need one. You'll make your mark here and leave something good, no matter what the state does with Sycamore. I'm onboard, and ready to roll my sleeves up and get to work."

"Good!" Gerona reached in his shirt pocket for his cigar case, taking out a cigar and a guillotine-style cigar cutter. He held the cigar under his nose and sniffed it. Then he cut one end and placed it between his front teeth.

"Let's get the hell out of here. I'll show you the residence that'll be at your disposal. Then we'll go to the one good Cuban restaurant in Indianapolis for lunch, followed by a tour of the city. Your first baptism of fire will be tomorrow when you met with the prison guards—I mean correctional officers, as they are now called."

CHAPTER 6

Mitch pulled out of the driveway and headed for Sycamore and his first meeting with the correctional officers. He had not prepared for the meeting and did not want to wing it. He decided that the best he could do was to formulate his address during the drive. But, try as he may, he could not clear his mind from the conversation he had with Kenzie last evening.

Kenzie was reading in bed when he got home from the hospital. Mitch quickly removed his clothes, reached for the newspaper that was on his bedstand, and slipped under the covers without a word.

"Oh, quiet tonight, are we," Kenzie said, putting her book aside. She rolled over to her husband's side and pulled the newspaper he was reading away from his face.

"Not really," he said with a smile, rumpling Kenzie's thick auburn hair. "Don't know if I can accurately capture for you what I've experienced today. In many ways, it's like I've been a character in a Kafka story. I need to sleep on it to digest what happened. I'll tell you over breakfast," he said, returning to his newspaper.

This time Kenzie jerked the newspaper out of her husband's hands, shook her head at him, and pursed her lips into a firm "no."

Mitch ruffled her hair again, and whispered in her ear, "OK, ma'am, we won't wait till the morrow. I'll spill the beans right now."

An Abbey Returned

"Good," Kenzie said, patting his cheek.

"You won't believe what Sycamore Hospital looks like," Mitch began. "It resembles a country estate in Victorian England more than a maximum-security correctional facility. It's a series of huge brick buildings forming a rectangle, all surrounded by tall trees and green meadows. It was built as an abbey in the early 1900s, by a religious order from Europe. However, they never occupied it. Since it was abandoned, the state took it over, and turned it into a prison to house criminals or those who were mentally ill and dangerous.

"When you go inside the building, you know immediately it's a prison. It's gloomy, impersonal, and crisscrossed with narrow hallways leading to offices, cells, and meeting rooms—all behind steel doors. What you notice most are the barren and drab concrete walls. The damn place reminds me of a bunker in Berlin during Nazi Germany."

"That's not so surprising. After all it's an old prison," Kenzie remarked, resting her head on Mitch's shoulder.

"It's more than just old; it's medieval, something out of much darker period in history. Do you know there are even catacombs under the place and a cemetery filled with deceased inmates on the grounds. The damn place is spooky!"

Kenzie chuckled. "I'm sorry. I know there's nothing funny but when you said it was spooky, you had a look on your face like a child who has been frightened by a ghost on Halloween. It's good to see you still have some child left in you. You don't show that often. Tell me about Guillermo, what plans he has for the hospital, and how you fit in."

"It was delightful to see him again after all this time. I did notice that he looked a little tired and his face was a bit puffy. But other than that he was still his old self: filled with energy, ideas, and embracing life in general. In spite of all his vigor, he's the most relaxing person to be around. He makes everything seem so natural."

"Natural. That's a strange choice of words. What do you mean?"

"The best I can do is to give you an example. As you know, Guillermo took the job to restore the hospital to a treatment facility, so the state would not have to close it. Well, just before our meeting, he'd learned he was misled and that the state has no intention of the keeping the place open. They are only using him, so they can buy time to complete the sale and make other arrangements for the patients."

"That's terrible!" Kenzie exclaimed.

"Yes, it is, but that's not how Guillermo views it. He did not appear to be upset that he'd uprooted his famly to accept a job that was doomed to begin with."

"It's hard to believe he wouldn't be distressed," Kenzie said, her eyes flashing. "After all, he was betrayed. That's a tough pill for most people to swallow."

"I agree, but Guillermo is not like most people." Mitch paused and tilted his head back as if he were gathering his thoughts. "He simply shrugged his shoulders and said that bureaucrats often say one thing and do another. He went on to say, in a very calm voice, that he'd been hired to reform the hospital and that's what he would do, in whatever time they gave him. And I said that I would join him."

"Hmmm."

"I'm well aware that this may be a very simple and unsatisfying explanation, but it's the best I can do. Remember, I told you that I needed to sleep on things before discussing them," Mitch said, a touch of annoyance in his voice.

"Oh, your mind is perfectly clear and working well, my love. You enlightened me on Guillermo; you reminded me that he's different than most people. There was really not much more to add. If you were to try to explain what makes him different, I'm afraid it would only make things more convoluted. You know he's charismatic and you're going to follow him wherever this job takes you both. That's exactly what you should do. What you have to do now is to make something good come out of your venture."

Kenzie paused, took a deep breath, furrowed her brow, and appeared deep in thought. After a few moments, she said, "Mitch I'm reminded what Scarlet O'Hara's father said to her about Tara in *Gone with the Wind*. He said that land was the only thing worth working for, worth fighting for, worth dying for, because it was the only thing that lasts.

"You should keep this in mind as you head down the path with Guillermo because, this sacred land that has been badly misused will be your dilemma." Kenzie turned off the light and buried her head in the pillow.

Mitch glanced at his wrist watch. It was 7:57 a.m. He would wait three more minutes so he could make his entrance to the meeting with the correctional officers at exactly 8 a.m., the exact time the meeting had been scheduled. He opened the door, slipped in looking straight ahead, and sauntered to a small podium in the center of the room. He took his favorite pipe, a Caminetto briar, and tobacco pouch from his coat pocket. He dipped his pipe into the pouch and filled the bowl. He tamped the tobacco with a pipe tamper, torched it with butane lighter, and took two short draws. He gently set the pipe on the podium and watched a ring of smoke rise to the ceiling. After the smoke disappeared, he turned around and faced his audience.

There they were, some fifty strong, mostly men, with a few women, sitting erectly in rows of straight-back chairs, arms folded across their chests, eyes focused straight ahead, stern expressions on their faces.

But what caught his eye were the rows of white socks lined up before him. Apparently the men's khaki trousers were a couple inches shorter than they should be, and completely exposed their socks. Never before had Mitch seen such a sight. In a strange way, the scene was somewhat intimidating. Out of the corner of his eye, he spied a tall muscular man dressed in black trousers and shirt with two gold bars on each shoulder. The man looked him over, then quietly left the room.

Mitch picked up his still smoldering pipe, and took a couple of draws in an effort to compose himself.

"I'm Dr. Gainer," he said forcefully. "I'll be working with you to implement a new treatment program at Sycamore Hospital. I do not work for the state or the hospital. My only role is to serve as a consultant to Dr. Gerona. I'm a psychologist and have previously worked with Dr. Gerona at a VA hospital. I also have a private practice in Cleveland, Ohio. My most recent employment was on an Indian reservation in Idaho. Presently, I am the business manager for my wife, a classical musician with an international reputation.

"My professional training in psychology includes a bachelor's degree from Boston College and a doctorate from Ohio State University. However my main training in psychology did not come from a book or a university. It came from a disabled gambler named Chinook Swindle, whose classroom was an Indian reservation and mining camp in Idaho."

Mitch picked up his pipe, came out from behind the podium, and strolled in front of the group, like a major inspecting his troops. "You may smoke if you wish," he called out. Immediately hands reached for cigarette packs and the room quickly filled with smoke.

Mitch returned to the podium, put his smoldering pipe in his coat pocket, and addressed the group.

"My first rule is to keep things simple, so we'll start at the beginning. Sycamore Hospital was founded as a place to treat mentally ill criminal offenders. However, it seems it was never that. Rather it became a place to warehouse such people. Treatment has been largely nonexistent. But that's all going to change now. Dr. Gerona and I want to turn this place around by making treatment the top priority."

Mitch paused as reactions to his words became evident in the officer's expressions. Skepticism was reflected in the assembled faces.

"This does not mean that security will be compromised. Security is and will remain a necessary part of treatment, so your roles will not be diminished. In fact they will be expanded and you will become partners in treatment."

Mitch paused again and looked at the group, most of whom were now puffing away, creating a fog so thick that only their white socks were clearly visible. He knew that his words had largely fallen on deaf ears. He'd expected this response. He would keep things short.

"Well, this is enough for today," he said. "I'll be back next week at the same time and I'll be meeting with you individually on the wards. Thank you and good day."

CHAPTER 7

Mitch and Kenzie were in bed enjoying their customary hour of reading before turning out the light. Suddenly, Mitch closed his 1,500-page hardbound biography of Poncho Villa with a thud. The loud sound startled Kenzie, who dropped her own book and sat up straight in bed.

"Mitch, what's going on?"

"Sorry for startling you. But tomorrow will be a day of reckoning for those who've dismissed me during my initial time at Sycamore."

"What are you talking about?" Kenzie gazed at her husband with a puzzled expression.

"I've told you that the correctional officers have chosen to harass me during our meetings. Since smoking is allowed, they purposely light one cigarette after another to deliberately fill the room with heavy smoke. In addition, they refuse to look at me, and completely ignore me when I'm speaking. What's even worse is their captain who, without explanation, does not show up for meetings with me."

"Just what are you proposing to do in this day of reckoning?"

"When I walk into the room to meet with the officers, they will all light up in unison. But instead of walking up to the lectern at the front of room as I usually do, today I'll stoke up a good Cuban cigar, and stroll among them, puffing away. When the smoke is so thick you can barely see, I'll give them an asinine written assignment, tell them to work on it for the entire period, and leave the room.

"Mitch! That's such an infantile thing to do; I really don't know what to say."

"You don't need to say anything. There's one thing I know for sure. Actions are stronger than words, particularly with this outfit. I'm banking that they will not like working on a nonsensical assignment in a smoke-filled room any better than I would. After all, they're working in a maximum-security facility where you can't even open a window. I have every reason to believe when I meet with them after that, I'll find less cigarette smoke and maybe some attitude adjustments. That's all I'm hoping for."

Kenzie shook her head and rolled her eyes." Pray tell, just what you are going to do with the captain?"

"I'm not sure," Mitch replied, as he began fidgeting with his hands. To steady himself, he reached for his Poncho Villa book, placing it on his lap with his palms resting on the cover.

"I've never met the man. He did made brief appearances at my meetings with the officers. Always standing alone in the back of room, he'd look around for a few moments and leave when the room got smoky.

"From what I gather, he's the Big Kahuna at Sycamore. As head of security, everything passes through him. He's an ex-marine and decorated war hero, who's tough as nails and smart to boot. The consensus at Sycamore is that he's firm but fair. He's clearly giving me the message that he's not going to cooperate with my efforts to develop treatment programs. For that, I have no choice but to confront him. I don't know how he'll respond, but suspect that it will be a battle."

"If you're going to be a combatant, you'd better get your rest." Kenzie playfully ruffled Mitch's hair and turned off her bedside lamp.

The next morning, Mitch stuffed a Beethoven cassette and a bottle of cranberry juice in his briefcase and rushed out the door. The cranberry juice and Beethoven's Third Symphony should make his drive to Sycamore more relaxing.

He slammed the car door and headed for his meetings with the correctional officers and their captain. After clearing security, he felt a rush of adrenaline, and dashed down the hallway, bumping into Guillermo, who momentarily lost his balance.

"Mitch! What's going on? You're as red as a beet."

Suddenly, Mitch found himself looking down at his shoes, wondering why in the hell he was so hyper. "I'm sorry, my friend. I was on my way to the meeting with the correctional officers, and not paying attention to where I was going."

"Let's have a cup of coffee," Guillermo said, placing his hand on Mitch's shoulder as he led him to his office.

Mitch stared at the tiny cup of espresso before putting it to his lips. "I guess Guillermo, I just lost it for a moment or so. All I could think about was confronting Captain Laggins. I'm scheduled to meet with him for the first time later today. But, I know he'll be standing in the back when I start my meeting with the officers. He'll look me over quickly and leave without a word. I want to confront him right there and have our first encounter with the officers present."

"Bad idea," Guillermo said with a chuckle.

"No shit! I don't know where that came from. I don't even know what I have to say to him. I know he'll just hand me some passive aggressive bullshit just like the officers do. I'm determined not to let him pull that on me!"

An Abbey Returned

"You know, Gavilan always told me the venue was the main thing that concerned him when he fought," Guillermo said, his eyes on the portrait of the Cuban boxer. "He truly believed that if he could've chosen where his fights were held, he never would've lost. He'd joking say that he'd have all his fights at the Palacio de Deportes in Havana. I don't believe he ever lost a fight there."

Guillermo paused and poured himself another espresso. "You're correct in your thinking that your first meeting with Laggins may well be a contest. You can't control that, but you can control the venue. Don't have it at the hospital. That's his territory. He's always victorious there. You change things.

"I'll have Ms. Bascom cancel your meetings—you go enjoy the sights of Indianapolis. Before you leave for Bloomington, drop in the Ding Dong Tavern around 4 p.m. It's just across the street from the hospital. You'll find Laggins standing alone at the end of the bar, having his after-work refreshments. You can have your meeting there."

"That's a good idea," Mitch said as he left the room.

Walking leisurely to his car, Mitch pondered what sights in Indianapolis he wanted see. He decided that he would start by visit the Indianapolis Motor Speedway, home of the Indianapolis 500, the most famous auto race in the country.

Since Mitch had little interest in automobiles of any type, particularly race cars, he did not find his visit to the famed speedway very consequential. The tour he took of the track and grounds was only mildly entertaining, and his brief walk through the museum even less so.

Since he remembered Vonnegut's mentioning war monuments in Indianapolis in his writings, he decided that would be his next stop.

Mitch found the Soldiers and Sailors Monument in the center of the city to be more than he expected. The obelisk-shaped limestone monument was about the same size as the Statue of Liberty. Resting on a raised foundation, surrounded by pools and fountains, it was stirring. He was in awe of the magnificent limestone and bronze sculptures decorating the base of the monument. He climbed the observation tower and was treated to a spectacular view of a city that he had obviously underestimated.

Mitch spent the rest of the morning in the Colonel Eli Lilly Civil War Museum, a museum of Indiana's history in the American Civil War, located in the basement of the monument.

After a Reuben sandwich and a thorough read of the Indianapolis Star in a nearby delicatessen, Mitch headed for the Indiana War Memorial. He took the newspaper with him because he found a lengthy complimentary article about Kenzie, complete with a striking picture of her standing in her emerald-green concert dress, holding her cello and bow by her side.

Mitch joined a guided tour of the memorial gathered at the entrance of the magnificent structure, built in the 1920s to honor Indiana veterans of the Great War. The guide mentioned that the design was based on the Mausoleum at Halicarnassus, one of the Seven Wonders of The World, which triggered a lively discussion about the Seven Wonders.

Mitch decided to skip the rest of the tour and went back to the main entrance. He came face to face with an enthusiastic docent who thrust a brochure in his face and told him, "Be sure and spend time in the Shrine Room on the upper level. It's breathtaking and inspirational."

Eager to get away from the woman, Mitch dashed up the stairway for a quick look at the room. Then he would get the hell out of here, and find another place to kill time before the dreaded meeting with the captain.

An Abbey Returned

The docent was right! The Shrine Room was breathtaking. He glanced at his brochure and learned that the room was 110 feet tall and 60 feet square, with a vast ceiling supported by 28 columns of blood red marble. Hanging in the center was the Star of Destiny. Below that below was an American flag; below that, the Alter of Consecration.

Mitch sensing a spiritual ambiance in the room, was drawn to the red marble columns. He walked over to a column and placed his hand on the smooth stone which felt cool to his touch. His mind drifted back to the night, several years ago when he and Farrell, his Indian friend, cut their thumbs with a knife and placed their bloody thumbs on Chinook's red granite monument to symbolize their lifetime bond with the man who had been their mentor and protector since they were children. Oh, how he wished Chinook were here to guide him, to advise him on his meeting with Captain Laggins.

Then, suddenly he reminded himself of what he already knew. Although Chinook had departed, his spirit had remained with him. All he had to do was to find it, buried in what Chinook had taught him over the years, using gambling as a metaphor to teach life lessons. Suddenly Chinook's words came to Mitch.

"Poker is all about gut feelings and patience. You have to know when to act on your gut. No one can teach you that. You have to learn it on your own. All I can say is, it has something to do with patience. Always try to slow things down rather than speeding them up when you get that feeling in your gut."

When Mitch took his hand off the column and turned around to leave the memorial, he noticed several people staring at him with solemn looks on their faces. He wanted to tell them that, yes, he'd had a spiritual experience about war. But it was not a war that involved soldiers, battlefields, and the like.

It was a personal war within him over what was right and what was wrong.

Mitch checked his watch when he got back to his car. It was now 2:45 p.m. He opened the glove compartment and withdrew a cassette of Vivaldi's "Four Seasons." Driving around Indianapolis with Vivaldi's relaxing music filling his ears would be a good way to kill the remaining time before his dreaded meeting.

The Winter section of Vivaldi's masterpiece was nearly finished when Mitch pulled into the parking lot of a long limestone building with a huge center archway. There, over the front door, hung a huge white sign that said The Ding Dong Tavern, in red, white, and blue letters.

Mitch sat in the car until the Vivaldi finished. As he wove his way through the cars parked helter-skelter around the building, he was thinking about the Shrine Room and how it was as spiritual and comforting to him as any of the great European cathedrals he had visited. He reminded himself to take Kenzie there soon. Then he opened the front door and entered the correctional officer's lair.

There were several tables, a shuffle board, a pool table, and a jukebox in straight lines before a long bar that nearly filled the room. The tavern was filled to the brim with officers, still in uniform, throwing down drinks, playing pool, cards, talking loudly, and laughing profusely. The deafening noise stopped the moment Mitch entered the room. He could clearly hear the Hank Thompson hit, "A Six Pack to Go," playing on the jukebox. By the time Mitch reached the end of the bar where Lynsford Laggins stood alone, the jukebox was now playing Hank's "Blackboard of My Heart."

Laggins reached for a shot of whiskey on the bar and dumped it, glass and all, into a schooner of beer. The shot glass hit him in the nose as he tipped his head back and swigged the alcohol down.

Mitch took a half a step backward and watched in amazement as Laggins finished his drink. Without thinking, he blurted, "You've brought back old memories, Captain Laggins. This is the first time I've seen anyone drink a depth charge since I left the mines of Nugget Valley years ago. You see, in Nugget Valley, a depth charge is an esteemed drink and only the very best miner is allowed to drink it. The bartenders will not make the drink for anyone else," Mitch said, in obvious awe of the tall, muscular captain.

Laggins started to say something but hesitated as if he was not sure how to respond. Finally he asked, in a deep commanding voice, "Did you, Dr. Gainer, ever drink a depth charge?"

"Never had the honor," Mitch replied, thinking he may have chosen an obtuse way of introducing himself. "I was a miner and, I think, a pretty good one, but clearly not one of the best."

"We'll fix that. I'll buy you one right now," Laggins said, motioning to the bartender.

"I appreciate your offer, but I must decline. I didn't earn a depth charge in Nugget Valley and it wouldn't be right to have one now. Besides I have to drive back to Bloomington. I don't drive if I've been drinking strong liquor."

Laggins threw his head back and started to laugh. He immediately repressed the laughter, leaned forward, and looked Mitch dead in the eye. "Sounds like you may be a man of principle, Dr. Gainer. Now tell me why in the hell are you in here?"

"I think you already know why I'm here. It's time we have a chat about the hospital, and this is as good place as any."

"Fire away," Laggins said, motioning for Mitch to take the empty bar stool next to him.

Mitch ignored the gesture, thinking if Laggins was going to stand, then he would stand. "It's like this," he began. "I came here as a consultant, with no specific power, to work with Dr. Gerona, and to help him humanize the hospital and implement sound mental health treatment programs—ones that should have been implemented years ago."

"Sounds like a big charge to me that may not be welcomed," Laggins said, motioning the bartender. "Bring me another drink, and give Dr. Gainer whatever he wants," he commanded.

"I'll have a club soda," Mitch told the bartender. He wished that he did not have to drive back to Bloomington so he could have a shot of top-shelf tequila. "I'm only in the area temporarily."

"Yes, I know you're here at IU with your wife Kenzie, the cellist. She's the talk of the whole state," Laggins said, eying his fresh drink.

Mitch did not know if there was a hidden meaning in Laggin's words. "Yes, I can tell you personally, from years of experience, she is worth all the talk," he said with a smile.

Laggins tipped his head back and threw another depth charge down the hatch. This time the shot glass slide off to one side and missed hitting his nose.

"Dr. Gerona and I are good friends and go way back. I worked under his supervision at a VA hospital and I can tell you that he an excellent therapist, and more than that, an excellent reformer. When he found out that I was here with Kenzie, he said he'd been hired to reform Sycamore Hospital. He needed help and asked me to join him to implement new treatment programs."

"What did he tell you about the status of Sycamore, and what he was facing?"

Mitch sensed immediately that Laggins knew the full story, so there was no point in beating around the bush. "Gerona was hired under false pretenses. He was told that he was hired as a last-ditch effort to reform the hospital, so it would not be closed. But he knew there was a good chance that the hospital would be closed, regardless of his efforts.

"On my first day on the job, he told me he'd just learned that the hospital was always going to be closed, and that he was really hired to appease the minority political faction who wants the hospital to remain open."

"I know the story. Those political bastards deal from the bottom of the deck," Laggins said. "I don't understand why he's staying around. His best efforts will be for naught."

"You don't know Gerona. He marches to the beat of a different drummer. He understands politics and knows he's been betrayed, but that will not stop him from doing what he was hired to do. He'll reform this place whether they close it or not."

"And what about you?"

"As long as I'm in the area and he's here, I'm with him all the way. It doesn't matter so much what the outcome will be. It's the effort that counts, and I'll give him the best I can offer."

Laggins placed his hand on Mitch's shoulder. "I've been where you and Gerona are now and you're right, it's the labor that counts. When I was with the Marines in Korea and later in Vietnam, we quickly learned that the politicians would not let us win. But, it didn't stop us from being Marines."

Laggin's words produced a period of silence when both men appeared to be searching for words. Finally, Laggins offered his hand and said softly, "Drop by my office when you're at the hospital and we can get to work."

CHAPTER 8

Mitch woke up famished, an hour before the alarm went off. He threw on a robe and hurried to the kitchen to prepare his favorite breakfast—sausage, large brown eggs over easy, hash browns, whole wheat toast, and espresso. When he finished cooking, he heard the alarm, a signal that Kenzie would be joining him soon.

"What's going on?" Kenzie appeared, rubbing the sleep from her eyes. "This must be a special day for you to prepare your breakfast feast. Usually you just tear out the door with a cup of espresso in your hands."

Mitch sat down the table, speared a piece of sausage, pointed it at Kenzie, and said, "Yesterday started for me with a rush of adrenaline. I couldn't settle down and was obsessing about my meetings with the officers and Captain Laggins. By the time I got to the hospital, I was so hyped up, I literally ran into the building. As I was streaking down the hallway, I bumped into Guillermo. I mean, I literally bumped into him, nearly knocking him on his ass."

"A great way to greet your mentor and best friend," Kenzie said, laughing.

"Fortunately, he headed me off before my meeting with the officers. He insisted that I take the day off and visit the sights of

Indianapolis, drop by the tavern where Laggins drinks after work, and meet with him there."

"What, a tavern? That doesn't sound like the best meeting place to me."

"Well, it was, but that's not the main thing I want to tell you about. When I was killing time, I visited the Shrine Room at the Indianapolis War Memorial. I was a mess of anxiety when I got there. But the room was very spiritual and I calmed down immediately. There were rows of tall red marble columns that were same color as Chinook's monument. For some reason, I walked over to one off the columns, raised my arm over my head, and leaned against it like I did the last time I visited Chinook's monument. I could hear his words echoing in my ear, reminding me to pay attention to my gut feelings and be patient.

"I was fine when I left there and I made my mind up that Chinook's words would be my approach to dealing Laggins. I would trust my instincts and be patient, and I was. Laggins was not what I thought he would be. Rather than being an adversary, he offered to help me make reforms to the hospital. Strange as it sounds, I felt a bond with him during our brief encounter."

Kenzie said nothing, but sat quietly at the table, ignoring her breakfast. She continued to gaze at her husband with a puzzled look on her face.

"When I walked into the tavern, all the noise stopped and they all stared at me as I walked up to Laggins. He was standing at the end of the bar, where Guillermo said he would be. To my great surprise, he was drinking a depth charge. When I told him that a depth charge was an honored drink in Nugget Valley, and that only the very best miners were allowed to drink it, he seemed to soften. After that, we had a very enjoyable conversation and he told me to drop by his office so we could begin working together."

"Just what is a depth charge?"

"You drop a shot of whiskey, glass and all, in a large glass of beer and drink it down on one gulp."

"It sounds awful," Kenzie said, wrinkling her nose. "Pray tell, who would want to drink such a concoction?"

"The best miners in Nugget Valley and the captain of the correction officers at Sycamore Hospital are the only ones I know of."

"What about you? Would you drink a depth charge?"

"Heavens no! Whiskey makes me crazy. Besides, I wasn't genetically gifted enough to be one the best miners in Nugget Valley."

"Are you sure that you are not overacting a bit, my love? Before yesterday, all you could say about the captain was that he was a hard nose, took over the hospital, ran things with an iron fist, and would be a problem for you. These were your words. Maybe you need to get to know him a little better before you decide exactly who he is."

"No, I don't think so, Kenzie. I haven't trusted my feelings in a long time and, as you know, I sure as hell haven't been patient. But that all changed now. I'm back in touch with my spirit.

"I know that Lynsford Laggins is exactly who I think he is." Mitch got up from the table, kissed Kenzie on the cheek, and said, "I've have to get to the hospital, dearest. I'll see you tonight. Have a good day."

As Kenzie watched her husband hurry out the door, she thought how fortunate Mitch was to be spiritual. It was something she could not be. She tried many times but just could not get it.

When Mitch reached the hospital, he looked at his watch, and saw he had a few minutes before his meeting with Laggins. He decided to stop by Guillermo's office to share his newly found optimism about the captain. When he opened the door to Gerona's office, he ran into Ms. Bascom, arms loaded with a stack of files.

"If you're looking for Dr. Gerona, he won't be in today. He's a bit under the weather and is taking the day off. He said if you need to speak with him, call him at home," the secretary called out, her face nearly hidden by the stack of files.

"Is he OK?" Mitch asked a look of alarm on his face. It was not like his Cuban friend and mentor to call in sick. It wasn't something he did.

"Oh, he's fine. Maybe it's a touch of the flu. He's looked a little peaked the last few days. He said he'd be in tomorrow." Ms. Bascom set the files on her desk.

"If he calls in, tell him that my meeting with Captain Laggins went well, and we're meeting again today, to start things moving," Mitch said, as he left the room. Try as he might, he could not erase the thought that things were not well with his friend and mentor.

When Mitch entered the captain's office he found him sitting at his desk, hunched over a box of photographs he was studying intensely. The captain did not look up, so Mitch took a seat in front of the desk. The walls were covered with framed pictures, mostly of Laggins dressed in his Marine Corps uniform accepting military awards, and standing over prized trophy kills, wearing hunting clothes, holding high-powered rifles. There was one framed letter. Mitch walked over to the wall to read it. He took a step backward and shook his head as he read the letter, written on presidential paper, and signed by President Richard M. Nixon, awarding the Marine Corps Commendation Medal to Lynsford Lee Laggins, posthumously.

"I sent the medal back but framed the letter. I keep it on the wall to remind myself each day that I'm damn lucky to be on this side of the grass," Laggins said, looking up from the photographs.

Mitch smiled and returned to his seat. This large powerful man, surrounded by military and trophy hunting pictures, reminded him of Earnest Hemingway. Not sure of what he wanted to say, he decided to be quiet and let Laggins set the stage for the meeting.

"You know, Dr. Gainer, I was surprised to see you walk into the Ding Dong Tavern last night." Laggins twirled a letter opener that looked more like a dagger in his hands.

"I apologized for that," Mitch offered weakly. "I had no business bothering during you during your leisure hours. I just wasn't thinking."

"Oh, I think you were thinking a lot, Dr. Gainer," Laggins said, cleaning his finger nails with the letter opener. "You had to know the Ding Dong is off limits to Sycamore personnel who are not correctional officers. Hell, they're afraid to drive by the place, let alone go in there. You walked right in the front door last night like you owned the damn place."

"That's not the way I felt, Captain. I knew I was treading on someone else's turf and it wasn't my idea, to tell the truth. It was Gerona's. He suggested that I meet you there."

"I like the Cuban," Laggins said, setting the letter opener down, and inspecting his immaculate nails. "He's got balls and he's smart. It's too damn bad he didn't come here earlier. If he would have, things may have been different now. It's too late now. It's just a matter of time until they close the doors."

"I know, but the doors are still open. Tell me about this place."

"Sycamore Hospital has never functioned as a hospital treating mentally ill people in the criminal justice system. It's always been a maximum-security prison to house the most deranged and difficult inmates."

"Why do you think that's the case?" Mitch asked, thinking that this man was lot smarter than he previously thought.

"All I can tell you is what I have seen since I came here, after I left the Marines in '68, and what I can piece together from talking with people who have been here for years."

Laggins retrieved a package of Red Man Chewing Tobacco from his desk drawer and loaded his mouth with the loose-leaf tobacco. "A habit I picked up in the hollers of West Virginia when I was a boy," he said, leaning back in his chair and placing his massive arms across his stomach.

"Those were the best days of my life. We had no money, lived off the land, built our own cabins, and knew few people who weren't kin. I learned early how to hunt and shoot with best of them. I also learned how to take care of myself, if I had to."

Suddenly a look of sadness came across his broad face, and he said, in a voice not much louder than a whisper, "Never went to school. Never had a chance to learn to read and write."

Mitch was stunned. How could a man who never went to school and could not read and write rise to the station of life where Laggins now was?

"Well enough of that," Laggins said abruptly.

"No, no," Mitch said cutting him off. "This is more important. I would like it if you would tell me how you were able to get where you are today, in spite of not knowing how to read or write. What you've accomplished is remarkable."

"When I was about fifteen, I got to know a man who came to the holler to hunt boar. He owned a trucking company in Charleston. I was big for my age, and he thought I was older than I was. He offered me a job driving trucks. Hell, I had never driven a car, let alone a truck. My father didn't even own a car. If we wanted to go somewhere, we walked.

"I threw some clothes in a gunny sack and left the holler for good. He took me to Charleston, and since I had no money, he fixed up a cot for me at the terminal. I lived there for the year I worked for him."

"What!" Mitch was grinning from ear to ear.

"The cot was just fine, and I wanted to save some money. Besides I was on the road most of the time and slept in the sleeper behind the seat. I wasn't at the terminals that much, only long enough to pick up another load and hit the road again."

Mitch was awestruck at what he was hearing. "Did it take you long to learn how to drive? After all you'd never driven before."

Laggins began to chuckle. "It's funny now that I think about it. The boss never asked me if I could drive a truck. As soon we got to Charleston, he told me that a driver was taking a load out and to jump in the truck with him. He said the driver would teach me all I had to know. All the driver said to me was 'My name is Slim. Throw your bag in the sleeper. You'll take over in two hours.' "

"That's unbelievable. What did you do?"

"I just watched what he did. I knew that he wouldn't tell me anything if I asked him. I've always had a good memory and I memorized every move he made. When it was my turn, I just got behind the wheel and took over."

"Weren't you frightened? Weren't you afraid you'd kill yourself of someone else?"

"No, I don't frighten easily. Oh, once when I was about ten, a wild boar charged me. I was leaning against a tree and only had one bullet in my .22 rifle. My heart was beating fast when he got within ten feet of me, which could've been a sign that I was frightened. But I pulled the trigger, hit him dead center between the eyes, and dropped him right at my toes.

"Compared to that experience, driving a truck for the first time was nothing."

"It was much more than nothing." Mitch said sharply.

"Not really, Dr. Gainer. Driving a truck is not that hard. All you have to do is shift the gears smoothly, not flood the engine, and pay attention to where you are going. Besides, I've been blessed with good motor skills, excellent hand eye coordination and peripheral vision, as well as steady nerves. If I didn't have these skills, I may have been in trouble."

"You said you only drove truck for one year. What did you do after that?"

"I was in a barber chair in Charleston and a Marine recruiter was in a chair next to me. He said he could tell I'd make a fine Marine, and to drop by the recruiting office next door when the barber finished with me. And I did. Later that afternoon, I was on a bus heading for Paris Island."

As he listened to Laggins, Mitch was reminded of that day, years ago, when he was not a whole lot older than Laggins had been, when he jumped on a bus in Spokane and headed for Canada, and an adventure that changed his life forever. "Weren't you too young to enlist in the Marines?"

"I just turned sixteen and I think the age minimum was seventeen, but I told them I was eighteen and they didn't question it. The Korean War was going on and they needed people. They weren't asking a lot of questions."

"What about your limited reading and writing ability? Did that ever hold you back while you were in the Marines?"

"That was never an issue. Reading and writing is not what the Marines are about," Laggins growled, his eyes turning a steely gray. "It's about being a soldier and one who knows how to fight to win at all costs. If I can say so myself, I was damn good at it. I took to it naturally.

"There was no uncertainty about what the Corps expected of you. All you had to do was to respond rapidly to all commands.

I liked the physical challenges, and I was victorious more often than not. I was best rifleman in my unit, and the first in every one of the drills they put us through in basic training.

"What I learned most of all in the Marines, Dr. Gainer, was how to lead men. The Corps rewarded me for doing that. I was dead set on being a Marine for life, but one day—for reasons, I still do not understand—I no longer wanted to respond to the commands. So when my time was up in Vietnam, I got out. There are times that I have regretted that decision. But it is what it is."

Even though Mitch would have liked to explore this topic more, he decided that he had questioned Laggins enough. He changed the subject. "I was thinking—as I listen to you talking about your life in the holler, driving trucks, and in the Marines—how much confidence in yourself you had at such an early age. It took me years until I reached that level of belief in myself. I wish I would've had that insight at such an early age."

"That I learned from my father. He always taught that I could do just about anything I wanted to do if I put my mind to it. He said, it's always up to you. That's what I've always done and for the most part have been successful. I know when things are out of my reach. If they are, I let them be. I'm a very simple man, Dr. Gainer, and I try to live my life that way."

"A simple man, Captain Laggins, you're not. You're one of the most complex people I've ever met," Mitch said, smiling. "I'll bet you even taught yourself how to read and write."

"Oh, I've learned a little, Dr. Gainer, enough to get by. But not without help. I still go down to the federal building and sit in on classes with foreigners who are learning how to read and write English as they prepare for citizenship. In fact I even help the teachers out. I have also, over the years, used private tutors to build my vocabulary and writing skills. You can't do everything by yourself. The Marine drill sergeants taught me that."

"Lessons learned," Mitch said. "Now I need you to teach me some things. How do I make my first changes at Sycamore Hospital? I want to do away with the rule that patients cannot rock in the ward rocking chairs. I want return the social workers to the ward."

"Teach you!" Laggins exclaimed. "Hell, you're the leader. Just command, command. That's all you have to do and they'll follow."

"Unlike you, Captain Laggins, I wasn't raised in the holler and didn't learn to live off the land. I know I'm the leader and they'll do as they're told. But that does guarantee success? Success is all I'm interested in. To get that, I need you to teach me how to live off the land here at Sycamore. There are as many wild boars here as there are in the holler."

Laggins roared with laughter, pushed back in his chair, and slapped his leg. "Damn good analogy, damn good analogy," he said, shaking his head. "I suspected you were a smart one the first time I saw you in action with the correctional officers. Now you've shown me you know how to use your smarts. I could tell by the look on your face that you were surprised when I used the word 'analogy.' That didn't come from the holler. That came from years and years of working crossword puzzles. Just tell me what you want to know."

"What's the power structure around here? Who really runs things?"

"That's a real good question," Laggins said, in a more serious tone. "On paper, the hospital superintendent is in charge of everything. The second level of command includes the heads of the various departments: administration, medical, security, housekeeping, dietetics, and maintenance. If you're really are interested in who really runs this hospital, I'll tell you in confidence."

"Please do."

"This place is run by security, and the various power gangs among the inmates. At present, that includes the blacks, the Latinos, the hillbillies, the skinheads, and the old cons who are just here pulling time."

"That is shocking!" Mitch got out of his chair, turning his back on the captain. He walked over to the window, placed his hands on the sill, and peered outside, as if he were searching for something.

Laggins waited until Mitch returned to his chair before continuing. "I'll give you a little history which I think will help you understand how things became what they are today. At the beginning, the hospital was run by the hospital superintendents, with total control, and a firm hand on things. Since the institution was also a working farm and produced woodwork, the inmates or patients were kept busy, working in the fields and making furniture. Security was less of an issue then, with the exception of inmates' occasionally running away.

"However, things changed when the institution moved away from farming and making furniture. The patients became idle. As the number of inmates with behavior problems transferred here from the prisons, courts, and state hospitals increased, security became more of an issue. The security staff increased significantly. Unfortunately. the inmates who came here tended to remain here for long periods because the prisons, courts, and hospitals didn't want them back. Sycamore Hospital became overcrowded."

"It sounds like Sycamore became a place to house 'difficult patients,' rather than treat them," Mitch interjected, thinking that Laggins would make a fine teacher. "What about the superintendents? You would think since they were physicians, they would have instituted treatment."

"They may have tried in the beginning, but I seriously doubt it. Over the years, they became political hacks and figureheads who were content to let security keep the peace. The general public paid little attention to Sycamore, except when they heard on the news or read in the paper that a patient was abused. They paid attention until things settled down. Then they went back to ignoring what is going on here. Sycamore is not really part of their lives."

"It strikes me as ironic that the last superintendent they hired is not a hack but probably the best person in country for the job," Mitch said, looking a trifle put out.

"You're right on that, Dr. Gainer. I was shocked they would hire such a competent person."

"Fortunately, corrections were not in charge of recruiting. It was Graciela Cevallos, the head of mental health, who recruited Gerona. She knew exactly how competent he was since she was one of his students at the Cleveland VA. If she wanted a stooge as superintendent, she would have never come after Gerona."

"Well that sure explains things," Laggins said, spewing tobacco juice in a paper cup. "They must have used her to give the public the impression that they were interested in making a sincere effort to reform Sycamore."

"It's long been my impression that when you listen to bureaucrats and politicians, you should pay as much attention to the exact opposite of what they are saying, as you do to what they are telling you," Mitch said smiling.

"But I don't think that's the case with Graciela Cevallos. I took some classes with her in graduate school. She's a real dynamo and very, very bright. I don't believe that she would be part of a scheme to set up a fellow Cuban, a man she holds in high esteem. She really believed that if anyone could change this place it would be Guillermo Gerona. Of that I'm certain."

"How did Gerona handle it when he found out that they were always going to close Sycamore?"

"To be honest with you, he dismissed it. All he said was something like, 'that's politicians for you. I'm going to do what I came here to do, for as long as I'm here.' That is the kind of man Guillermo Gerona is."

The red telephone on the desk rang. Laggins reached for the receiver, then held it to his ear briefly before hanging up. "Sorry Dr. Gainer, duty calls, "he said, reaching for his hat and rushing out of the room.

CHAPTER 9

Today, Mitch would show Kenzie the sights of Indianapolis and honor her request to take her for a drink at the Ding Dong Tavern. She would drive in early in the morning from the university, and they would spend the night at his Sycamore residence. He was sitting on the sofa, reading the New York Times, eagerly awaiting her arrival.

Kenzie, her arms loaded with musical scores and an overnight bag, burst in the front door. She put the music and bag on a sturdy oak table.

"Mitch, this furniture is incredible. Is it Amish furniture? I know there are some Amish in Indiana. I'll bet it's handcrafted and antique." She sat in a rocking chair and gently rocked back and forth.

"You'd better be careful. This is one of the same rocking chairs on the wards. As I told you, inmates are not allowed to rock in them. If they not allowed, than neither are you. After all, we're on hospital grounds and rules must be followed," Mitch said, smiling.

He shook his finger at her and flopped in the other rocking chair and began rocking as hard as he possibly could. "I may not be able to change much around here, but I'll put an end to that rule. It's criminal not to let human beings rock in rocking chairs."

The telephone rang. Mitch let it ring, hesitant to answer because he was not due at the hospital until tomorrow morning. He did not want any interruptions on the special day he had planned for Kenzie. But as it was not in his nature to let phones ring, he picked up the receiver.

"What! Is he OK? Give me the address!" Mitch scribbled the address down on a note pad, hung up the receiver, and hugged Kenzie, tears welling in his eyes.

"Guillermo's taken ill. We need to go to Methodist Hospital now. Will you drive?"

When Mitch and Kenzie arrived at the hospital, they were met at the main desk by Ms. Bascom. "You must be Kenzie," she said, holding out her hand. "I greatly admire your music."

"Thank you," Kenzie said, taking the woman's trembling hand in hers.

"This is Donna Bascom," Mitch said to Kenzie, looking a little annoyed. "She's Guillermo's administrative assistant." Turning to Ms. Bascom, he asked, "Have you seen Guillermo? Is he OK?"

"Yes, he's going to be just fine. Right now, he's in his room sedated, sleeping peacefully. You can't see him now. They won't allow visitors until tomorrow so he can rest. He told me to tell you he would call you then."

"What happened?" Mitch noticed that Ms. Bascom's usually bright face was now gray. She looked exhausted and appeared to be unsettled.

"Come, Ms. Bascom," he said taking her arm and leading her to a nearby sofa. "Let's sit here a moment. What happened?"

"Well ... well ... we were going over some reports," she stammered. "He was chuckling over some badly written sentences when suddenly he reared back in his chair, clutched his chest, and gasped for air. And then, foam came out of his mouth and he turned gray and slumped in his chair. It was horrible!" She burst into tears.

Kenzie took her in her arms, dried her tears, and patted her on the back. Ms. Bascom quickly composed herself and continued with her story.

"I'm sorry for the outburst. At first I thought he was dead but I found a pulse. I loosened his tie and shirt so he could breathe better and called for an ambulance. A doctor was in the building and he rode to the hospital with us and gave him a shot and some oxygen."

"I take it he had a heart attack," Mitch said, noticing that some of the color had returned to Ms. Bascom's cheeks. "He's fortunate that you were there. You're a remarkable woman. You really know how to respond to an emergency."

"I've had plenty of experience," Ms. Bascom said. For the first time, a slight smile appeared on her face. "At first, the doctor thought he had a myocardial infarction but tests showed that he has angina pectoris. Fortunately, there was no damage to his heart.

"The doctor said that he is healthy and strong. He'll have to slow down, change his diet, and throw away those smelly Cuban cigars that he sneaks out to smoke every chance he gets. They'll probably keep him here until tomorrow, then discharge him."

"Can we see him tomorrow?" Mitch asked.

"I doubt that he wants any visitors, Dr. Gainer. I suspect that's why he told me to tell you he would call you in the morning. Knowing him, he'll call early, before you come to the hospital for your meeting with Captain Laggins. He's a strong man and he wants to let you know he's in still in control of things."

"He certainly is a strong man, and you too, are a strong woman, Ms. Bascom. See you tomorrow," Mitch said. Maybe what he thought was a complete disaster would not be so bad after all.

An Abbey Returned

"It's been a pleasure meeting you, Ms. Bascom. I hope we see more of one another," Kenzie said, taking Mitch's arm as they left the hospital.

When Mitch turned the key to start the engine, he said, "I'm beat. Why don't we go back to the house and relax. We can do Indianapolis and the Ding Dong another time, when things are brighter."

"Agreed."

"We can pick up some Chinese food and a couple bottles of plum wine."

"Sounds good," Kenzie said, putting her hand on Mitch's.

The Chinese food, plum wine, and a radio station playing endless Mozart set the tone for conversation. Mitch began,"I thought that Guillermo might be in bad health when I first saw him. He looked tired and washed out, but he insisted that he was fine. He did act like his old self. It had to be a real strain on him to give up his practice, and uproot his family to take a job that turned out to be a scam. This certainly contributed to his angina. The whole damn thing makes me angry as hell. It's just not fair!"

"I know. The main thing is that he's going to be OK. That's what we have to focus on. What can we do to help him?

"There's not much we can do, other than wait for his call tomorrow. If he said he'll call me tomorrow, he will. He'll tell us what he needs, what he's going to do, and how we can help him— if he actually needs any help."

"Are you worried about what changes this means for you?"

Mitch poured another glass of plum wine. He stared into the glass for a few moments before taking a drink. "You're a very insightful woman. You ask me questions that I need to consider, but don't want to answer."

"Why would you say that?"

"Because I don't wanted to make this about me. It's about Guillermo."

"Yes it is. But it's also about you. Guillermo's illness changes everything for you. You're not being selfish if you have concerns about how this affects you."

"It affects you, too, because I've brought you into it. I know that I can't abandon Guillermo and that means I can't abandon Sycamore. It means I'll be covering for him until he gets back, and that will involve more time and commitment. That's not fair to you. We're here because of your residency. I feel I will be taking time away from that and it worries me. It makes me feel like I'm on a fool's errand, when I should be focusing on what I came here to do—to experience your residency with you."

Kenzie began to chuckle. "Maybe you should take some lessons so we can rehearse together, and both really experience my residency."

Mitch began to laugh. "I guess my tendency to melodrama shows itself again. The only valid thing I said was feeling that I may be on a fool's errand. Guillermo's illness means if I am, I am by myself."

"No you're not, Mitch. I'm there with you, and have been since the moment you told Guillermo you would come to Sycamore Hospital. You just need to finish the job. Let's go to bed. I want to feel you next to me."

Ms. Bascom was right. The telephone rang as soon as Mitch pulled back the covers and got into bed.

"Guillermo! I'm glad you called."

"I hope I didn't get you out of bed. I wanted to catch you before you go to the hospital."

"You didn't. You know I'm an early riser." Mitch was surprised and pleased that Guillermo spoke in a strong voice. He certainly did not sound like a man who had just had a heart attack.

"I'll be leaving for Miami as soon as I can make arrangements. Benita and the family are at our vacation home."

"That's good," Mitch said, knowing that his friend would not want to talk about the real reason he was going to Miami. "I'll hold the fort down until you get back."

"That's what I want to talk to you about, Mitch. I'm afraid I've gotten you into a pickle and I'm sorry for that."

"You didn't get me into any pickle," Mitch snapped. "I knew what I bought into. It's not over, Guillermo. In fact, I think we're just beginning. Now you tell what you want me to do."

"Is Laggins on board?"

"I think so. I have a meeting with him to implement some changes."

"Good. You need to work with Graciela Cevallos. She's the only power base we've got."

"I meet with her after I see Laggins."

"No, meet with her before you do anything else."

"Got it."

"The nurse will be here in a few minutes so I'll have to sign off."

"Before you do, I have a couple of questions for you. "When will you get out of the hospital?"

"This afternoon or tomorrow."

"How are you traveling to Miami?"

"I'll either fly or take the train."

"Are you giving up your cigars?"

"No!"

As soon as he hung up, Mitch turned to Kenzie. "I'm cancelling my meeting with Laggins. Let's go back to Bloomington. I need to get out of here so I can think things through, and decide what I need to do next."

Mitch was unusually quiet on the ride back to Bloomington. When they were halfway there, Kenzie turned on the radio and found the "Bolero." "There's one of our favorite pieces of music, Mitch," Kenzie said playfully.

"It certain is," Mitch said, his mind drifting back to that night in Halifax, in his room above the Irish tavern Brogan's Bog, where he and he Kenzie met and made love for the first time. It was the highlight of his life.

"What have you been thinking about?"

"Guillermo told me that before I do anything, I need to meet with Graciela Cevallos. He didn't tell me why he wanted me to meet with her. All he said was that she was the only power base we had."

"If I remember right, you told me she was one of his students at the VA, and the one who hired him for this job."

"That's her. She's the director of mental health for Indiana and a real sharp cookie. But it bothers me that I don't know why he wants me to meet with her. He's never said, or even hinted, that she would be a part of our work at the hospital."

"Maybe she's always been involved, and he just did not tell you."

"No, Kenzie, that's not his style. If that were the case, he would have told me. Guillermo is not secretive. He's upfront about everything. That's what I like about him. Enough shop talk," he blurted, turning off the radio. "The first thing we're going to do when we get back to our place is put on 'Clair de Lune,' go to bed, and read.

CHAPTER 10

After three stops at different convenience stores to ask for directions, Mitch found the small restaurant called Inocencio's. The restaurant stuck out like a sore thumb in this semi-industrial area bordering downtown Indianapolis.

When Mitch opened the restaurant door, he was overwhelmed by the sounds of rumba music and the smell of heavy cigar smoke. Feeling slight beleaguered, he remained in the doorway and took in the scene. There was a small bar with a Cuban flag on the wall behind it, several small tables, and booths. A large ceiling fan twirling slowly gave the restaurant a tropical flavor. It was an immaculate and pleasant place.

"Dr. Gainer."

Mitch closed the door and came nearly face to face with Graciela Cevallos. He felt foolish standing in the doorway, and really did not know to say, so he just smiled.

Graciela returned his smile. "This place takes a little getting used to but, as they say, the food is good. Dr. Gainer, this is Inocencio Melendez, the proprietor."

Mitch shook the hand of the tall man with a full head of wavy black hair and a thick mustache. He wore a baby-blue guayabera, the traditional Cuban short-sleeved, embroidered linen shirt favored by Guillermo. "It's a real pleasure to meet you, sir. You have a fine place here."

"The pleasure is mine, Dr. Gainer," the man said, in a heavy Cuban accent. "Follow me please." The dapper proprietor led them, as if he were leading a conga line, to a room in the back of the restaurant.

"This is our VIP room," he said, seating them across from each other, at the end of a table set for eight. "May I offer you a drink?"

"Sounds good. I'll have a mojito," Graciela said.

"I'll have a Bucanero, no glass please," was Mitch's reply.

Inocencio clicked his heels, closed the door, and left the room.

"I hope it wasn't a hassle, finding Inocencio's. I know my directions are not the best," Graciela said, flashing a big smile.

"No problem at all," Mitch said, tongue-in-cheek. "Your directions were just fine, and besides, I'm pretty good at sniffing out restaurants."

Graciela broke out in laughter. "How many stops did you have to make for directions?"

"Only three pit stops, at convenience stores," Mitch responded with a grin.

"When Inocencio came to Indianapolis, from Little Havana in Miami—where he had been the best chef in the area—he wanted to open a small restaurant for the local Hispanics. He did not want it to become a tourist trap, so he chose a location where there were no restaurants, and in an area where people would not look for restaurants. Inocencio often said he knew that once one person came through the door and tasted his food, they would invite another person, and that person would invite another person, and so on. In his words, 'My restaurant is by invitation only.' That's why I invited you to Inocencio's for our meeting."

There was a rap on the door and a young Latina with a fresh yellow rose in her hair and an ear-to-ear smile appeared with their drinks. "We're serving Ropa Vieja today," she announced, flashing her sparkling white teeth.

"We're very lucky. Inocencio is serving Cuba's national dish. It is his specialty and he's received many awards. It will go good with your Cuban beer."

"That's what I'll have," Mitch said, thinking he would have instead preferred a Cubano sandwich, his favorite Cuban food.

"This is delicious, truly delicious," Mitch exclaimed, after taking his initial bite of the robust Cuban stew.

"Ropa Vieja literally translates to old clothes," Graciela began. "The story goes that once a penniless old man shredded his clothes and cooked them because he did not have enough money to feed his family. He prayed over the boiling concoction and a miracle occurred, turning the clothes into a rich, tasty, meat stew. The recipe originated in Spain some 500 years ago, and travelled to the Caribbean and Cuba with the Spanish. People say the shredded beef and vegetables resemble a heap of colorful rags."

Mitch glanced at his plate. "I can see why they say that. It is an attractive and colorful dish, easy to look at. With a little imagination you could see a lot of things in it." He set his fork down. He was trying hard not stare at the sparkling dark-brown eyes with their long lashes that lit up Graciela's face like a neon sign. It was a slightly narrow face, with smooth olive skin, high cheekbones, a square chin, and provocative lips. Her broad smile made her face warm and inviting.

"Are you saying Ropa Vieja is like a Rorschach test?" Graciela asked, in a teasing fashion.

"Why would you ask me that?" Mitch dropped his fork and sat up straight in his seat.

"If you think back to your days at Ohio State, you'll figure it out," she replied, still being playful.

Mitch broke out laughing. "I always thought you were a clever lady. Now I know for sure that's what you are. You're referring to the one class we took together as graduate students. If I remember correctly, we never spoke to each other, or had any interaction. It was a class in projective tests, taught by the acclaimed psychiatry professor, Dr. Wellford Gork."

"You're spot on," Graciela added. "Dr. Gork asked you to evaluate the Rorschach, and your response was classic."

"I wouldn't use that word," Mitch said, shaking his head. "Foolhardy describes it much better."

"It's anything but that, Dr. Gainer. I can still the look on that pretentious professor's face when you answered him. He turned red, gasped for air, stuttered, and fled the classroom. In fact, I can remember exactly what you told him. You said, 'the test may have some value if the patients would interpret the results, rather than the psychiatrists.'"

"I knew I could blow everything if I told him what I really thought. After all, Dr Gork was the most powerful professor in the department and could make it so I would not get my doctorate. With one stroke of the pen, he could have labeled me unsuitable for the degree and recommend that I be asked to leave with a master's degree in hand."

"Then why did you do it, when you know how he would or could respond?"

"Like I said, I may have been foolish, but not stupid. Chinook had taught me, as a kid, to always be honest in your answers. But he also taught me to think ahead to what reaction my honesty may bring before responding.

"As I said, I knew my response would make Dr. Gork livid. I also believed that he was a vindictive bastard who would keelhaul me if he could. But I also knew he could not do anything before the end of the term, and he would have to turn in a failing grade for me, to justify my elimination from the program. He knew I was an A student. He could not justify a grade lower than a B, just for my remarks.

"If you recall, on last day, I asked, in front of the class, if he would explain to us the new process students could use for appealing grades they thought were unfair. And I also let him know that I would use this process, if I thought it was necessary. I even hinted that it might be a good idea to seek legal counsel as well.

"He shunned me and gave a B, which is what I thought he would do. I earned an A, but didn't appeal it because of my foolishness in answering his question. I should have told him that I preferred not to answer the question, and let it go at that."

"I'm very impressed, Dr Gainer. You did think it all out. I do recall your asking about the appeal process, and Dr Gork getting red-faced again, telling us to go ask student services. I'll admit I always wanted to talk you about your response to Dr Gork, which I and the other students applauded.

"I apologize for bringing this up now but mojitos, even one, do make me a trifle playful. If you don't mind, I'll ask you another question before we get to work."

There was rap on the door, and the waitress entered with two doncellitas, a Cuban after-dinner drink with crème de cocoa and heavy whipping cream, topped with a maraschino cherry. "The meal is with the compliments of Mr. Melendez. He's asked me to give you this, Dr. Gainer," she said, handing an envelope to Mitch.

Mitch opened the envelope, read the note, and announced, "Well, I guess I've met Mr. Melendez's standards. He has invited me to invite another person of my choice to Inocencio's," he said, raising his glass to Graciela. "You said that you had another question. I'll be glad to respond if we drop this 'doctor' business. Call me Mitch, and I'm going to call you Graciela. I've always like the name, and you have given me the first chance to use it."

"Agreed. I like Mitch as well," Graciela said, raising her glass. "I'm interested in who this Chinook was who taught you so much when you were a child."

"It's very difficult for me to explain Chinook to you since he was many things to me," Mitch said, in a serious tone. "On the surface, he was a lame, alcoholic gambler named William Swindle who owned a brothel in the mining camp where I was born and raised. He became Chinook when an Indian chief found his mother giving birth, behind an old boxcar on an Indian reservation. His mother knew she was dying, and asked the chief to take her son. He did and renamed the boy Chinook, after the warm, dry wind that was blowing when he found him.

"Later Chinook seriously damaged his leg when he fell off a freight train he'd 'hopped,' leaving the reservation. As a result, his damaged leg became shriveled and was shorter than his other leg, causing him to walk in a scissor-like fashion. He wore a high-heeled boot on the leg and used a cane.

"Although he was impaired, he clearly was not disabled. He had this magnificent cane, with a solid-gold coyote-head handle, which he used as a weapon. He could move as quickly as anyone I've ever known, and could hike mountain trails with the best of them.

"He took me under his wing when I was a young, lonely, somewhat isolated child. He protected me and taught me life lessons that I still rely on today. He was a very spiritual man and introduced me to the Indian ways, and taught me to look within myself, rather relying on others for answers. Best of all, he taught me about people from all walks of life: how to 'read' them and how to interaction with them.

"When we buried him in the sacred Indian ground, he did not leave me. It's like he's always with me. I can close my eyes and see him. I can ask him a question in my mind, and I can hear him answer. When I'm in a tight situation and need help, I can ask myself, what would Chinook do? What would Chinook tell me? What did he teach me? I always find my answer when I summon him in my mind, just like when I summoned him in person when I was young. I know that didn't answer your question, but it's the best I can do."

"That was a perfect answer, Mitch. And quite beautiful, I might add. You're very fortunate to have Chinook in your life."

A silence fell over the table and they looked into each other's eyes for a few moments. Graciela suddenly turned her eyes toward her watch, and announced, "it's getting late and I have to be back to office before closing time. We'd better address what you wanted to discuss with me."

"I'm afraid, Graciela, I don't have an agenda," Mitch said, a sheepish look on his face. "I called you because Guillermo told me that before I do anything at Sycamore, to meet with you first, because you were the only power base we have. He didn't tell me why I should meet, with or what we should discuss—only that I should meet with you. He was quite insistent."

Graciela smiled and rolled her eyes. "That sounds like Guillermo. He likes to operate in the gray areas. I guess that's what we'll have to do. I don't know why he wanted you to meet with me. I'm not connected with the hospital. I'm the state director of mental health and my role was to find, and submit to the governor, a top mental-health person to take over Sycamore for an interim period. When I submitted Guillermo's name, the governor accepted it, and instructed me to offer him a contract. That's all."

"Why would they do that? You would think that someone in the Corrections Department would do the hiring."

The smile disappeared from Graciela face and she spoke with a strained voice, as if she was trying to force the words out. "Mitch, I'm angry as hell. I know now they used me. When the indictments accusing staff of patient abuse and worse came out, the state was going to close the institution, and would have, had there not been a public backlash. People protested that they were only closing it to cover up criminal offenses. Others were arguing that Sycamore should not be closed, but run as a hospital, not as a prison. They wanted it managed by top-level mental-health professionals, as well as better-trained correctional officers.

"The compromise was that the governor authorizes a national search for a highly qualified, experienced mental-professional to lead the hospital as superintendent. Because the people did not trust the Department of Corrections to do the hiring, the governor wanted someone in the Mental Health Department to conduct the search, and oversee the hiring process.

"When they approached me for the job, I was hesitant to consider it because I was aware of the politics involved. I had some fears that they were only 'paying lip service' to treatment to appease the public, and only wanted a 'baby sitter' until they could make arrangements to close the place.

"They assured me that was not the case, and there was a reason for a national search for the highest qualified person. He or she would have their full support to reform the hospital, and to develop quality mental health treatment. They also said that this was a 'last ditch effort,' and if these treatments could not be established within a reasonable period of time, then Sycamore would be closed."

Graciela's voice weakened and became throaty. Mitch felt empathy for this woman who was struggling to tell a tale that appalled her. He also felt uncomfortable about this unexpected spark she'd triggered in him. It crossed his mind that this meeting he thought was wonderful, might just turn out to be unfortunate.

Graciela took a drink of water that seemed to sooth her voice, and began again. "I was tempted to ask them to operationally define what they thought was a reasonable period of time, and I should have, but I didn't. I trusted that they were going to give the person a legitimate chance at reforming the institution. The only person I knew who could do that was Guillermo, and that's why he's the only person I contacted. And then I found out, after I talked him into taking the job, they had no intention reforming Sycamore and were going to close it all along," she said, her voice breaking.

Graciela slowly lowered her head and, resting her forehead in her hands, began to weep softly. Mitch reached across the table and took her hands in his. "I think I know why Guillermo wanted me to meet with you. He knew you were hurting, and wanted me to reach out to you because he couldn't."

Graciela dropped her hands and raised her head. "I'm sorry, Mitch. I don't usually make such a spectacle out of myself," she said in her normal voice.

"You didn't make a spectacle out of yourself," Mitch said, still holding her hands. "You've been betrayed, and to be betrayed is the one of worst things. You're a strong woman and you're handling it well. Let's put our heads together and figure out what we're going to do about it. Because if you were betrayed, Guillermo was betrayed. If he was betrayed, then I was betrayed, too."

"But I talked him into taking this job, and moving, and causing him to have a heart attack," she said, sobbing.

"That's utter nonsense and you know it. No one talks Guillermo into anything. This was a great challenge for him, and he was excited to meet it. You know he's a reformer at heart. He saw this as his last opportunity before retiring. He wanted to share it with me and that's why I'm here.

"As far as his heart issues go, it has nothing to do with you or this betrayal. It was obvious to me when I saw him, before any of this happened, that he was ill. Of course, he denied it. But the good thing is that it can be remedied. He may have to watch his diet and cut down on his cigars, but there is no reason why he can't come back all the way."

"I'm not sure what we can do, Mitch. There is a part of me that would like to get revenge, but I know that's not the answer, and would only make things worse."

"You got that right," Mitch said. "Chinook told me when I was a kid to never seek revenge, because it will bite you in the ass every time. When Guillermo told me to contact you for a meeting, he did say that you are our only power source. Why would he say that?"

"Well, I don't know that power would be."

"Guillermo wouldn't have said it if it were not true. Like you said, he likes to operate in the gray areas. I suspect that was the reason he did not tell me what your power source was. It will be up to us to find it.

"For starters, I want you to support me in the reforms I'm going to make at the hospital. Let the powers that be know I am carrying out Guillermo's plan, and that things are the same now as when he was here. We need to publicize this, and may consider letting the media know that changes are being made at Sycamore. Guillermo told me that we had to have the support of the captain of the correctional officers to accomplish anything. We now have it, so I think things are going to move quickly."

"That's great. But you know they're going to close the hospital, and I think it will be sooner rather than later."

"Sniff around a bit and see what you can find out. Downplay things. Give them the impression that you're not concerned about the hospital's closing. You're only concerned about keeping things rolling along at Sycamore. That will confuse the hell of them because they will expect you to be in shambles, and instead you'll be acting as if things are business as usual.

"There is a bit of a mystery about this closure. Why, all of a sudden, are they in a hurry to close this place? If they intend to use it as a typical state institution, they would want a more orderly process, to implement the change. There would be no need to hurry.

"Maybe they want to sell it to some private company. You know this is a valuable piece of property which, I think, would be in high demand. You could make this place an upscale resort, turn it into high-priced condos, apartments, or even a hotel. It would make a fine golf course.

"See if you can find out the legal issues. Does the state own it outright? Did they take it over for taxes, and can they sell to the private sector? See if you can find out what they really want to do with the property. But do it in Sherlock Holmes fashion. Be subtle and follow the clues. I know damn well that there is something fishy about this."

"You're a trip, Mitch Gainer," Graciela said cheerfully. "Before you go, will your wife Kenzie be performing while she's at IU? I'd love to see her in concert. She plays my favorite instrument, and I think she's the very best cellist."

"I know she'll be playing the fiddle with Tullamore Due, an Irish band. She toured with them when I first met her. There'll be a major concert at IU soon and I'm certain she'll play a warm-up concert in the area before she goes back on tour. I'll see that you get tickets," Mitch said, acutely aware that he was married to a superstar.

"Just remember, Mitch," Graciela said, as she gently removed her hands from his, "the powers that be have always governed Sycamore with malignant neglect—treating the place as if it does not exist, completely ignoring all activities that go on, including treatment. This is disgusting, but it does create opportunities for you to develop any programs or make any changes that you wish, without interference. You have a free hand. Use it. Let's stay in touch. You keep doing what you're doing at the hospital, and I'll support you," she said, taking her racing gloves out of her purse. When she opened the door to leave, she abruptly turned around, smiled, and blew him a kiss.

After Graciela departed, Mitch stood as the table for several moments, arms folded across his chest, wondering just what he had gotten himself into.

CHAPTER 11

Mitch was sitting at his desk, staring at the pile of documents stacked there. He had come to office early so he could review the material, in preparation for his important meeting with Captain Laggins. But rather than reviewing the documents, Mitch was searching for a reason to call Graciela Cevallos. He knew that he had no good reason to call her, but he simply could not get her off his mind.

Since their meeting at Inocencio's, Graciela was constantly in his thoughts. He knew that he had feelings for her. This alarmed him and took him back to a time several years ago, when he was smitten for an Episcopal vicar named Abigail that led to a passionate kiss in her church office, then ended quickly with a visit from the bishop and the vicar's leaving the area. It was an experience that he did not care to repeat.

He viewed his attraction to Graciela as a potential threat to his marriage. He had taken Chinook's words to heart when he was young. Chinook had told him marriage was like being in a poker game that you must not to lose. If you did not think you could win, you should never marry, because if you lost, the results were devastating, and long term.

Mitch remembered those words as he got up and headed out for the meeting. He would not act on those feelings. Nor would he call her. He would dismiss her from his mind.

Mitch found Captain Laggins sitting at his desk, with a shoeshine brush in one hand and his boot in the other. He looked up, acknowledged Mitch with a nod, and began vigorously brushing his boot. Apparently satisfied with his work, he inspected the boot thoroughly, then put it on. The brush went back into his desk drawer.

"It's a practice I developed in the Marine Corps. Unless I'm in the field, I never report for duty in shoes or boots that are not highly shined."

"Neither do I," Mitch said, pointing to his highly buffed Bass Weejuns. Both men began to laugh.

"I suppose you have pennies in those penny loafers."

"Certainly, an Indian head penny in each," Mitch replied.

"That's good, very good. I like that," Laggins said, smacking his lips together. "I'm sorry I had to run out on you, without explanation, last time. It was necessary, I assure you."

"Nothing to be sorry for. When duty calls, you have to respond immediately." Mitch watched Laggins load his cheek with a wad of Redman Chewing Tobacco. The aroma of the leafy tobacco filled the room. Mitch was surprised that its fragrance was on par with his best pipe tobacco.

"I'll explain things to you now," Laggins said, leaning back in his desk chair. "If you remember, I told you that Sycamore is really a prison, run by security and the various power groups among the inmates. It's essential that the power structure remain in balance. If it's out of whack, bad things can happen."

Mitch nodded.

Laggins adjusted the tobacco in his mouth with his tongue and continued. "There is a snitch hotline where the patients can relay information to security, so we can maintain this delicate balance, and avoid a crisis.

"When the red phone rings," he said, pointing to the larger of the two telephones on his desk, "I know that something is afoul and I'd better get my ass in gear, locate it, and defuse it. In the situation last week, there was a loose knife on a ward where a new patient was operating a bootleg repair operation."

"What in the hell is a bootleg repair operation?"

"In a prison, Dr. Gainer, thing are pretty much the same as on the outside. Inmates have few personal possessions, and those they have are highly valued. These possessions—say a watch, a chain, a pendant, a radio—may need repair from time to time. There is usually one patient who can fix them, so he starts a repair business. All the patients bring their items to him. They usually pay him for his services with cigarettes, tobacco, and items they can purchase at the commissary. When another patient, usually a new one, starts another repair business, a turf war begins, and someone gets hurt.

"That's what the telephone call was about. They were alerting me that there was a loose knife on the ward."

"I can see why you rushed out of our meeting."

"You have to move quickly and quietly. I appreciated your not questioning me about the call. Nor did you bring it to anyone else's attention, or make a big deal about it. People panic easily around here."

"I knew you would tell me, if you wanted me to know," Mitch said. "Besides, although you moved quickly, you did not seem to be alarmed, and acted as if it was business as usual."

"It was business as usual," Laggins said, with a chuckle. "There was an easy fix. I immediately handcuffed the patient who'd started the new business, confiscated the tools he had in a cigar box, and marched him with a squad of officers to solitary confinement. I purposely left the ward unintended. When we returned several minutes later, the knife was sitting on the officer's desk. In the end, the patients got an attitude adjustment, we got the knife back, and more importantly, peace was restored without anyone getting hurt."

"How often do you get situations like that?"

"At least once a week, more often when the weather is hot, or when something unusual is going on in the institution."

"I'm puzzled about one thing, Captain Laggins. "If the patient had the knife, why didn't he use it? I assume it's because someone snitched on him."

"It's not that at all," Laggins said, putting more tobacco in his mouth, causing his cheek to puff out like a balloon. "The patient never intended to use the knife. It was a signal to me to stop the illegal repair service, and keep the peace.

"If the patient wanted to hurt him, he would do it in more subtle ways. We would see nothing and find him dead or badly injured. Remember, Dr. Gainer, the gangs are not stupid, and they don't want to start something that will bring the hammer down on them all."

Laggins pulled a large bronze key on a chain from his pocket, and held it in front of Mitch's face. "This is the only way out of this place. I have the key and the patients don't. They're locked in and have no way of defending themselves against the forces that run this place. If a riot broke out—and one could've over the bootleg repair services—the patients would remain locked in their areas. They would either be starved out or removed by force.

"The best scenario for them, if the force comes in after them, is that they come out on stretchers rather than in body bags. So for the patients, the best solution is to send me a message, and, like the sheriff of Dodge City, I'll see that order is restored, without any blood being shed."

"Is that always the case?"

Captain Laggins sat up straight in his chair and looked Mitch in the eye. "There's never been a drop of blood! Not on my watch! The patients trust me. They know I'm firm but fair, and don't lie to them.

"I'll admit that they have some fear of me. There have been occasions, not many, when they had firsthand knowledge of my combat skills. And even the meanest and strongest among them want no part of that. So they're content to let me be the sheriff of Dodge City, and call on me often to keep the peace in this pressure cooker that could blow up at any minute."

Mitch was in awe of this large powerful man across from him. "I do believe you would have done very well in Tudor England. You would have kept your head without severing the heads of others, even in the court of Henry the Eighth."

Mitch hesitated and gathered his thoughts. "I have a hard time understanding why a man such as you would tolerate your correctional officers not allowing the patients to rock in the rocking chairs on the wards. It seems to be beneath you."

"Well, Dr. Gainer, it's like this," the captain began. "When I took over Sycamore, I found the correctional officers to be inept at best and atrocious at worst. It was my job to get them in shape, and quickly. The worst of the lot needed an attitude change, so I focused on them first. A couple of sessions, out behind the barracks, did the trick."

"'Out behind the barracks'—what is that?"

"It's a term I picked up in the Corps, when we had to take a few men who just didn't get it, out behind the barracks, for a private discussion: sometimes with a little persuasion and sometimes with a demonstration. It's something that should be implemented only when all else fails."

Suddenly the captain banged his fist on the desk. "Those officers who didn't belong here, the worst of the worst, suddenly realized that this was no place for them and left. Those who stayed realized that things would be different and that patients would be treated with fairness, respect and, most of all, would not be mistreated or abused in any way," he said loudly, small leaves of tobacco and spittle flying from his mouth.

"You put an end to the abuse, didn't you?"

"You're damn right, I did. It hasn't raised its head since I took that first group out behind the barracks, and it won't. If I even get a hint of it, the offender is out of here on his ass. It's one strike and you're out, if you're under my command." Laggins replenished his tobacco supply in his mouth.

"I know, Dr. Gainer, it's difficult for you to understand why the patients are not allowed to rock in the rocking chairs on the wards," Laggins said, in his normal voice. "You, no doubt find it absurd, and you may even think it's abusive. But I can assure you, it's neither. It serves its purpose."

"You're right on that. I do think the whole damn thing is absurd, and frankly unnatural. What in the hell do you do in a rock chair but rock? What other possible purpose could it serve?" Mitch asked.

Laggins leaned back in his chair and folded his arms around his massive chest. "I suspect, Dr. Gainer, you assume I run this place with an iron fist, but nothing could be further from the truth. Everyone must buy in, or things will go to hell quickly. The officers lost a lot of authority when I took over, and I had to give them something under their command so they would understand that they still had some clout around here.

"The chairs are treasured by the state because they are relics of the past that display the excellent woodwork done here at the hospital. They are worth a considerable amount of money, and the state is flooded with attractive offers from private businesses who want to buy them. As you've noticed, the chairs are kept in immaculate condition by the officers.

"When the officers first took over control of the chairs, they prohibited the patient from rocking in them because they were fearful the chairs would be damaged. Apparently some of the 'crazy' patients were rocking so hard, the chairs tipped over.

"The officers take a lot of pride in the chairs, and receive a lot of kudos from both the public and officials who come to the hospital. Since the officers took charge, the chairs have been the 'show items' of Sycamore, and many people visit the hospital just to see them."

"This is amazing," Mitch said. "Maybe I should leave things alone. Maybe I'm trying to fix things that are not broken."

"I wouldn't say that, Dr. Gainer. You asked me to show you how this place operates and that's what I'm doing. You're getting valuable information that most people don't bother to get, so you can make better decisions about what needs to be done here. As far as the rocking-chair issue goes, you now know it serves a purpose.

"The authoritarian and control needs of the officers are focused on the chairs, and not the patients. All I know is that the interactions between the officers and the patients have improved. There are fewer issues on the ward that could result in physical abuse, and I believe it has a lot do with the officers' taking control of the chairs."

There was a period of silence in which both men seemed to be immersed in their own thoughts. Finally Captain Laggins said, "You mentioned, Dr. Gainer, that you want to discuss putting the social workers on the wards."

"I see things a little differently now," Mitch said. "When I first came here, I was astonished to see that the social-service staff was not actively involved with the patients on the wards. How can they do therapy if they are not where the action is? I assumed they were on the losing end of a power struggle with the officers over patient management, and were driven off the wards. I now realize that is not the case.

"The powers that be never wanted the social workers on the wards treating patients, and that's why they gave them correctional officers to begin with. The expectation was that they would make a minimal effort, or lip service, at treatment, and do reports for the legal system—move paper work.

"Since they're closing this place down, it's too late for me to put them on the wards. All that would do is disturb the delicate balance you talk about, and do more harm than good. If I had more time, I would put them on the wards and work them into the process. But that's not to be, Captain Laggins. This has been a very informative meeting. I thank you for your honesty. You've been a great teacher. See you next week." Mitch got up from his chair and left the room.

CHAPTER 12

Graciela Cevallos skillfully wove in and out of the heavy morning traffic, maintaining a speed exactly five miles above the legal limit. A lover of fast cars since adolescence, she always slipped on driving gloves when she got behind the wheel. Her driving skills were respected by the racing teams at the Memorial Speedway. They not only befriended her, but occasionally let her drive their racing cars on the fabled track.

She always felt free and unrestricted when she was behind the wheel of her canary yellow Corvette. But that's not how she felt today. Today, she was tied up in knots. She was recoiling from the spark she'd felt for Mitch Gainer when they met at Inocencio's. It put her in a tizzy because she knew she longed for something from him that she would never get.

And what was also as disturbing was the telephone call from the Department of Corrections commissioner, calling an emergency meeting on the status of Sycamore. She knew this was a sign that the end of the hospital was coming, and she would be facing the biggest failure of her professional career.

Graciela made a quick stop in the women's room to splash cool water on her face in an attempt to snap out of her funk. She freshened her makeup, threw her shoulders back, and left the restroom with a spring in her step. When she went into the commissioner's office, she was greeted with the same scene as always—five men dressed in dark-blue suits, wearing nondescript ties, sitting silently at the end of a long empty conference table. The commissioner sat at the head of the table; his assistants sat two on each side.

Since she knew she was merely the audience and not a participant, she took a seat nearest to the door, leaving a noticeable gap between her, and Commissioner Simpson and his crew of toadies. As soon as she sat down, the commissioner, a gangly emaciated man who was known as "The Skull" by the state's inmates, rose and faced Graciela. She leaned forward to meet his gaze.

"Commissioner Simpson's eyes were deep-set and barely visible, his cheeks were hollow, his lips were puckered, and the skin over his jaw appeared to be stretched so tight, so you could nearly see the bone. There was not a hair on his head, and the only semblance of color was in the tiny dark bags under his eyes.

When the commissioner was in his heyday, he had been known as "The Enforcer" because he was an expert in martial arts, and did not hesitate to aid the officers in quelling any prison riots that may occur. But unfortunately he lost that title, and the respect that came with it, when Lynsford Laggins came on the scene. They'd had a dispute that was taken off hospital grounds and settled behind the Ding Dong Tavern. The end result was that The Enforcer was taken to the hospital by paramedics, while Lynsford Laggins threw down a shot of Wild Turkey and snapped his left index finger back into joint.

The commissioner turned his eyes away from Graciela and focused on the table. He began to speak in a thin, raspy voice. "The governor will not join us today. He was called away to a meeting in Gary, and sends his regrets. However, he has asked me to convey the decision that he has made regarding Sycamore Hospital.

"After many hours of meetings and discussions, he has decided that Sycamore will be closed. All staff are to continue functioning as they are now, until such time as arrangements for patient transfers will be determined." With that being said, the commissioner stood and left the room, followed by his assistants.

Graciela flashed the commissioner a contemptuous smile as he walked by her. It was her way of letting him know exactly how she felt about the so-called meeting, without using words. It was something she had learned from her father.

When the door closed and the silence settled in, Graciela remained in her chair, deep in thought—not about the appalling way she had been treated at the meeting, or the commissioner, or even the betrayal she experienced in her job. Her mind was filled with her father, Mateo. She could see herself as a young child, sitting on the floor at his feet, watching him roll leaves of smuggled Cuban tobacco into long, perfectly shaped cigars in his garage, after putting in a full day of hard labor on the Miami docks. She would walk with him, hand in hand, as they delivered the much sought-after cigars in Miami's Cuban section.

The cigar sales became so profitable that Mateo quit the docks, and was able to start a small business importing legal items. When she was not in school or in bed sleeping, Graciela was with her father at his ever-growing business. She was not just a kid who tagged along behind him as he went through his daily duties. Rather she was his pupil and he was her teacher. He told her at the very beginning, "Graciela, my business is, to me, the small world. I can teach you many things in this small world that will help you when you leave, as you will, and go into the big world."

Mateo systematically taught her about all aspects of his business, starting with bookkeeping and accounting, and moving her through the ins and outs of selling, customer service, personnel, and finally how to negotiate business deals.

When Graciela was in junior high school, Mateo would let her sit in meetings as a note keeper. By the time she was in high school, she was in meetings as a full participant, and was viewed in the community as Mateo's business partner. But what she valued most of all is how he taught her to always keep her emotions out of the business, to maintain an even, low-keyed temperament at all times, and to always focus on the facts, not speculation.

But today, Graciela was having trouble keeping her emotions under wrap. She was angry as hell and a part of her would have liked to smash the idiot commissioner, the governor, and all his henchmen, but that would be revenge. There would be no gain in that. There is only one thing to do, she told herself as she got up. She would focus on what options she had left, if for no other reason than to let them know she was still around.

A glance at the clock on the wall told her it was after five. Her first step would be to go to Andre's, a local watering hole for attorneys and high-level government workers. Justin Overholt, the star attorney of the Attorney General's office, would be sipping his after-work martini. He could fill her in on what had been going on with Sycamore Hospital.

By the time Graciela stepped outside the building and melted in the crowd of workers hurrying home, she realized why she had gotten so angry at the meeting. It wasn't the commissioner, or the way she was treated, or the decision the governor had made to close the hospital. It was because she knew that the closure would force her to work closely with Mitch Gainer, after she had made her mind up it was best to distance herself from him. This is what she wanted, because she knew this spark between them could only lead to pain for her.

That they had connected on a much deeper level at Ignacio's had surprised and shocked her. She knew he was a happily married man, married to a beautiful world-famous cellist. The facts were there to see. There was no future for her with Mitch Gainer, only frustration at best and pain at worst—that had to be avoided. But she really could not avoid him. It was her duty, her moral obligation to set her feelings aside, and do what was best for Sycamore. That meant contacting him and helping him find the best way out of a bad situation.

When she opened the door to Andre's, she spotted Justin, sitting by himself in a corner booth, with his nose buried in the New York Times, sipping a martini. It would be a lot easier if she had a spark for him instead of Mitch Gainer. But that was not the case. Justin, a lanky good-looking man whose youthful face belied his years and earned him the nickname of "the world's oldest teenager," had an unending crush on Graciela. She'd ignored his advances for the two years she had been living in Indianapolis.

Nonetheless, they had developed a friendship, and she admired his mind, and the fact that he was the "star" prosecutor in the Attorney General's office. Jason had ignored lucrative offers from prominent law firms throughout the country, choosing public service instead. In her mind, he was the only attorney she knew who was completely honest and always did what was morally right.

Graciela flipped Jason's newspaper with her finger and sat down opposite him in the booth.

"Graciela, I knew you would be here. That's why I'm hiding my face in the New York Times. This will discourage colleagues from joining me, so you will have a seat and privacy," he said, in his surprisingly deep voice.

"That's very considerate of you, kind sir," Graciela said, her eyes riveted on Cheryl, the owner and the only bartender.

She was standing at the cash register, ringing up a customer's charges. "Love watching Cheryl operate. She has the best hand-eye coordination of anyone I've ever seen. She also has such a quick mind.

"You come here, look at the menu on the blackboard behind the bar, and tell the waitresses what you want. They write it down on a slip of paper, or on their hands, and take it in the kitchen. You get your meal, eat it, walk up to the bar, and when Cheryl sees you, she opens the cash register, and tells you what you owe her—without any paperwork involved. All in her head, and she is spot on with what you ordered and what the bill is. Too bad she doesn't encourage talking. I always wanted to ask her how she does it. She's one of the most efficient people I've ever seen. I wish my father could see her in action. He'd be very impressed."

"It's hard to talk when you're always on task. Cheryl is all business, and we could sure use more like her at the AG's office," Justin said, motioning to a waitress. "Bring the lovely lady a mojito, and another martini, on the rocks, with two blue-cheese olives for me."

Graciela took a sip of her drink, and immediately came to the point. "Justin, what's going on with Sycamore Hospital?"

"You know I'm not a gossip, and don't like relaying what I hear, but I'll make an exception for you because you're special."

"Don't get syrupy. Just tell me what happened at the governor's office," Graciela said abruptly.

"If you insist," Justin said, rolling an olive around on his tongue. "It seems that our governor has landed a big fish filled with cold, hard cash, in exchange for Sycamore Hospital and grounds."

"Who's the fish?"

"His name is Squire Young, and he is the CEO of a newly formed corporation called War Horse."

"Squire Young? I don't know that name. Who is he and since he's paying with cash, is he clean?"

"Very few people have heard of him. He's from Great Britain, and has made his money in the casinos in Europe and, surprisingly on an Indian reservation in Idaho. He also breeds priceless Friesian horses and owns both a NASCAR and an Indy racing team. The answer to your question "is he clean,' is yes. Not even one minor blemish.

"Rumor has it if the gambling laws change in Indiana, they would build a Los Vegas style casino and resort. Since that's a long shot, they'll probably end up building a luxury resort that could easily be converted to a casino, if, and when, the laws are changed." Justin frowned as he watched Graciela reach for her purse, signaling her exit.

"Thanks, Justin, you're a good friend," Graciela said, before she dashed toward the door. Jason held up his glass and stared into it, thinking that there was really little difference between Cheryl and Graciela. They were both on task all of the time and neither said much.

CHAPTER 13

Mitch was at his desk, reliving the invigorating three-day retreat he and Kenzie had spent in a log cabin in Brown County, not far from Bloomington. There they immersed themselves in nature, hiking in the forest, and enjoying the solitude. It took them back to when they were managing Chinook's Mother Loft in Nugget Valley, where they'd spent their spent their best moments in the forest, near the waters of pristine Alpine Lakes. The telephone rang.

"Mitch, it's Graciela!"

"Are you all right? You don't sound like yourself. Did something happen?"

"Yes, something happened. I'm fine," she said, in a much calmer voice. "I didn't mean to alarm you. It's just that I need to talk to you, as soon as I can, about Sycamore. Could you meet me at Inocencio's for lunch around noon, so we can discuss things?"

"I'll be there with bells on."

"Welcome back to Inocencio's, Dr. Gainer," the dapper proprietor said, with a firm handshake and a pat on the back. "Dr. Cevallos is waiting for you in the VIP Room."

Mitch was reminded of Guillermo when his nostrils filled with the fragrance from the large cigars that smoldered in ashtrays, while the diners, mostly men, devoured Cuban cuisine. As he followed Inocencio to the back of the restaurant, he was aware that people were glancing up from their food, and were probably wondering who he was to be getting such special attention.

Inocencio opened the door and waved him into the VIP room. There she was, dressed in a black business suit, wearing no makeup or jewelry. What was most surprising to Mitch was that her usually immaculately styled hair was in disarray. Her eyes were focused on a full glass of red wine on the table in front of her. But, she was still a beautiful woman. That she could not change.

Graciela looked up and flashed him a smile—not her usual ear-to-ear smile, but a very small smile, from the corners of her mouth.

Mitch took a seat across from her but said nothing. After a few moments, Inocencio snapped to attention. "I'll give you a few minutes to settle in. Then I'll send a waitress in for your orders," he said, clicking his heels and leaving the room.

They sat there in silence, Mitch studying Graciela's face while she studied the red wine. Mitch slowly reached across the table for her hands. Just before he touched her, he hesitated, as if he were going to pull back. When their hands clasped together, Graciela's eyes moved from the red wine to Mitch's face, and she smiled broadly.

There was a rap on the door and one of Inocencio's gorgeous young Cuban waitresses, wearing two red roses in her hair, appeared with a tray of drinks and appetizers. "Inocencio sends some appetizers—a mojito cocktail with fresh strawberries for Graciela, and a Bucanero for Mitch.

"Today is our food from the islands. Our special is mofongo. It's a traditional dish from Puerto Rico, and is made with fried plantains stuffed with garlic shrimp, roast pork, and vegetables." The waitress put the food and drinks on the table.

"That's what we'll have," Mitch said, plucking a rose from the waitress's hair. "May I borrow this, Miss? I promise to return it intact after the meal." He carefully placed the rose in Graciela's hair just above her right ear.

"Certainly, sir," the waitress said, smiling as she left the room.

"I can't believe you snatched the poor girl's red rose," Graciela said, shaking her head.

Mitch took a swig of beer. As he swirled the ice-cold liquid his mouth, he became aware he had just done a stupid adolescent thing, and now had to try to explain why. "It was the best thing I could do with what I had to work with, to brighten things up a tad." He looked at the table.

He paused a few moments, looked at Graciela's face, and continued, "And, it's worked. The color is back in your cheeks, and your eyes are sparkling again. Now let's set that aside. Tell me what has happened that has caused you so much distress."

Graciela reached out and patted Mitch's hand. "My feelings are jangled," she said softly. "I'm angry and I'm sad, but mostly I feel stupid, and that's what bothers me the most."

"Stupid, you're not," Mitch said, this time with a smile. "It just doesn't fit you. Let's take the anger first. Why are you angry?"

"The governor has authorized the sale of the hospital. That isn't what bothers me so much, because I always knew that was highly probable. What bothers me most is that I brought Guillermo on, and through him you, into an impossible situation, when I should have known better."

Tears filled her eyes. "I'm sad. Sad mainly because my stupidity has wasted Guillermo's health and your time."

Mitch stood up, took his handkerchief out of his pocket, and reached across the table to wipe the tears from her eyes. He dropped the handkerchief, took Graciela's face in his hands, and kissed her forehead.

There was a rap on the door. Mitch quickly sat down while Graciela sat straight in the chair. The smiling waitress twirled through the door like a dancer, and placed the scrumptious Puerto Rican meal before them.

Apparently, Mitch's kiss on the forehead had put an end to conversation. The meal was consumed in silence, only broken finally when Mitch announced, "This food is truly outstanding."

Graciela laid her knife and fork on the plate, took the red rose from her hair, and placed it on the table. "There is something I need to say." her voice quivered. "I want it all with you, Mitch." She reached across the table and touched him on the cheek, her hand shaking as she caressed him.

Mitch immediately pulled back, his head spinning. He was fighting for control. Kenzie's face was flashing before his eyes, and he knew this was his moment of decision. Whatever he decided to do would have lasting implications that could not be erased.

He moved closer to Graciela, took her hand, kissed it, and held it close to his cheek. After a few moments, he gently placed her hand on the table and sat back in his chair. He took a long look at this stunning, desirable woman. He opened his mouth to speak, but before he could get a word out, Graciela interjected.

"You can save your words. I already know what you're going to say. I'm sorry I put you in this position." She reached for her purse and got up from the table.

Mitch took her his arms, held her tightly, and kissed her deeply. He could feel her long fingernails digging into his back as they clung together in this lingering embrace until Mitch sat her in her chair. He picked up the red rose, placed in her hair, and returned to his seat. No sooner had Mitch sat down, then there was a knock on the door, and the smiling waitress appeared with dessert, followed by Inocencio.

"This is budin de pan," the waitress announced, setting the desserts on the table.

"It's Puerto Rican bread pudding, very spicy, tasting both sweet and salty," Inocencio added.

Mitch took the rose from Graciela's hair, and placed in the waitress's hair. "Thank you, Miss, for the use of the rose. It greatly enhanced our meal," The smiling girl bowed.

"May I offer you an after-lunch drink?" Inocencio asked.

"No thank you," Mitch and Graciela both replied,

"Well, I'll leave you two to your business. I hope to see you more often, Dr. Gainer."

"You will. That's for sure. Your food and hospitality are second to none," Mitch said, standing and shaking the proprietor's hand.

After Inocencio left, the two snuck quick looks at each other. Mitch finally spoke. "Just like you, Graciela, I too want it all, but what I want and what I'll get are two different things. When I was a kid, I was rescued from a dysfunctional childhood by a gambler named Chinook Swindle, who taught me many things that today form the code I live by.

"Since he was a gambler, one of the best, he always explained things in gambling terms. He emphasized that life was like an unending series of poker games, some with big pots and some with small; some important, some not so much. Many times, he told me that the biggest poker game I would face was marriage, and if I sat down at that game, I had to win, because if I lost, it would tarnish me for the rest of my life.

"He also said if I did not think I could win, I should not sit down at the table. That's what he chose to do. Well, I've sat down at that table, and I hold a winning hand, but if I follow my feelings for you, I'll no longer have that."

"Well put," Graciela said, this time with a smile. "Your mentor was a wise man and I like his pedagogical approach. His counsel as regards marriage seems harsh but creditable. I would put our circumstances another way. If we follow our feelings, we'd be playing two ends against the middle. Both of us would get burnt."

"It reminds me of that line in a Johnny Cash song—'I don't like it but I guess things happen that way.' That pretty much sums it up for me." Mitch scratched his head.

"That certainly brings things into proper prospective. There's not much else to say." Graciela folded her hands in front of her, looked to the side and announced, as if she were talking to a person sitting beside her instead of across the table, "It's time we move on, Mitch."

When Graciela turned away from him, Mitch suddenly felt that he'd done something horribly wrong. She looked so vulnerable and he felt so responsible. He was fighting the urge to rush to her, take her in his arms, and comfort her. He started to speak but pulled back because he felt tongue-tied, not knowing what to say.

Graciela reached for a glass of water, took a sip, and looked directly at Mitch, her eyes flashing. "At the meeting, if you can call it that, with the commissioner, I was degraded and ignored. He simply announced that the governor had made the decision to close the hospital, and walked out of the room. After the meeting, a friend told me in confidence, that the governor has received an offer, in cash, from a group of businessmen to buy Sycamore. They want immediate occupancy, which probably explains the sudden closure."

"You said the commissioner did not mention the sale, just said the hospital was closing?" Mitch asked.

"Yes."

"That seems a little odd to me. Maybe they don't want to publicize the sale. You say a group of business men are going to pay with cash. That's unusual. Who are they and what are they going to do with the hospital?"

"They're a corporation called War Horse, from Los Angeles. They want the property to build a luxury resort and casino, if the gambling laws in the state are changed. Their CEO is Squire Young. He made his money in casinos in Europe, and on an Indian reservation in Idaho. He also breeds Friesian horses and owns NASCAR and Indy racing teams."

"Squire Young!" Mitch exclaimed, doubling his fist and smashing it into his other palm. "Do you know if he's English?"

"Yes, he's from Great Britain." She was taken aback by the intensity of Mitch's response.

Mitch folded his arms around his chest, and rested his chin in his now-red palm. "I know Squire Young. Know him well. Hell, I hired him to run the casino at Chinook's Mother Lode on the reservation. Thanks to him, we were able to change what was a corrupt and ineffective gambling hall into one of the finest and most honest casinos in the west. He's a genius, a real Renaissance man who graduated from Cambridge, and has a doctorate in theology from Harvard Divinity School.

"He was raising Friesian horses on some land he leased from the tribe when I came to the reservation. I remember he was getting $50,000 stud fees for his show horses that were in high demand in the movies and circuses.

"He built a beautiful horse farm with stables and an outstanding English Tudor manor, which he left to the tribe when he moved everything to Los Angeles, to be close to Hollywood. If the state is going to sell the property to a businessman, they could not have picked a better one than Squire Young. He has high moral fiber and will make good use of the property. That's for sure."

Mitch had the feeling his words were falling on deaf ears. The faraway look in Graciela's eyes suggested that she was thinking about something else. He knew if he stopped speaking that she would, in her own time, reveal what was really on her mind.

After several minutes, Graciela spoke, "I'm sorry, Mitch. I haven't been attentive."

"I would have never guessed," Mitch said, laughing.

"I've been obsessing over the sale. I'm not obsessive by nature, so this is all new to me. It's very unsettling."

Graciela paused. After taking a deep breath and another drink of water, she continued. "I'm not upset about Sycamore being closed, or the way they used me, or the way I was treated when they made the decision to close the place. That comes with the job, and although I don't like it, I understand it.

"It's because they're selling Sycamore for cash to businessmen who want to build a luxury resort with a casino. The state will get that bundle of cash, which they will immediately find ways to waste, and what do the people get? Nothing. It's just not right. There are a lot of better uses for Sycamore," she said, her voice rising. "I hate to admit, but I would sabotage the deal if I had a chance."

"If it's the sale that's really vexing you, then I think that's the first thing we need to focus on." Mitch paused. "The evolution of Sycamore has been a mystery to me. Think about it—it was constructed as a monastery, complete with catacombs, by a religious order from Europe who, for unknown reasons, did not bother to occupy it. Then the state took it over and turned it into a hospital for the criminally insane."

"Yes, it is unusual, but what does that have to do with the sale?" Graciela asked, appearing a trifle annoyed.

"If I remember right, the hospital has been in existence since 1915. That's many years ago and who knows how the property was transferred then. You should check the records to see what documents exist."

"Mitch, that seems to be a waste of time," Graciela snapped.

"Settle down, Missy," Mitch chortled. "There's a method to my madness. I told you Chinook was my mentor, and when I was young, he willed a piece of property to me. It was sacred Indian land that he had won in a dice game. It's the same land that the tribe eventually built the casino on.

"Like Sycamore, it was very valuable, highly coveted property. Chinook spent his life protecting the property so that one day, he could give it back to the Indians, to whom he believed it rightly belonged. He was on his deathbed when he willed the property to me. He made me promise that I would protect the land as he had, and one day return it to the Indians."

"That's a tall order for a young boy." Graciela's voice softened, as did her eyes. She moved her chair closer and leaned forward toward Mitch.

"You're not just kidding; in many ways it's been the major focus of my life. I left, or rather fled, Nugget Valley when I was eighteen. I'll tell you more about that some other time. I want to Canada and wound up in Halifax. Since I was unsure if I could protect the property, I had an attorney transfer to the property to the tribe.

"I thought that settled things, until years later when I was contacted by Sadie, a friend, or more like a sister, to Chinook. She asked me to come to the reservation because an Indian drug lord had taken over the casino and was terrorizing the tribe. When I got there, she told me that Chinook had arranged for her to put any documents signed by me, transferring the property to the tribe, in a safety deposit box. The documents were not to be recorded until she thought it was a good time to actually transfer the property.

So I still owned the property. That's why I took the casino over and, after we got the mess straightened out, I finally transferred the property to the tribe."

"What an amazing story!" Graciela reached across the table and grasped Mitch's hand.

"That's only the half of it. You put your feelers out and find out what's gone on with the property from the very beginning. We'll go from there." Mitch kissed Graciela's hand. "One thing for damn sure, I'm going to have a helluva time keeping my hands off you," he said, reaching for the check.

CHAPTER 14

Graciela was wound as tight as a drum when she left Inocencio's restaurant. The butterflies in her stomach were a signal that she needed to settle herself down, the sooner the better. She slipped on her racing gloves and headed for the Indianapolis Motor Speedway. A high-velocity ride around the famed track for a couple of laps would do the trick. She would be back in control again.

"Well if it isn't Missy Graciela." The tall muscular black security guard came out of the guard shack, opened the gate, and waved Graciela through with a sweeping bow.

Graciela rolled down the window and slipped two crisp twenty-dollar bills in the large hand of the onetime teammate of Oscar Robertson at Crispus Attucks High School, when they were dominating Indiana basketball.

"It's great to see you, George," Graciela said, thinking how unfortunate it was that a severe automobile accident had robbed George of a promising career in basketball, leaving him with a security guard job at the speedway after high school graduation.

"Now you put that little yeller Corvette through the paces," George said, with a big smile as he went back in the guard shack.

Graciela felt sensations of euphoria as she drove the car onto the famed track. She was one with the car, as she effortlessly shifted the gears, gently easing the accelerator to the floor. With a steady hand, she kept the speeding vehicle on course. But with her eyes focused on the yards of asphalt flashing past, Graciela became mesmerized. She lost sight of the first turn until it was upon her. To avoid hitting the wall, she turned the steering wheel sharply. The car began to skid. Losing control, she was thrown sideways; her face and head hit the driver's side window. Spinning on the track like a top, the car finally came to rest on a grassy area just off the asphalt.

Graciela lay crumpled in her seat, dazed and breathing deeply, aware of the sickening taste of blood. She searched her mouth and discovered that one corner of her upper lip was torn. When she leaned forward to reach for a tissue in the glove compartment, she was hit with a wave of nausea and a mouthful of saliva. Fighting off the urge to vomit, she found a tissue and dabbed her mouth. She leaned back in the seat and closed her eyes. As the nausea subsided, she ran her hands over her face and head, searching for blood. Relieved not to find any, she knew she was OK—sore all over, but OK.

The engine was still idling. Graciela put the car in gear and eased back onto the track. Blocking the unfortunate incident from her mind, with both hands firmly on the wheel, she pushed the Corvette from zero to over one hundred miles an hour in what was for her, a record time. She was looking forward to the next curve which she negotiated with great finesse. Her confidence was now high. She knew that she was driving faster than she ever had had before. And what was even better, she was enjoying it more than ever.

When Graciela left the track and drove to the gate, George came running out of the guard shack, clapping his hands. When he reached her car, he was hooting and dancing around in circles.

"That's sure one fine show you put on, Missy," George said, leaning in the front window. "Starting out like a demolition derby driver and finishing like Mario Andretti. I didn't know you had it in you."

"Stop it George," Graciela said, laughing. "You know damn well, I'm lucky I didn't roll my car and kill myself on the first turn. That's the worst mistake I've ever made behind the wheel."

"No, no, Missy, you got it all wrong. That's just show business. That's all it is. See you next time." George opened the gate, gave Graciela a salute, and jogged back to the guard shack.

Graciela took a sip of wine, and studied her face in the bathroom mirror. Other than a small scrape on her cheekbone and above her eyebrow, everything was intact. When she bent down to get into the hot bubble bath, she felt a slight pain in her shoulders and neck. Settling down in the hot water, she watched the fragrant bubbles gather around her. As she took another swallow of wine, Graciela began to laugh. She still had her racing gloves on. Setting the glass down, she peeled off the gloves and hurled them across the room.

The combination of the fragrant bubbles and hot water were so soothing to her aching body. Soon she was in a state of tranquility, something that she had not experienced in a long while. She had been living in a state of tension, stressing her being mentally—and now physically, with the near calamity at the race track.

Her mind flashed back to when she was a child and had dashed into the traffic without looking, only to have her father pull her to safety at the last moment. All he said to her was, "This has been a bad experience, not to be repeated. Usually there's a reason for it. You can learn many things from it."

She could not distinguish between dashing out in traffic as a child and driving recklessly on a dangerous racetrack as an adult.

They were one and the same: bad experiences, not to be repeated, and to be learned from.

Graciela drained the tub and wrapped herself in a towel. She knew exactly what happened to her—she had allowed herself to get too emotional over situations that she could not control. She could not allow that to happen again. It was too perilous. What she needed now was a good night's sleep. She would head for bed after making a quick call to Justin, asking him for more information on the Sycamore sale.

Graciela woke up the next morning feeling rejuvenated. The soreness had diminished. The abrasions on her face were barely noticeable after a dab or two of makeup. All she had on her schedule this morning was several telephone calls, and she could do that at home. She could relax there until her lunch meeting with Justin about the hospital sale.

Justin Overholt was reading the Indianapolis Star and nursing the first of his two daily luncheon martinis at Andre's. When he looked up from the sports page to take a sip of the marvelous drink that always calmed his nerves, he spotted Graciela walking toward his table. He felt a wave of excitement, something he felt each time he encountered Graciela. He could not curb his desire for this woman, even though he knew she would always be beyond his reach. If he was relegated to be her "errand boy," so be it.

"I knew you'd be in a good mood this morning. I watched the last inning of the Reds-Cardinals game last night, when Johnny Bench smashed a homer in the last of the ninth to win the game," Graciela said, as she took a seat in the booth.

"It was great. The Big Red Machine is the best in baseball, and it all starts with their catcher. Johnny Bench is young, and the best catcher who has come to the majors in years." Justin took another sip before setting his glass down. "Would you like a cocktail before lunch?"

"No thanks. It's too early for a mojito and I have too many things to do today." Graciela took the menu for the waitress who'd stopped by their table. "I'll have a Reuben sandwich and iced tea."

"I'll have the same, except scratch the iced tea and bring me another martini." Jason handed the waitress his empty glass. Knowing that Graciela was not one for small talk, he immediately came to the point. "The most accurate statement I would make about the sale of Sycamore Hospital is that it is convoluted. Having said that, the bottom line is that the state has the legal right to sell the property."

"That's why they're selling it as fast as they can for cash, so they don't have explain anything to the public," Graciela added.

"You're correct as usual," Justin said, eyeballing the fresh drink before him. "Things were handled in a shoddy fashion from the very beginning. An order of Trappist monks produced a handwritten title to the property in 1906, and it was recorded. The Abbey was completed in 1915. As you know, the monks never occupied the property. The state took it over as a hospital for the criminally insane in 1915."

"Under what grounds did the state take it over so quickly?"

"That's where things get fuzzy," Justin said, taking another sip of his drink. "There is some indication of a lease, where the state would've paid an undetermined amount, to lease the property on a yearly basis. Whether or not the lease was executed is unclear."

"What about taxes? Were taxes paid on the property?"

"There's no record of that."

"That's astonishing," Graciela said, shaking her head. "Did the state claim the property for nonpayment of taxes?"

"Well, they have now. That seems to be their best solution, since the state learned that the order of monks was disbanded in the late 1920s. They've completed all the paperwork, and want to push the sale through as soon as they can."

"So what you're saying is that the property just sat there in limbo all those years."

"Yes, I guess you could say that. They apparently did not see a need to formalize things until now, when they decided to sell the property."

"When will the sale go through?"

"It will take a little time. They're being very careful to deliver a clean title to the hospital."

"Can the state's claim be contested?"

"Yes, but that would cost a lot of money, and I don't think you'd win in court. Why? Are you thinking of doing that?"

"Heavens, no," Graciela exclaimed. "Just want some idea of how much longer we have at Sycamore before it's sold."

"A lot would depend on the buyer or buyers, and their attorneys who would insist that all steps be taken to assure a clean title."

"Lunch is on me," Grace said, picking up the check.

"OK. Call me if you need anything else."

"I will. Thanks, Jason." Graciela patted his hand and left the booth.

Jason stood up and with sad eyes, watched her leave the restaurant. He picked up his glass from the table, and signaled to the waitress to bring another drink.

CHAPTER 15

The applause died down in Recital Hall, Indiana University's most historical performance space. Mitch and Kenzie left their seats and followed the crowd toward the exit.

"Your student really gave a tremendous performance tonight. I love the Bach Cello Suite No. 1. She certainly did it justice," Mitch said, as they stepped outside the building. "Of course, she's had a magnificent teacher," he added, squeezing Kenzie's hand.

"My teaching had very little to do with her performance. She's a very talented young woman, as are all the other students in the program. This is a difficult program to get into. They only choose the most talented."

"Do you think she has a chance to make it as a concert performer?"

"She certainly has the ability, but I'm not sure if she has the focus that will take. She's a very emotional person who is easily distracted. This greatly impacts her ability to play. When she's upset with her boyfriend, she can barely play the right chord." Suddenly, Kenzie changed the conversation. "Mitch, I want to ask you something."

Mitch sensed that the "something" had to do with Graciela Cevallos. *Thank God I did not get involved with her, or did I?* Mitch swallowed hard, and said weakly, "Certainly."

"You've always been an open book to me, but not so much when it comes to Graciela Cevallos. Would you please explain to me why?"

Mitch stumbled on a small branch on the sidewalk and nearly lost his balance. "There's nothing to explain," he said, fumbling for words.

He knew immediately by the look on Kenzie's face that she didn't buy that. He knew his only choice was to come clean. "Just what is it you want to know about Graciela?"

"Not just Graciela, Graciela and you," Kenzie snapped.

"It's not what you think. I'm not involved with her."

Kenzie immediately cut him off. She stopped walking, put her hands on her hips, looked him directly in the eye, and said, "Now why would I think that? You tell me."

Mitch glanced both ways. He felt a sense of relief that they were alone on the sidewalk. "I feel very foolish and adolescent," he said, looking over Kenzie's shoulder as if he were speaking to someone behind her. "Since Guillermo got sick and I had to take over, Graciela has been working closely with me at the hospital. You know she is a friend of Guillermo, and the one who brought him to the hospital in the first place."

"Stop being nonsensical, Mitch. You know I know all that, but what I don't know and want to know, is what your feelings are for this Graciela woman."

"I don't want you to think I'm downplaying this, but something happened that shouldn't have happened, and I don't exactly know why," Mitch said, his voice wavering. "Graciela and I had a meeting, about the sale of the hospital, over lunch at Inocencio's. She was extremely upset about the whole situation, particularly Guillermo's illness. She feels responsible for that because she is the one who brought him to Sycamore. I held her and we kissed, which shocked both of us. That was the end of it."

"The end of it! It's only the beginning!" With that, Kenzie stomped down the sidewalk, leaving Mitch standing there, his hands in his pockets.

Later, as Mitch toweled off after a hot shower, he decided that now was the time to put an end to this debacle, before it spun completely out of control. He knew Kenzie would be in bed reading, so he strode into the bedroom, reached down, and then, as gently as he could, lifted the book from her hands.

"Just what do you think you are doing?" Kenzie bolted up from the pillows, her eyes flashing over her half-frame reading glasses.

"If you can leave me high and dry on the sidewalk, I sure as hell can take your book," he said, smiling in spite of himself. "This whole thing is getting silly. I feel stupid," he said, holding her hands.

"You should feel stupid," Kenzie snapped. "That's the first candid thing you've said. I ask you one question, to tell me your feelings about this Graciela woman, and you tell me that she was upset, that you held her, kissed her, and you both were shocked—but you don't know why it happened. Although I don't condone what happened, it's not my main concern. It's how you feel about her. Now will you answer my question and tell me how you feel about this Graciela woman? I sense you've been hiding that from me."

"First let me say, I have not consciously been hiding Graciela from you," Mitch said firmly. "That's ridiculous."

"Sometimes you say a lot when you're saying nothing."

"So that's what you're thinking. Because I don't talk about Graciela, I must be hiding something," Mitch said, obvious annoyed.

"That's right," Kenzie said serenely. "You're an open book, Mitch. You know that, and when you close that book, it suggests that there is something you don't care to share with me. Or maybe even share with yourself."

Mitch left the room. He returned a few moments later with two bottles of beer. "This is a good time to have a cool beer," he said, handing a bottle to Kenzie, who accepted it without comment. "You're too damn smart, Kenzie Fairfax. You make me feel like a dunderhead. Certainly I've been hiding my feelings about Graciela from myself and if I'm doing that, I've been hiding them from you are well.

"So here goes, I'll tell you exactly how I feel about Graciela Cevallos. I like her a lot. She's very bright, creative, and pleasant to be around. As you know, she did an internship under Guillermo at the VA, and was a couple of years behind me at Ohio State. We took a psych class together, and although we did not know each other or speak then, we remembered each other."

Mitch paused, took a swig of beer, sat the bottle on the night stand, and deliberately remarked, "Graciela intrigues me and I am attracted to her. We both were very upset about what happened to Guillermo, and how we were being betrayed by the hospital. I think these emotions were obvious that day, and resulted in the embrace and kiss. It was a spontaneous thing, without much thought."

Mitch sat silently on the edge of the bed, his hands folded together on his stomach. After staring at his hands for a moment, he went on. "There's more. After we kissed, she said to me, 'I want it all with you, Mitch,' which shocked the hell out of me. All I said was that was not going to happen. She said she knew it, and that really was the end of things. There was nothing more to say."

"Oh, I think there was more to say, Mitch. Did you ask her what she meant when she said she wanted it all with you? That's a pretty strong statement."

"No I didn't," Mitch replied, shaking his head. "It didn't seem to matter what she wanted. Nothing more was going to happen anyway."

"I tend to believe you—that nothing more was going to happen between the two of you. But, one thing bothers me, and that is, if she said she wanted it all with you, what she was really saying was that she wanted you all to herself. And that means without a wife, and that means without me."

"That's preposterous! I don't know exactly what she meant, but she didn't mean that. She knows better. She knows who I am, and what you mean to me, and that I'm happy with our marriage, and don't want anything else. I think she was as shocked as I was when we kissed. She knows that there can never be anything between her and me. She knows you're the only woman for me." Suddenly, Mitch took Kenzie in his arms, held her tight as they slipped under the covers.

Mitch stood at the stove, spatula in hand, waiting for the precise moment to flip the cheese and olive omelet. He gently nudged the spatula and lifted the omelet from the sizzling skillet. With a flip of his wrist, he turned the omelet over and dropped it back in the skillet. He looked at his watch and after ten seconds, he picked up the spatula again and deposited the huge omelet on a plate. He sat down at the table, doused the omelet with Tabasco sauce, and reached for his fork.

"You certainly are skilled at preparing omelets. I have thought many times you missed your calling as a short-order cook," Kenzie said, as she came up behind Mitch who was taking his first bite. She leaned over and kissed his neck. "You certainly wore me out last night," she whispered in his ear.

"That's what you call passion," he said looking up and shaking a fork full of egg at her. "It'd not my fault you're a sexual dynamo and I know which buttons to push."

"Oh, you're so romantic," she said, sitting down at the table. She reached for his fork and took a bite of his omelet. "This is delicious," she said, smacking her lips together. "Would you make me one? Hold the olives and cheese and add anchovies and tomato."

"Anchovies! Are you kidding? You don't put anchovies in omelets."

"Don't you remember that little café on the Left Bank where we ate breakfast? Their specialty was an anchovy omelet. That was what all the intellectuals from the Sorbonne had for breakfast."

"Yes, now I remember," Mitch answered smiling, as he mixed the ingredients for the new omelet. "I guess I had blocked that out because the snooty intellectuals and anchovy omelets both were obnoxious. I'll hold my nose and cook your omelet. I only have one concern. I read somewhere that anchovies may be an aphrodisiac, and if they are, I'm not sure it would be a good idea to slip one to a sexual dynamo like you. After last night, I need all the energy I have left to face the tigers at work today."

Kenzie looked up from her plate. "This anchovy omelet is a good as any I had in Paris. I want to have some students over for brunch sometime. Your anchovy omelet would go great with the champagne. If you'd be our chef, I'll reward you handsomely," she said, winking at Mitch, who was now standing at the end of the table, arms folded across his chest, watching her eat. "Sit down for a few minutes before you leave. You can fill me in on what's going on with the hospital."

Mitch pulled out a chair and sat down. "You know, I'm always amazed at how much of chow hound you really are. You're wolfing that omelet down in no time."

"Only with your cooking, my love. Now tell me what's going on at Sycamore."

"Well, I'm glad you asked," Mitch said. "You know, I don't bring my job home with me, but I need to run some things by you."

"Sounds good. Pour me a fresh cup of coffee and I'll lend you an ear."

"Something you said awhile back has stuck with me," Mitch began. "You told me that my biggest quandary at Sycamore would be the land. And, you're right. This land, this place, was sacred, but somehow, it was transformed into something it should never have been—a prison hospital. And I say 'hospital' in name only. It's really been a dysfunctional maximum security prison.

"As I see it, my main focus will be to do the best I can to make Sycamore a more humane place for those trapped in the criminal justice system. If I can accomplish this, then maybe the horrendous stigma that hovers over Sycamore can be replaced with something more benevolent. I've already seen signs that we're moving in the right direction. Graciela has been a huge asset, since Guillermo is out of the picture, as has Captain Laggins.

"The changes that are necessary will take time. Unfortunately, I've just learned that the state is selling Sycamore to a group of businessmen who want to turn it into an upscale resort and casino. It's a cash sale with immediate occupancy, so our time is cut short."

"What! You mean to tell me what originated as a holy place and mysteriously became a prison hospital is now going to become a luxurious resort and casino. That's bad karma to say the least," Kenzie said.

Mitch leaned back on his chair and smiled at Kenzie, who was flushed in the cheeks. "Kenzie Fairfax, you're a real beauty when you're angry. The fire just pours out and you just sparkle."

"Stop that nonsense," Kenzie said, throwing an annoying glance Mitch's way.

"That's not nonsense. Remember beauty is in the eye of the beholder. I'm just calling it the way I see it." Mitch got up and led Kenzie over to the sofa. He took her in his arms and kissed her on the forehead. "I'm damn glad I have you, my love. You've brought me up once again. The news of the sale cut through me like a sharp knife. I was ready to limp out of Sycamore, lick my wounds, and say the hell with it. But thanks to you, I got my grit back.

"There aren't many moves left for me at Sycamore, so I have to be sure they're the right ones. Let me sound this out with you."

"Sure," Kenzie said, now smiling. "But first tell what I really look like when I'm angry? I know it's not beautiful."

"I've already told you the truth. If it would help you, watch Jennifer Jones' last scenes in *Duel in The Sun*. That look on her face, filled with passion and determination, is what you look like when you're angry. That's all I have to say."

"I'll watch it if you watch it with me."

"That's the first thing we'll do when things are over with at Sycamore. But since they're not, we had better get to work."

Mitch paused for a few moments, then continued, "Do you remember that the VA Hospital where I did my internship had a series of tunnels beneath the main floor of the hospital? And that they were being used by the agency for the blind for mobility training?"

"I sure do. That was one of the best programs they had at the hospital."

"You know there are catacombs beneath Sycamore that could be used for the same purpose," Mitch added.

Kenzie responded with a quizzical look.

"Kenzie, I would not consider this if the state agency's blind clients or their staff would be jeopardized in any way. The catacombs are separate from the hospital and no one would have any contact with the inmates."

Kenzie took a long look at her husband before speaking. "This is a noble idea, Mitch. And with merit but, to be honest, it's unrealistic. In the first place, Sycamore is not like the VA hospital. As you've said many times, it's a hospital in name only and really is a maximum security prison. It's not an appropriate facility for mobility training for the blind. The risks greatly outweigh the rewards."

Even though Kenzie spoke in a soft and warm manner, her words stung Mitch and he felt a flash of anger. Ignoring his feelings, he said calmly, "I only take issue with one thing you said. Whatever I proposed is not a noble idea. I don't know what it is but it sure as hell isn't that."

"Say what you will, but to me, you're a noble crusader who always tries to do something that's good and righteous. Unfortunately what you propose is simply too difficult. I just don't think you'll be successful this time," Kenzie said, taking his hands. "But, I know you're going to bring the blind to Sycamore anyway, so tell how you're going to do it."

"It's a very simple plan, Kenzie. A simple plan," Mitch replied. "First I have to run it by Captain Laggins. If he thinks it's too risky and could put the clients in danger, or will not support it for any reason, then that's the end of it. If he supports it, and I think he will, then I'll try to sell it to the agency. They'll either buy it or they won't. Like I said, 'It's a simple plan!' "

"I have more questions about this so-called simple plan that I'll defer for now. However, I would like to ask you one thing. What do expect to gain from this?"

Mitch got up and poured himself a fresh cup of coffee. When he returned to the table, he stared at the cup before saying, "I joined Guillermo to bring treatment programs to this hospital.

If I can bring a blind mobility program, then I would have the satisfaction of at least bringing one new program to Sycamore. It also could bring something positive to the hospital, some good will. That's what the program did for VA in Cleveland. That could happen here."

Kenzie leaned over and kissed Mitch on the cheek. "I think that you will do it, Mitch." When she returned to her seat, she took his hands, and told him, "There is another thing you could do, something far simpler than your simple plan. I just learned that there is a small order of Trappist monks from the Amish country who are looking for some place near Indianapolis to develop a vineyard. Why don't you see if they would be interested in coming to Sycamore? There is plenty of unused farmland that could be put to good use. Think of the image a group of monks tilling the soil, wearing hooded robes, would create."

"Great idea," Mitch exclaimed, leaping up from his chair. "I'll do both. See you tonight," he said, grabbing his brief case and heading out the door.

CHAPTER 16

Mitch leaned back in his chair, placed his feet on the desk, and looked intently at the telephone. Fighting the urge to reach over, pick up the telephone, and call Guillermo was sucking the energy out of him. He really needed to hear his friend's voice—out of the question because of Guillermo's wishes for no telephone calls during his convalescence. He knew there was no choice except to wait for Guillermo to call him, when he was ready.

The telephone rang. It was Ms. Bascom telling him that Graciela Cevallos was on the line. "Tell her that I can't take her call now. I'm in a meeting with Captain Laggins and will call her when it's over."

Captain Laggins was loading a fresh wad of chewing tobacco in his cheek when Mitch walked in his office and sat down. The sweet aroma of the leafy tobacco filled Mitch's nose. When the captain sat the tobacco on the desk, Mitch reached for the package, opened it, and took a whiff.

"I've always loved the smell of chewing tobacco," he said setting tobacco on the desk. "It's reminds me of standing by the shaft at the main station of the Hawk Mine, waiting for the cage. I was squashed in with a pack of miners, mouths stuffed with chewing tobacco, some so full that tobacco juice would be running down their chins. Strange as it may seem, Captain Laggins, it's the thing I remember the most of my days in the mines. The rest is just a blur."

"Funny, the things you remember," the captain said in a serious tone. "What I remember most about my father is the way he could roll a perfect cigarette, using only one hand."

"That's really a feat," Mitch commented. "When I was in the mines, the miners always rolled their own cigarettes. They were always trying to roll one with one hand. I only saw one man do it, a hillbilly from the Ozarks. The cigarette was anything but perfect. In fact it was a squashed-up mess held together by a glob of spit. It was the best he could do, and he couldn't do that all the time."

"I've been hearing rumors that things may be coming to an end here," Laggins said, raising his eyes upward. "Do you know anything?"

"Yes, that's what I came to talk about. There's nothing official yet, so keep it under your hat. Sycamore is going to be sold to a group of businessmen who plan to develop an upscale resort and casino."

Captain Laggins frowned but said nothing.

"It's reported to be a cash sale with immediate occupancy. We're to carry on as normal until we get official word from the governor's office that the sale has been finalized. I have no idea when that would be, but I assume it will be sooner than later. There are a couple of projects I want to do before we have to leave, and I need your input and support."

Captain Laggins appeared chagrined and responded with a nod.

"I want to add one new treatment program," Mitch proposed. "Since we won't have sufficient time to develop a new program with our staff, I will have to bring a functional treatment program to Sycamore.

"When I was at the VA hospital in Cleveland, there were a series of tunnels beneath the main floor. They had a program with the agency for the blind, to use the tunnels for mobility training for the visually impaired. The program was very successful, and the VA Hospital got a lot of kudos for hosting it.

"The catacombs here would be ideal for such a mobility program. I want to develop one. What do you think?"

Laggins squirmed and looked at the ceiling for a few moments. "You know, it's awful dark down there. It might be dangerous for them. I'm afraid they would be stumbling around in the tunnels. They could easily be injured if they crashed into the sharp rocks that are buried in the walls of the tunnels."

The captain paused and scratched behind his ear. "I don't know, Dr. Gainer. I'd hate to see those blind folks get hurt. They have enough troubles as it is."

"You're right, Captain Laggins. It's very dark in the catacombs, as dark as the Hawk Mine, but I think there is adequate lighting. As far as crashing into the walls, I don't think that would be a problem. Remember they will be supervised by trained and sighted mobility instructors who will teach them how to travel with their guide dogs and canes.

"The first thing the agency would do is inspect the setting from top to bottom, to identify any barriers before they begin the training. If they think the catacombs will be dangerous, they won't use the facility."

"The first thing they'll teach their clients is how to position a long thin cane in front. They'll then teach them how to move the cane in a sweeping fashion when they walk, so they can identify what is in front and beside them.

Mitch paused, giving the captain some time to take in what he just said. "What I'm really concerned about are the patients. Would they pose any danger to the clients?"

"Hell no," Laggins bellowed, straightening up in his chair and leaning over the desk, nearly coming face to face with Mitch, who was taken back. "The patients like people from the outside and always treat them well. But it's not an issue because the catacombs are not part of the hospital. The blind folks would have no contact whatsoever with the patients."

"So I take it your main concern would be their safety in the dark tunnels."

"Yes. I sure don't want those poor blind folks getting hurt."

When Mitch heard the captain's response, he knew he had his support. "I'll contact the agency and offer the catacombs for mobility training. I'll arrange a time for them to inspect the facility. They will meet with you, and you will take them through the catacombs. If you both see eye to eye, then we'll have a program."

"Agreed!" Captain Laggins got up and offered his hand to Mitch.

"Welcome aboard, Captain Laggins. Welcome aboard," Mitch said, giving the captain a firm handshake. "I hope that you will be down there in the catacombs during the training, to keep an eye on those blind folks so they will not get injured."

"One more thing," Mitch said as they sat down again. "Since Sycamore was originally intended to be a spiritual place, would you have any objections if we provide a local order of monks some land to plant grapes for a vineyard?"

"Not at all. That's a great idea," Laggins said with a smile, for the first time since the meeting began. "It's always seemed to me to be a waste, having that much fallow land on the grounds. It'll be good to see it being used, particularly by the monks who are an industrious bunch. They would really tend to the soil."

"Good, I'll start the process immediately."

After the meeting, Mitch hurried to his office to call Graciela. When he opened the door, he was amazed to find her perched in a chair, reading the newspaper.

Graciela looked up from the paper. "There's an article on Squire Young in the Indianapolis Star, with a picture of him posing with a racing car. Is this the man you know?" She handed the paper to Mitch.

"It sure is," Mitch replied, studying the picture. "He looks the same as he did when I last saw him, several years before he became the Baron of War Horse Racing Team. But there's no mention of his purchasing Sycamore, or coming to Indianapolis, only that he believes his team has a great chance of winning the Indy 500 this year. He's quite a man. I look forward to seeing him again, only I wish it was under better circumstances."

Mitch returned the paper to Graciela and pulled up a chair next to her. He took a long look at her and was taken aback by what he saw. Where had the usual sparkle in her eyes gone? Where is the vibrant smile? Her lips were tightly sealed as if she were holding something inside. What was even worse, she looked fragile.

"I want to talk with you about the sale," Graciela said, in a flat voice. "I met with Jason Overholt and he said that there was a title recorded for the property, by Dettelbach Abbey in 1915. He also found paperwork for a lease between the abbey and the state, but he does not know if it was ever finalized. There's no record of any taxes being paid on the property. The state has now taken it over, for nonpayment of taxes, so they can complete the sale."

"What about Dettelbach Abbey? Wouldn't they still own the property?"

"The state learned the order was disbanded in the 1920s, so the property has essentially been in limbo since then."

Mitch shook his head. He started to say something, but changed his mind.

"The bottom line is that Sycamore will be sold, and our work is over with. All we can do now is to help the staff make a good transition."

Suddenly Mitch bolted up and took his seat behind his desk. "Not so fast," he snapped. "There are a couple of things I want to do before this ends. The first is to bring a new treatment program to hospital, a blind-mobility program, using the catacombs.

"And since Sycamore was built to be to a holy place for monks, I want to bring some here to till the soil and grow some grapes."

Graciela stiffened in her chair. Her face flushed, and she glared at Mitch. "What! Why would you want to bring an order of monks here? What possible good would that do? That's an absurd idea," she exclaimed, her voice shaking.

Graciela's words hit Mitch like a blast of water from a high-pressure hose. Her emotions propelling the words surprised him, and left him speechless.

After several moments of uncomfortable silence, Graciela said weakly, "I'm sorry. I shouldn't have spoken to you like that."

"No need for that," Mitch said, with a half smile. "I'll answer your question. I learned there is an order of Trappist monks in Amish country who are looking to start a vineyard. Since this place was built for monks to begin with, it seems to me only right to give them access to some of our fallow land. We could publicize it, and I think it would create public interest, and give Sycamore a much better image. In a small way, it could influence how the new owners would utilize the property. I don't see any downside to having the monks here."

Graciela slumped down in her chair. She avoided looking at Mitch, said nothing. She appeared to be lost in her thoughts.

Mitch felt an impulse to rush to her side, throw his arms around her, and comfort her. Instead he said, "Graciela, I think there is more to this than your objecting to monks coming to Sycamore. What is it?"

Graciela looked up, dabbed her eyes with a tissue, and cleared her throat. "When you mentioned the monks, it made me extremely angry. All I could think about is what happened to me when I was a child, in my Catholic grade school," she said, in an agonized voice.

"When I think back to my childhood, I guess I was what you'd call a tomboy. My brother was a couple of years older than me, and I always wanted to be with him and his gang. We frequented the beach, went fishing and snorkeling. I even played on their beach volleyball and soccer teams. Hanging out with my brother and the church was my life.

"I was always at the top of my class in school. Since I was doing so well, Father Jose, our parish priest, arranged an academic scholarship to the most prestigious Catholic school in Miami. I wanted to stay in the public school, but my father insisted that I go to the Catholic school, where I could get a better education.

"I knew from the first day when I learned I had to wear a uniform that it was not going to be the place for me."

"What did the uniform look like?"

"It was a big green, black, and white plaid jumper, worn over a starched white blouse. We also had to wear a matching ribbon in our hair, black patent leather shoes, and knee-high white stockings.

"I remember the first day I wore the uniform. One of the sisters took me aside, and told me that my hair was too long to wear with the uniform. It did not look good. I had thick, wavy hair down to my waist. She pointed her finger at me, and said my hair should not touch my shoulders."

"Did you cut it?"

"No. I was very proud of my hair. It was beautiful, just like my mother's. She used to brush it each night before I went to bed. I wore my hair waist length until I graduated from college."

"I suspect the sister may have been jealous of your hair. I think that nuns are required to wear their hair closely cropped. She may have resented it."

"If I were to describe the school, I would just say that it was a very uncomfortable place to be. For the most part, the sisters were competent teachers, and the curriculum was sound. However, the structure from which they operated was so regimented that most creativity was squeezed out. That made the classes dull and uninteresting.

"But worse of all to me was the slow pace that permeated everything at the school. This was particularly true of the students who dawdled in the hallways between classes. Although it was annoying, it was not a problem because I was very agile, and could easily zigzag my way through the herd of girls clogging the hallways.

"The sister, the one who disliked my hair, accused me of running in the halls and stairways, and being rude to the other girls. I tried to explain to her that was not what I was doing, but she would not listen. She just shook her finger and me, and told me that she would be watching me."

Suddenly Graciela paused and closed her eyes. She folded her hands in a prayer-like fashion and continued in a somber voice. "One day I was going down the stairs. The girl in front of me slipped and fell. The next thing I knew someone seized me by hair, put an arm around my neck, and jerked me off the stairs. She dragged me into the girls lavatory, screaming at me that I had knocked the girl down. I started kicking and tried to break away, but she was too strong. Then she leaned over my face and shrieked, "I'll wipe that lipstick from your lips!"

"What!" Mitch bellowed, stiffening in his chair.

"I had really red lips when I was a girl. I guess she thought I was wearing lipstick but I wasn't. She grabbed some paper towels and began rubbing my lips. My lips began to bleed and my mouth filled with blood as she rubbed harder and harder.

"Then the door burst open and the janitor rushed in. He pulled her off me, and when he did, her veil came off, exposing her shaved head."

Graciela was panting when she finished. For a moment Mitch thought she was going to hyperventilate. Holding her head in her hands, she began weeping softly.

Mitch felt the rage inside him subside, replaced by an overwhelming feeling of sadness. As he leaned over to comfort her, he felt a tear fall from his eye for that innocent young girl with thick, wavy hair who'd been violently victimized for no good reason. When a tear dropped from his other eye, he knew it was for the poor misguided lady of the cloth who had either lost her way, or had never found it.

Mitch held Graciela close and stroked her hair until she stopped sobbing and looked up at him. Using his silk pocket square, he gently wiped away the tears. After carefully folding the handkerchief, he returned it to his blazer pocket, and said softly, "I'm terribly sorry that happened to you when you were a young girl. It makes me both angry and sad because it's the kind of thing that can leave scars. No wonder you're angry at the church!"

"I'm not so sure angry is the word. 'Forsaken' better suits how I feel about the church. I'm not sure the church abandoned me, or I abandoned it," Graciela said, in a reflective tone. "At first, I wasn't really angry about what happened. I felt relieved that I did not have to go back to that awful place where I never wanted to be in the first place. Now I could go back to the public school with my friends, where I really belonged.

"As I got older and recalled what happened, I started to feel angry, and began distancing myself from the church. I had always loved church, and always been involved, but gradually I began to fade away—coming late for Mass, sitting farther back from the altar, and finally only showing up at the end for communion. I stopped going completely when I was in high school."

"That's really too bad you had to give it all up, because of a few misguided and ignorant people. It's sad but understandable. You were traumatized as child. That leaves scars that can last a lifetime." Mitch sensed that he was bordering on pontification, which was something he abhorred. "Are you adamant that bringing the monks to Sycamore is not a good idea?"

"'Ambivalent' better describes how I feel about it. And my feelings have nothing to do with what's going to happen. You're going to give the monks some land, they will grow grapes, and I will support you all."

Mitch took a long look at Graciela before saying softly, "Would you tell me something? If I would have told you right off that I was going to bring some monks to Sycamore, would you have told me how you felt?"

Graciela thought for a few moments then replied, "No. You probably would have sensed that I was not overly enthusiastic, but I would have supported your decision."

"Even though your response surprised me, and was not music to my ears, I'm glad I asked you what you thought. You needed to get some things off your chest, and my query certainly triggered it. It was a good thing, I think."

"Thank you, Dr. Sigmund," Graciela said, grinning from ear to ear. "I suppose this means I'm moving closer to gaining closure on this issue."

"Yes, madam, and I think you'll move even closer if you will consider contacting the monks, and initiating their coming to Sycamore. Now can we move on to the blind mobility program? How do you feel about that?"

"I think that's a dynamite idea," Graciela said, tongue in cheek. "But you had better work with Donaldo Perriman, the Director of Rehabilitation Services for the Blind and Visually Impaired. I'm afraid he's a bit of a male chauvinist. A couple of years ago, we had a tussle with him, when he insisted that one of our visually impaired mental-health patients be arrested for selling pencils on the streets without a vendor's license.

"Perriman runs an excellent program, but working with him personally can be a challenge. He's outspoken, can be obstinate, and does not like interacting with women he feels are independent or aggressive."

"I'll work with him. His personality is irrelevant to me. All I care about is if he runs a good program," Mitch added.

"He does that. He's at the top of his field."

"It's all settled now. Remember, Graciela, this is our last hurrah, and we better give it our best shot."

Mitch walked Graciela to her car in silence, and gave her hand a squeeze when she opened the car door. When she closed the door and started the engine, Mitch felt a sudden urge to do something, but what? By the time he reached his car, he knew what he needed to do. He'd call Squire Young.

When Mitch reached the outskirts of the city, he pulled in the parking lot of a ramshackle greasy spoon whose only saving grace was that they served the best hamburger in Indiana. He entered the crowded restaurant, placed an order for a hamburger to go, got some change from the cashier, and went outside to the telephone booth, next to the front door.

Mitch dialed information, got the number for War Horse, dialed, and dropped the coins in the slot. After a few rings, a pleasant woman's voice answered. "War Horse. How may I help you?"

"I would like to speak with Mr. Young."

"Whom shall I say is calling?"

"My name is Mitch Gainer. I'm a friend of Mr. Young."

Five minutes later, Squire Young came to the phone. "Mitch, this is a pleasant surprise. How may I help you?"

Squire's offhand response told Mitch that he did not wish to speak with him and was simply putting him off.

After a long pause, Mitch said, "I've heard that your group purchased Sycamore. I wonder what plans you have for the property."

"That's pure conjecture, Mitch. I looked at the property one time," Squire said curtly. Mitch immediately sensed that Squire was not being forthcoming. There was no reason to continue the conversation.

"I know you're busy so I won't take any more of your time. I'll give you a call when I'm in town, and we can meet for lunch."

"Sounds good," Squire said, as he hung up the telephone.

CHAPTER 17

With a flip of her hand, Kenzie spread her cards on the table. "Fifteen two, fifteen four, a pair is six, and a run of three is nine," she announced. "That puts me out, and you, my dear husband, are skunked."

"A thorough drubbing," Mitch conceded, removing the pegs from the ivory and inlaid-walnut cribbage board he inherited from his grandfather Angus. He carefully placed the pegs in a small compartment on the back of the board, picked up a dusting cloth, wiped the board clean, and gently placed it in a bright-blue velvet bag.

"With the two skunks, I won eight games tonight, and you won two." Kenzie recorded the outcomes in a leather note book. "That means I lead the cribbage series of our marriage, 1447 games to 1420." She puffed her chest.

"Enjoy it while you can, Missy. The tide will turn, and you'll get your comeuppance eventually. Consider tonight a gift," Mitch said playfully. "I gave at least three games away because I wasn't paying attention. My mind was on tomorrow when I take Donaldo Perriman, a blind man, into the catacombs."

"That's right! Tomorrow is the day you're meeting with the head of the blind agency to set up the mobility program." Suddenly

Kenzie paused. A puzzled look came over her face. "Mitch, you casually mention the catacombs, but you never say anything about them. Tell me, what are they like? They mystify me."

"They mystify me as well," Mitch began. "Simplistically stated, they are a series of man-made tunnels, small compartments, and rooms that the order built beneath the main floor, to be used for rituals and internment of their members. But they're much more than that. If you go there and experience them, you'll know what I mean."

Mitch paused, sat on the sofa, leaned back, and placed his arms behind his head. "Every time I've been down there, I felt like I was intruding on an extraordinary, or even sacred, space that was only meant for those who built it. Even though it's a part of the building, it seems detached, with a secretive entrance and a bunker-like quality."

"It sounds eerie." Kenzie sat next to Mitch.

"I guess you could say that. I'm not sure I would. I'd just say different and leave it at that. The walls and ceilings are lined with rocks, making it seem like you're in a cave or a cavern. In fact the first time I was there, it reminded me of the tunnels of the Hawk Mine when I was kid in Nugget Valley."

Kenzie raised her index finger at Mitch. "That must have brought back some good memories for you. I know how nostalgic your time as miner is."

"But what's really puzzling is they embedded the rocks with sharp edges in such a way that the edges stick straight out. You don't want to bump into the wall. If you do, it's like bumping into a cactus or thorny desert plant or tree. You're likely to come away with a cut or an abrasion. I can attest to that. The first time I was down there, I stumbled and hit the wall with my forearm. I scraped the hell out of my arm, drawing blood."

"Do you think that's a suitable place to teach blind people mobility training? Do you know what it's like to be blind, and have to feel your way around? I've never told you this, but when I was in Paris for a concert, on my first tour, I was invited to a meal afterward. As soon as we sat down at the table, the lights were turned off. The chef announced that we would eat the meal in total darkness, and would be served by blind waiters, who remained present during the meal to assist us."

"That's astounding! You didn't know beforehand you would be eating in the dark?"

"No. I was only told that we were invited to a special meal, prepared by one of the top chefs in Paris."

"Well, I bet it was all that and more. What was it like?"

"It was an unbelievable experience. I'll never forget the menu. We were served confit de carnard, balsamic roasted vegetables, a warm red-beet salad, mashed pumpkin, and Tannat wine. My main worry was that not being able to see, I would soil my best concert dress.

"Heaven forbid, you get duck grease, red wine, and mashed pumpkin on your emerald-green concert dress," Mitch chuckled.

"Stop it," Kenzie said, nudging Mitch in the shin with her foot. "They played Debussy, Ravel, and *Saint-Saëns* in the background. I slowly began to relax when the waiter handed me a bib, and whispered in my ear to concentrate on using my sense of smell, to identify the food. The aroma was scrumptious, and I was easily able to identify each item on the plate. Focusing only on the appetizing smells, I slowly moved the fork, with a small amount of food, to my mouth. To my surprise, not one time did I come close to spilling any food. In fact, I was able to cut a piece of duck with my knife, with little difficulty."

"That doesn't surprise me. After all, you're a super star with superb hand-eye coordination. As you said, you identified the food through your sense of smell. Once you did that, you no doubt created a vision of it on the plate in your mind, so you didn't need your eyes to get it to your mouth."

"Is that so, Mr. Deductive Reasoning," Kenzie said, a broad grin on her face. "I wouldn't go that far. All I know is that I didn't have a lot of difficulty eating. And, as I said, the food was delicious, which dominated the whole experience. I remember savoring each bite, and holding it in my mouth for what seemed to be a long time before swallowing.

"After we finished the meal, they turned the lights on, and served a tarte tatin and Grand Marnier. The chef then told us that he served the meal in total darkness because he thought it might make the food taste better. We would be using all of our senses to focus on the meal. He also thought it would make us more aware of blindness. And, he was right in both cases. To a person, we all said the food tasted better, and that we gained some understanding of what it was like to be blind."

"You're a very fortunate woman, Kenzie Fairfax, to have had such an astounding experience," Mitch said, taking Kenzie's hand and kissing it. "I'm sure it's something you'll never forget. I'm surprised you've never mentioned it until now."

"I think I'll have a glass of wine before we turn in," Kenzie said, getting up from the sofa. "Would you like one?"

"No thanks. I'm fine."

When Kenzie returned, she took a sip of wine, and sat on the sofa. Finally she spoke. "Mitch, I remember feeling completely overwhelmed when I caught a flight to Prague immediately after the meal. I've haven't had any further contact with the chef or any of the people I dined with.

"I've thought about the experience from time, but never felt the need to talk to anyone about it. I can't imagine saying to someone, 'hey, let me tell you about a meal I ate in dark in Paris.' That would be trivial, and what I experienced was not. It just came back to me when you were talking about the blind people, and the sharp rocks in the walls."

"I know that and I'm glad it did. I'm not insensitive to the perils the catacombs present for the blind. Believe me, if it's really dangerous, there will be no program," Mitch said firmly. "Can I ask you something?"

Kenzie nodded yes.

"You know this blind business is new to me. Like you during the meal, I'm just feeling my way along. If I need some assistance along the way, can I turn to you? You know things about blindness that I don't."

Kenzie threw her arms around Mitch and kissed him full on the lips.

CHAPTER 18

The next day, Mitch was at his desk, with his feet up, skimming the sport section of the Indianapolis Star to see how his favorite team, the Detroit Tigers, did in their game with the Cleveland Indians. He shook his head when he read that the Tigers lost the game, 8 to 7. He smiled slightly when he read his favorite player, Norm Cash, had hit a home run. He loved to watch 'Stormin Norman', standing in the on-deck circle, swinging three bats over his head. When his turn came, he dropped two bats to the ground, strode to the plate, and swung from his heels. What he like most about Cash was that he got the maximum out of every trip to the plate. Every swing of the bat brought excitement, regardless whether he hit he ball or missed.

He'd become a Tigers' fan when he was living in Ohio, and listening to Ernie Harwell announce the games. It was Ernie's soft Southern voice on the radio that was so important. Ernie could gently and concisely bring the game—and even Tiger Stadium, to life—while giving listeners a history lesson on the team and baseball in general.

Mitch preferred to listening to Ernie's broadcasts to being at the ballpark or watching the games on television. He purchased the most powerful radio he could so he could hear Ernie, no matter where he was living.

He quickly recognized that he was not a typical Tigers fan. When the Tigers won, he showed no emotion and reacted in a matter-of-fact fashion, as if was the way that things should be. But when they lost, particular if it were an important game, he became slightly depressed, and sometimes even a little surly. It bothered him, and he wondered if this was a generalized trait, or if he responded to other life situations in the same manner.

There was a rap on the door. When Mitch opened the door, he came face to face with a brawny man dressed in a dark blue suit and burgundy tie, holding a stout Blackthorn walking stick with an ivory knob. The man thumped the walking stick on the floor and announced, "I'm Donaldo Perriman, ten minutes early for our meeting."

Mitch stepped back and offered his hand. "I'm Mitch Gainer. It's a pleasure to meet you. I appreciate your being ten minutes early. It's also my custom as well."

The two men shook hands. Mitch reached for Perriman's elbow, and began to lead him to a chair in front of the desk.

"I appreciate your gesture, Dr. Gainer, but it's unnecessary. I have travel vision," Perriman said, in a gravelly voice. Gently easing his elbow from Mitch's grip, he began tapping the floor in front of him with the walking stick, moving it from side to side. He strode across the floor like a ballroom dancer and took a seat at the desk.

When Mitch returned to his seat at the desk, he studied the broad face with the slightly flattened nose, square jaw, wide lips, prominent cheek bones, and a high brow topped with wavy salt-and-pepper hair, worn in a pompadour style of the 1940s. This man is a throwback, Mitch told himself. A real man's man.

Perriman laid his walking stick across his lap and kept his right hand on the ivory knob. "My right eye is glass," he stated matter-of-factly, twisting the walking stick in his hand.

"My left eye has enough vision so I can get around with my walking stick, in lieu of the typical long white cane used by most people. I do not recommend the walking stick to my clients or other visually impaired folks, since there is a price to pay if you use one," he said, pulling up his pant leg, showing Mitch the bruises, abrasions, and scars on his shin bone.

"Nonetheless, there are many advantages to the walking stick—the best one being it's handy in self-defense, if the need should arise." He suddenly flipped the stick in the air like a baton, and snatched it by the tip, pointing the ivory knob directly at Mitch, who pulled back in his chair.

"That I know for sure," Mitch stammered. "I once had a friend, a mentor named Chinook, who had a game leg. He had a walking stick like yours, with a gold coyote-head handle. People viewed the walking stick as a lethal weapon in his hands. Did you ever have to use it?"

"A couple of times," Perriman answered. "Once in a subway station in New York City, when a man tried to jerk my briefcase from me, and another time in Chicago, when a man was kicking a homeless man lying on the sidewalk. A solid rap behind the knees with the ivory knob settled the issue in both instances," Perriman said, setting the stick beside his chair.

"You know, Mr. Perriman, you remind me so much of Chinook. Like him, you have an obvious impairment, but not a disability."

Perriman glanced at Mitch's shiny brass name plate, and commented, "Thanks for the complement, Dr. Gainer. Tell me what Chinook's impairment was?"

"Chinook was abandoned by his mother at birth on an Indian reservation in Idaho. He was raised by the Indians. When he was a teenager, he fled the reservation, and hopped a freight train. It was wintertime, and the grab bar he was holding onto was covered with ice. He lost his grip when he tried to pull himself into the box car. His leg slipped under the car, and was run over by the one of the wheels, shattering it to pieces, and leaving him crippled."

"That's a tough one," Perriman said. "In my case, it came from a game of Mumblety-peg, when I was also a teenager."

"Mumblety-peg! That's the old game played with pocket knives," Mitch said. "I haven't heard that name in years, not since I was a kid."

"That's the one." Perriman suddenly placed his walking stick directly in front of him, leaned forward in his chair, and pulled the ivory knob into his chest, griping it firmly with both hands. "We were playing in my backyard, and this particular game involved making trick throws. In the most difficult trick, you laid the knife flat on the back of your hand and flipped it up in air as high as you could, in such a way that the blade would stick in the ground when it landed. No one in the neighborhood had ever done that, including me. But since I had done it once in practice, I was confident I could do it in a game, where it really counted."

Suddenly Perriman appeared uneasy and paused for several minutes before continuing. "I've never told this story to anyone before, including my wife. I don't understand why I'm telling this to you, a person I've just barely met, but since I've started, I'll finish. I threw the knife from my hand as hard as I could. The knife went higher in the sky than any other knife I had thrown. When I looked up to see where it was, a burst of wind came up, and the next thing I knew everything went black. I felt a horrible explosion of pain in my right eye.

"When I regained consciousness in the hospital, they told me my right eye was gone and I was lucky to be alive. They did not tell me why my eye was gone. They did not have to. I knew why. The knife blade struck me right in the middle of my right eye!"

Mitch slumped down in his chair, shivers ran down his back, his breath shortened, and he could feel his heart beating hard. He wished that he could say something to comfort this man or maybe to comfort himself, but he knew that was not possible. He did not know the words, and even if he did, what happened to this man was beyond words. Best to be silent.

"When I think about that day, and that game of Mumblety-peg, I only focus on one thing. If the knife had missed me, it would have stuck in ground. I would have made a perfect throw, and been a hero in my neighborhood. That's what I remember.

"But it didn't end there, Dr Gainer. The worst was yet to come. There was an infection in my right eye and it spread to my left eye. After a few months, I lost the sight in that eye and was blind. Fortunately, a few years ago I regained some sight in the left eye. With treatment and medication, the doctors were able to increase my sight to the travel vision I have today."

As Mitch listened to Perriman speak of being blind, and getting some sight back later, Mitch thought of Eric Hoffer, the longshoreman philosopher, whose book, *The True Believer*, had a profound effect on him. Hoffer, too, had been blind as a child, and gained his sight back later.

Perriman set his walking stick beside his chair. "I'm interested in why you want to bring a mobility program to Sycamore Hospital. It seems to be a strange fit, particularly since this place is more like a prison than a hospital."

"That's a very good question," Mitch said, with a smile. "Your comment that this place is more a prison than a hospital unfortunately has merit. That is what we're committed to change, and we are making progress. As part of that change, for the first time, we are offering our facilities to other treatment programs in the community.

"The VA Hospital in Cleveland, where I worked, had tunnels that the blind agency used to teach mobility training. It was an excellent program and benefited both the hospital and the agency. There is no reason why we cannot develop a similar program here, since we have all the facilities.

"I don't know if you're aware that Sycamore hospital was originally built to be a monastery by a religious order from Europe. For unknown reasons, they did not occupy it. The state took it over in 1915, and made it a hospital to treat people in the criminal justice system.

"Beneath this floor are catacombs that have never been used. They would be an exceptional place for mobility training. They are separate from the hospital and would give your group the autonomy to develop your program without any interference. Use of the facilities would, of course, be pro-bono."

Perriman did not respond, but reached again for his walking stick. For a moment Mitch thought that he would be heading for the door. He was greatly relieved when Perriman laid the stick in his lap, and said, "Catacombs, you say?"

"Would you like to take a tour?"

Perriman nodded yes.

"Good," Mitch said. "Captain Lynsford Laggins will accompany us. He's in charge of security, and he can address any concerns you have in that area."

Captain Laggins led the group down the main corridor, with Mitch and Perriman walking in cadence behind the ex-Marine. Mitch was surprised to feel Perriman gently take hold of his elbow as they followed Laggins to a paneled section at the very end. Laggins reached in his pocket for a ring of keys. Choosing a large cast-iron key, he placed it in the keyhole in the center of panel, twisted it, and the huge walnut door swung open.

"This is the original key," Laggins said, holding the key in the air. "Still works slick as a whistle." He pointed at a large electrical switch on the wall of a small room with a stairway in the center.

"This is the main switch for all the lights in the catacombs," he said touching the switch. "The lights in this room stay on 24-7. Follow me," he barked, pointing at the stairway. "Hold onto the banister. The stairway is narrow and steep, so watch your step. You'll enter the catacombs at the end of the stairway. The walls are lined with sharp rocks that could easily cut you, so be sure and walk in the middle and away from the sides."

Mitch glanced at Perriman to gauge his reaction to Laggin's orders. The blank expression on Perriman's face suggested that they did not leave much of an impression. If they did, he was keeping it to himself.

Perriman suddenly dropped Mitch's elbow, lurched ahead of him, and followed Laggins down the winding stairway without the assistance of the banister. They reached the catacombs with words or incidence.

Shortly after they entered the catacombs, Mitch heard the ripping sound of cloth tearing. His heart beat rapidly as he looked up and saw that Perriman had stumbled into the wall and slashed his coat sleeve, his shirt, and his right arm on a sharp rock. Blood soaked his shirt and coat sleeve.

Mitch rushed to his side, took hold of his upper arm, examining the gash near his shoulder. Perriman jerked his arm away and barked, "It's nothing. Just a scratch." He reached for a handkerchief in his back pocket and pressed it on the cut.

"What happened?" Captain Laggins turned around, and walked back toward the two men.

"Donaldo cut his arm on one of those sharp rocks," Mitch answered. *It's all over with before it's really begun. I should've listened to Kenzie. She knew it wouldn't work. Why am I so goddamn stupid?*

"Those damn sharp rocks," Laggins muttered. "I don't know why in the hell those monks placed them in the walls like that. They're nothing but a hazard. Let me see your arm, Mr. Perriman," he said, reaching for Perriman's arm.

"No need for that," Perriman declared. "Let's continue with the tour. I want to see the catacombs. I think they may be just what I've been looking for years."

"First, Mr. Perriman, I need to check that cut on your arm," Laggins insisted. "I keep a medical kit in a room just ahead. We can do it there."

The two men just stood there, looking at each other, and said nothing. Finally, Perriman nodded, and Captain Laggins led the way to the small room. In the middle of a table was a well-worn U.S.M.C. medical kit.

"Let's get you out of that coat," Laggins said, taking Perriman by the shoulders. "My God, this man is brawny, more powerfully built that any Marine I served with," he remarked to Mitch, as he struggled to help Perriman out of his coat. "Dr. Gainer, take a seat, and open the medical kit, but don't touch anything."

Mitch opened the medical kit, and watched the two men grapple with removing the coat from Perriman's broad shoulders. He took a closer look and was surprised as what he saw. In addition to the usual bandages, sterile gauze, tape, scissors and tweezers, there were scalpels, hypodermic needles, surgical sutures, a needle holder, and a fine-toothed forceps.

"Have a seat, Mr. Perriman," Laggins folded the coat and set it on the table. "Do you work out regularly?" he asked, as he reached for a pair of scissors and began cutting the sleeve of Perriman's blooded-stained shirt.

"Twice a day," Perriman answered.

Laggins dabbed some gauze on the cut. "This is a clean cut that will need a couple of stitches. I can save you a trip to the doctor, Mr. Perriman, and can stitch it up here, if you like."

"What!" Mitch leaped up from his seat, and glared at Captain Laggins. "You're no doctor! Clean the cut and we'll take him to a doctor immediately." Mitch sat down when he realized that both men had ignored his words.

"Where did you learn to stitch wounds?" Perriman asked.

"When I was in the Marine Corps at the battle of Chosin Reservoir, in Korea. Our medic went down and I had to take over. After that, any time our medic went down—which was often because fingers were continually frostbitten—it became my job. It was the best thing I ever did in that horrific war. It's far better to save people than to knock them down."

"Stitch away, Captain Laggins," Perriman said, smiling at the ex-Marine who put on his surgical gloves and reached for his surgical tools.

Mitch was impressed with Laggin's finesse at pushing the round needle into the skin, pulling the surgical string through, tying the knot, and cutting the string in one fluid motion. In no time, Laggins sealed the cut with four neatly placed stitches.

"You're right," Mitch said to Laggins, when the captain finished bandaging the wound. "We didn't need a doctor. You certainly know your stuff."

"Unfortunately, I've had a lot of practice in my life." Laggins wrapped his tools in a cloth, and returned them to the medical kit. He turned to Perriman. "Mr. Perriman, keep that covered for a few days, then come by my office, and I'll take out the stitches. That cut will heal fine."

"Thanks, Captain Laggins." Perriman shook the captain's hand. He put his jacket without looking at the torn sleeve, and said to Mitch, "Can we get back on the tour? I'm anxious to see the rest of the catacombs."

"Let's do it," Laggins barked, taking the lead. He turned to Mitch, bringing up the rear, and called, "be sure that Mr. Perriman stays in the middle of the path and away from the walls."

"I appreciate your concern, Captain Laggins, but it's unnecessary. I don't make the same mistake twice," Perriman said, tongue in cheek.

The men walked in silence until they reached the stairway leading to the exit, when Perriman said, "Like Captain Laggins, I too, was in a battle with the Marines during war time. Only mine was during the Second World War, and my battlefield was in a bar. I was there, having a drink with a friend, when a group of Marines on leave came in. They were drunker than hell, hollering and screaming, raising hell. One of the Marines called me a coward, a draft dodger, and thumped me in the chest with his finger. I couldn't see much in those days, and didn't see his punch coming. It hit me flush on the mouth, splitting my lip, knocking out one of my front teeth, and stunning me.

"I remember grabbing him under his arms, putting my head under his chin, and lifting him off his feet. I drove him across the floor and into the jukebox. When we hit the jukebox, we slipped to floor. I could barely make out his face, but it was enough of a target, so I nailed him with everything I had. That ended it. I pushed him off me, and he laid on the floor, flat on his back, out for the count.

"The bartender called the cops. They thought I started the fight, and were going to arrest me for hitting the Marine, who was still on the floor. When the cop came close enough to put on the handcuffs, he waved his hand in front of my eyes. He knew then I could not see. Suddenly everything changed. The cops left without arresting anyone, the Marine got up from the floor, shook my hand, and we all sat down, got drunk, and closed the bar down."

"You certainly distinguished yourself in battle, Mr. Perriman. If you bring your program here, I'll be happy to serve under your command," Captain Laggins said, with a salute.

Perriman turned to Mitch. "Dr Gainer, I accept your offer to bring the mobility program to Sycamore on one condition—that Captain Laggins will be available to assist us in the training."

Mitch looked at Captain Laggins, who smiled. "You've got it. It's a deal, Mr. Perriman. When do you want to start?"

"Next Monday," Perriman replied.

"Oh, by the way, Mr. Perriman, go to any clothing store you want, and buy a new suit, shirt, and tie. Send the bill to me," Mitch added.

"Thanks, but no," Perriman said. "I've been buying my own clothes my whole life, and I'm too old to stop now."

CHAPTER 19

Graciela Cevallos was not looking forward to her meeting at St. Aloysius Abbey to discuss the order's coming to Sycamore Hospital. But she was very much looking forward to the three-hour drive though the back roads to the abbey, located in Shipshewana, a small town in Amish country. Today she would break in her brand new Italian lambskin racing gloves.

After putting them on, she made a couple of fists, opened her hands, and placed her palms on the hood on her prized possession: her canary-yellow Corvette. She was ecstatic because the specially ordered yellow gloves from Rome matched the car's color perfectly.

Settling behind the wheel, Graciela kept her eyes focused solely on the winding country roads. Oblivious to the passing scenery, her mind drifted back to when she'd walked into the governor's office yesterday afternoon, to discuss some new policies in her department. The governor was hunkered over his desk, his nose buried in a stack of papers. After five minutes—when he did not acknowledge her or even look up—she calmly walked to his desk, sat her policy book on top of the papers he was looking at, and stated, "Governor, I wish to inform you that I'm resigning my position. Tomorrow will be my last day." With that she walked out.

She smiled when she thought how she had never done anything that impetuous before. She'd known she was going to leave the agency as soon as things at the hospital were settled. To do it in such an impulsive fashion was so unlike her. But she had to admit it felt good. After all, she had been ignored from the very beginning. Perhaps it was fitting that she was ignored at the end. She rushed to her apartment, called Jason Overholt to tell him what she had done, and asked him to keep an eye on her apartment because she would be driving to Miami as soon as she met with the Trappist monks.

How she longed to get back home, among her people, and speak Spanish again. She would find something to do, but it would never be working for someone else again. She would be her own boss. Knowing that she had good business sense, she would find her niche.

The sign, "Welcome to Shipshewana, Indiana, Home of Indiana's Colossal Flea Market," appeared too soon for Graciela, who wanted to keep driving the country roads. She eased the Corvette down the main street, and settled behind a black horse and buggy. There were more buggies parked on the street than cars. The sidewalks were filled with Amish people, dressed in their traditional black garb.

Turning right at the Amish-Mennonite Museum, Graciela followed the road out of town for three miles, to a thick wooded area. When she pulled into a small parking lot at the edge of the woods, she could barely see the abbey behind a red sandstone wall. Peering over the wall, she saw the top of a church spire, and the roofs and chimneys of two buildings. She walked toward the ornate wooden gate, under a sandstone arch with a huge cross in the middle.

The gate swung open, and a small hunched-over man in a hooded black habit appeared. When he saw Graciela walking toward him, he faced her, elbows close to the sides of his frail body. His bony hand was stretched sideways, palm up. Speaking in a voice barely above a whisper, he said, "I'm Abbot Arthur. Welcome to St. Aloysius Abbey, Dr. Cevallos. You picked such a fine day to visit. I suggest we have our discussion in the garden."

Graciela followed the wobbly cleric, careful not to bump into him, down the winding path through a small grove of trees, to an open area next to the stone wall. The grass was so thick and soft, Graciela wanted to kick off her shoes and go barefoot. In the center was a luscious, rectangular garden filled with geraniums, pink daylilies, purple coneflowers, sedum, Russian sage, black-eyed Susans, petunias, coleus, and begonias. The flowers' fragrance was intoxicating, and Graciela suddenly was glad she'd made to the journey here.

She took a seat on a concrete bench, next to a statue of St. Francis of Assisi, and watched the abbot bend down and struggled to pick a large ceramic flagon of brown liquid that had been basking in the sun. Certain that he would drop the flagon, Graciela fought an urge to reach out and help him. This, she sensed, would offend him. There was nothing to do but hope he could bring it to the bench without incident. And that he did, in spite of losing his grip on the handle several times. Finally, staggering and stumbling, he dropped the flagon on the bench. To Graciela's surprise, it did not shatter.

"We'll treat ourselves to some sun tea, to celebrate this beautiful day," he said, reaching for a wooden box the size of a small suitcase, beneath the bench. With shaky hands, he opened it, took out a silver tray, and two antique-pewter tankards. Holding the hinged lid of the flagon open, he waved it above the tankards. Although the flagon was moving from side to side, he was able to fill the tankards to the brim, only splashing a moderate amount of tea on the tray, and none on the bench.

When the abbot reached down and started to hand one tankard to Graciela, she gently took it, and said, "Thank you, Abbot Arthur. This will be a real delight. I haven't had sun tea since I was a child. It was my father's favorite drink. I remember many hot muggy days in Miami, sharing sun tea with him, while watching him hand-roll his Cuban cigars."

She took a drink and smacked her lips together. "This brings back so many good memories for me. I'm glad to share this with you in this beautiful place."

Abbot Arthur smiled and squeezed Graciela's hand. They sat there, quietly absorbed in the sun tea, watching the humming birds feed on the brightly colored flowers, particularly the petunias and daylilies.

Graciela sat her tankard on the bench and faced the abbot, whose face was nearly hidden in the black hood. His eyes were closed, and she was unsure if he'd fallen asleep or was meditating. After waiting a few moments, she said softly, "Abbot Arthur, we have some fertile unused farm land at Sycamore Hospital that would be most suitable for planting a vineyard."

The abbot's eyes opened wide and he sat straight up on the bench.

"Since your order is well known for its excellent vineyard and wine," Graciela continued, "we would like to offer that land for you to plant and maintain a vineyard. There are also unused buildings that could be converted to a winery, if you so desire."

The abbot pulled off his hood, and took at long look at Graciela. He put his hood back on, saying, "Please, Dr. Cevallos, elaborate on the offer."

Graciela smiled at the face that disappeared in the hood. "The offer is very simple and straight forward. There are no hidden agendas. You bring your monks to Sycamore to plant, maintain, and harvest the grapes. Any profits that may occur are yours, as well as any expenses involved in the process. The land is provided free of charge—no lease or rent."

"What happens if the state sells the property? I've heard rumors that the property may be sold."

"That may happen. If it does, you will receive adequate compensation for your efforts."

"One final question, Dr. Cevallos. Tell me, what does the state gain from such an agreement?" the abbot asked, in a pleading voice. "It's not apparent."

"I understand your concern, Abbot Arthur. Let me say there is a desire to have the hospital utilize all its resources, as it did in the past. There was a time when the unused farm was producing crops that were not only feeding the patients, but the community as well.

"Sycamore was viewed a valuable resource by the community, and not looked down on, as it is today. A vineyard run by the Trappists would go a long way to restoring that image. You would be a welcomed and much-needed group who could bring the hospital back."

"Come, Dr. Cevallos, let us visit the church before you depart." Abbot Arthur took Graciela's arm and led her toward an ornate Romanesque style red sandstone church with a stunning steeple. To her surprise, he was no longer wobbly, but was now walking with a firm step. When they reached the steps of the arched doorway, Graciela suddenly pulled back and cried out, "I can't go in there, Abbot Arthur! I just can't!"

Graciela's words so alarmed the abbot, he lost his balance on the steps and started to fall. With Graciela's help, he steadied himself, and they both sat on the steps. The abbot was shaking; Graciela put her arm around him to comfort him. "I'm very fearful of falling," he said. "Last year I fell on these stairs and broke my hip. My bones are brittle and I'm afraid if I fall again, I'll be in a wheelchair for good."

"I'm sorry. I didn't mean to startle you. The words just came out," Graciela said.

"There's no need to apologize, Dr. Cevallos but, if you will, please tell me what on earth would cause you to say such a thing?"

Graciela took a long look at the gloomy face before saying, "It goes back to something that happened to me when I was a child." She then told the abbot, in vivid detail, about her Catholic school experience, and how it made her lose her faith—not in God, but in the Catholic Church.

When she finished, Graciela expected some response, but the abbot appeared to be more interested in watching the humming birds gather nectar than he was in her. Finally his eyes pulled away from the birds, and he reached in his pocket for his rosary. Holding it loosely in his palm, he looked at Graciela, and said, "Follow me."

She fell in line behind him as he led her into the sanctuary, down the aisle, to the huge crucifix behind the altar.

Graciela knelt, and said, "In the name of the Father, and of the Son, and of the Holy Spirit. Amen." After Abbot Arthur heard Graciela's confession, he returned his rosary to his pocket, and said, "I've heard your confession; now you can have communion."

Graciela was not sure she'd confessed to anything, but it didn't matter. All she knew was that she needed the body and blood of Christ, so she cupped her hands.

After receiving communion, Graciela followed Abbot Arthur to the door. When he opened the door, he reached again for his rosary, handed it to Graciela, and said, "I'd like you to have this. I have a feeling I won't be needing it much longer."

"Thank you, Abbot," Graciela said, squeezing the rosary tightly in her hand. "I seem to have lost mine somewhere along the way."

She started at the steps, then suddenly turned around. "Oh, by the way, I neglected to ask if you accept our offer to come to Sycamore Hospital."

"Your offer is accepted with great pleasure," he replied, a broad grin on his face.

"Good. Dr. Mitch Gainer will contact you to work out the arrangements."

When Graciela pulled out of the parking lot, she glanced in the rearview mirror, and took what she knew would be her last look at St. Aloysius Abbey. She felt an overwhelming sense of freedom, gained as she left the church. Communion had cleansed her and had brought her back to where she once was, and would always be.

There was only one thing left to do before she could put everything behind her. She had to contact Mitch Gainer to tell him the Trappist monks would be coming to the hospital. *I'll stop by Sycamore, then tell him when I get to Indianapolis. No, I don't want to see him. I'll stop on the way and call him. That's what I'll do.*

When Graciela reached the outskirts of Indianapolis, she pulled into a service station. After filling her gas tank, she spotted a telephone booth. As she dropped the coins in the slot, she had an irresistible urge to see him one more time.

"Mitch, this is Graciela."

"Graciela! It's good to hear your voice."

"I visited St. Aloysius Abbey and met with Abbot Arthur."

"How did it go?"

"It went well. I'm just outside the city. Could you meet me at Inocencio's in an hour? I'll fill you in."

"I'll be there."

"Welcome to Inocencio's, Dr. Gainer. It's a real pleasure seeing you again."

"It's good to see you," Mitch said, shaking the debonair proprietor's hand.

"Dr. Cevallos is powdering her nose and will join you at the table. Follow me, please." Inocencio led Mitch to the VIP Room. He pulled back a chair, announcing, "I just returned from a holiday in Portugal, and brought back some excellent port. The waiter will bring a bottle and some hors d'oeuvres for your enjoyment. "

Mitch was eyeing a deviled egg topped with caviar and a jalapeno stuffed olive when Graciela entered the room. She smiled, took a seat at the table, and reached for a wine glass. "I think I'll pass on Inocencio's tray of delicacies, but I can sure use a glass of wine."

"Been one of those days?" Mitch asked, as he poured her wine.

"What about you? Aren't you having some?"

"Unfortunately, I have to drive to Bloomington tonight. I never drink any alcohol if I have to drive. I've witnessed too many horror stories involving drinking and driving, starting with my father."

"That's admirable."

"There's nothing admirable about it. It's simply that if I were to drink, even a small glass when I knew I'd be driving, I wouldn't enjoy it. I'd be conflicted, so there would be no point. And one thing is for sure, I don't like being in conflict."

When he said that, he became aware he was in conflict right now—in conflict, because this superficial banter they were engaging in was, to him, meaningless. He knew that the only real conversation he wanted with this woman would involve revealing his feelings toward her. That frightened him. He knew he would fill the air instead with idle chatter which, in the end, would be dishonest.

"This is excellent port," Graciela said, sitting her glass down. "Inocencio is a real connoisseur of wine."

"Yes. He said he just brought this port back from Portugal." Mitch noticed that Graciela seemed to be avoiding eye contact. Her usual broad smile was replaced by a close-lipped frown, and her demeanor was one of melancholy. "How did things go with the abbot? Is he coming onboard?"

"Things went very well. He's accepted our offer with great enthusiasm. I told him that you would be contacting him to work out the details," Graciela said, her voice cracking. Tears were forming in her eyes.

"Graciela, what is it?" Mitch reached for her hand. She immediately pulled away.

"Mitch, I turned in my resignation this morning. I will be leaving tonight."

"What!"

"Things are over for me here. When I met with Abbot Arthur, I went in the church, and he offered me confession and communion. I took both for the first time since the incident with the nun. It cleansed me, Mitch, and brought me back to where I'd been. And that's where I want to be, back with the church I went to as a child, and back with my people in Miami."

Mitch was dumbfounded. Finally, after much hesitation, he asked, "Are you really going tonight?"

"Yes. It's better for me to get on the road. There's nothing left to stay for. My friend Jason will close my apartment and ship my stuff to me."

"You're driving, I take it."

"Certainly. That's how I travel. That's how I came here, and that's how I'll leave. But Mitch, I have to tell you something. Being with you is the best thing that ever happened to me, even though it was over with before it really began. I want you to know I'll never forget you, because you have a place in my heart." She picked up a napkin, wiped the tears from her eyes, and rushed out of the room.

Mitch slumped in his chair, fighting back tears. He was dismayed because he could not bring himself to validate Graciela's feelings, and let her know that he cared for her. He felt a strong urge to run after her and tell her how he felt, but it was too late. He'd had his chance and blew it. For that, he felt shame.

CHAPTER 20

Mitch was leaning back in his chair, feet on his desk, sipping a cup of espresso. Listening to the haunting melody of Ravel's "Bolero" on his cassette recorder, he was reflecting on what had happened since he met with Graciela Cevallos at Inocencio's.

He was pleased that the transition of the mobility program and the religious order to Sycamore had gone smoothly. The fields were filled with men in black hoods, tilling the soil. The catacombs were occupied by people, with limited or no sight, learning mobility skills.

Although he was delighted with the way things had gone, he was still on guard. It was too quiet. He had not heard a word from his superiors, or anyone else, about these two vastly different groups suddenly being a part of Sycamore. Even Ms. Bascom had said nothing. But there had to be an undercurrent, and he was going to be prepared for it.

Mitch had long disciplined himself not to fret about things he couldn't control. Even though the sale of Sycamore was totally out of his control, he feared it would happen at any moment.

He'd wanted to talk to Guillermo before the inevitable sale. Now, he felt an urgent need to do so, as soon as possible. But he clearly did not want to break his word, not to contact Guillermo during his convalescence. He had no choice, if he wanted to communicate with his absent friend.

When the music's final refrain faded away, Mitch reached for the telephone. "Captain Laggins, this is Mitch. Meet me at the Ding Dong Tavern after work. There's something important I need to talk to you about."

Mitch spotted Captain Laggins standing alone at the end of the bar. Glancing at the tables filled with correctional officers, he thought how different things were now. Instead of being rebuffed, as he had been when he first entered the Ding Dong, now he was greeted with smiles and raised mugs of beer. Even those playing pool and shuffle board interrupted their games to give him a warm welcome.

Mitch sat on the stool next to Laggins, threw a twenty-dollar bill on the bar, and signaled the bartender. "Bring the captain another depth charge and I'll have a club soda."

"Dr. Gainer, one of these days, you'll have to have a depth charge with me," Laggins said, dropping the shot glass into the huge glass of beer.

"I will, I promise. Kenzie will be with me, and she can carry me out, if need be."

"That's good; she can have a depth charge too. If it's necessary, I'll carry both of you out."

Mitch laughed and shook his head. "Tell me, Captain Laggins, you're always standing at the end of the bar. Do you ever sit on a stool or at a table?"

"Never! When I'm at the Ding Dong Tavern with my people, I'm still on duty. I can monitor everything that's going on from my perch here. If there are any signs of trouble, I can nip it in the bud, before it even begins."

"You remind me of Squire Young," Mitch said, in a serious tone. "He's the man heading the group who wants to buy Sycamore. I think I've told you about him. He ran a casino for me when I was on the reservation."

"Yes, I remember."

"Well, he used to stand at the corner of a balcony above the gaming floor. I can still see him there, arms folded across his chest, scanning the floor below, like a beacon light. He never missed a thing, and said many times that he could run the whole operation from the balcony he called the 'bridge.' In fact, when he trained a manager to replace him, he would seldom let the man go on the gaming floor, insisting that the man spend his time on the bridge, watching what was going on below."

"He was wise. He knew the key is to be aware and know when to act, and when not to."

"You said a mouthful."

"Speaking of Squire Young, I just got a tip that the governor is livid that the blind and monks are at Sycamore. He is blaming Graciela Cevallos, and has fired her."

"He didn't fire her," Mitch snapped. "She quit. If he wants to blame anyone for it, it should be me. I'm the one who brought them to Sycamore."

Captain Laggins chuckled and tapped Mitch on the arm. "I knew it was you who brought them. There's no way Graciela Cevallos would do that. She's not one to interfere, and besides, she does not work for us."

"In truth, I'm not sure she thought it was a good idea, particularly bringing the monks on board, but she helped me just the same. She's a damn good woman. Oh, by the way, how are the monks and Perryman doing?"

"I think you know the answer to that, Dr. Gainer. They're top flight, absolutely top flight. The monks are some of the best workers I've seen. They work silently and never take a break, including Abbot Arthur. I worry that the abbot is going to drop dead in the field one day. He's so damn fragile, and appears in bad health, but he keeps pace with the rest. In fact he leads them.

"Donaldo Perriman runs a real tight ship. He's a great teacher and, above all, a great motivator. I think if he told the clients they could run through the catacombs, they would actually do it."

"Is he using you in the teaching?"

"Is he using me in the teaching?" Laggins roared. "Hell, he's got me blindfolded, using a cane, leading the group through the catacombs. It tops any mission I led in Korea. I can tell you that."

The image of the burly captain leading the clients was too much for Mitch, and he broke out laughing. "How are your arms? Have they made contact with the sharp rocks?"

"Do bears shit in the woods? Thank God, I still have a heavy leather flight jacket I won in a poker game in the Corps. It serves as a great buffer. My arms are just fine."

"Sounds like Perriman has you going beyond the call of duty. Are you sure you want to do that?"

"Dr. Gainer, you told me to assist Perriman in the program, and that's what I'm doing," Laggins said, a stern look on his face.

"Tell me, Captain Laggins, do you enjoy working with the blind and visually impaired?"

"Yes, I do. I'm learning a lot. I want to help these people, and Perriman is showing me how. And besides, he'll come to the Ding Dong and enjoy a depth charge with me."

"Well I'm giving you another assignment," Mitch said abruptly. "Things are coming to a head now. It's time that I contact

Guillermo to make final plans. I'll be going to Miami next week to see him, and I want you to take over while I'm gone."

"Will the brass like that? You know I don't have a degree." Laggins laughed.

"They'll have to. You're the only one around here who can do it. Everyone knows that, so there'll be no issue. I'll even give you the title of acting superintendent, if you want it for your resume."

"Forget that. I've never liked the term. It doesn't fit me in any way."

Mitch signaled the bartender, and handed him another twenty-dollar bill. "This is for a round of depth charges for Captain Laggins and Donaldo Perriman, the next time they're in here together." Turning to Captain Laggins, he slapped him on the back. "I'll see you when I get back. If you have any problems, call Kenzie. She'll help you."

CHAPTER 21

Mitch was sitting on the balcony of his Fontainebleau Hotel suite, enjoying an exquisite view of the ocean. He was sipping on a piña colada, and had just snipped the end of a bootlegged Cuban cigar he bought from the Miami airport cab driver. As he lit the cigar and took a deep drag, he thought back on his best days in Cleveland, when he would smoke a cigar and watch the lake freighters make their way in and out of port. There was something about being around water—whether it was the ocean, a lake, a river, a stream, a waterfall, or even a pond—that always created a tranquil mood. In spite of making such a big fuss about staying in such a posh hotel, when a simple motel near the airport would have been just fine, he was damn glad he was here. He knew he was now in the best frame of mind for his grand finale with Guillermo.

Somewhere in the middle of his second piña colada, Mitch's thought again about his encounter with Kenzie, after he'd met with Captain Laggins. He could see her, in her pajamas, sitting on the sofa, reading her students' compositions.

"Mitch! You're finally home. I was starting to be concerned. You usually call me when you're going to be late like this. What's going on?"

"I had a meeting with Captain Laggins at the Ding Dong Tavern after work. I know I should have called you, but I got caught up in the moment."

Kenzie laughed and set her papers aside. "You got caught up in the moment. That's your excuse for being irresponsible." She got up from the sofa, threw her arms around him, kissed his neck, and whispered in his ear, "Well you're home now. That's what I want. That's what I've always wanted."

"That's no excuse. That's just what happened. I'm sorry for that."

"You should be," Kenzie said, smiling.

"Do you want an earful now, or do you want to finish grading your papers?"

"The papers can wait. Fill my ears."

"Good. Let me get a beer. Do you want anything?"

"I'll have a glass of wine. There's some chardonnay in the refrigerator."

Mitch returned with the drinks and sat next to Kenzie. "I'm finishing things at the hospital because I sense the end will be coming soon, and the place will be sold.

"Things are going very well—the program for the blind and the monks have settled in. They've all been accepted, and even welcomed by the staff. Now it's time for me to contact Guillermo, to tell him that things are coming to the end. I need to call him and tell him that, but I keep putting off the call. I just don't want to do it."

Kenzie moved closer to Mitch, and rested her hand on his thigh. "I know it's hard for you to call your friend, your mentor, and tell him that things have not worked out as he hoped."

"It's not that."

"Well what is it?"

"When I last saw Guillermo in the hospital, he emphatically told me not to contact him while he was recovering. He made a strong point for me to wait until he contacted me. I did not like it, but I agreed."

"Now I understand, Mitch," Kenzie said sympathetically, "you feel like you'll be breaking your word, if you call him."

"Yes, but I know I have no choice but to call him, and tell him I'm coming. I can't just pop in his house, unannounced. It's very important that I see him."

"When do you want to see him?"

"The sooner the better."

"I have a solution, my love. You shouldn't make the call, but I can. We're a team, Mitch, and when Guillermo gets you, he gets me. He knows that."

The third piña colada and the butt end of the Cuban cigar took hold. Mitch wobbled to his feet, and headed for the satin sheets of the hotel's Louis XIV bed.

Mitch handed the address to the driver, and jumped in the back seat of the cab. He was feeling refreshed, having had the best night's sleep in months.

"The address is in Little Havana. It's a short drive from here." The driver set the meter. "It's a popular tourist area where many Cuban refugees live. They have a lot of good restaurants, shops, and fruit markets. The music and nightlife is great, and there are many beautiful women. I could introduce you to one if you like."

Mitch smiled, shook his head, and muttered, "No thank you."

The cab stopped at a small bright pink house, at the end of a cul-de-sac in a quiet neighborhood, near the tourist section. Mitch jumped out, thrust a twenty-dollar bill at the driver, and rushed down the sidewalk to the front door. As soon as he reached for the doorbell, the door opened, and Guillermo appeared.

Mitch was stunned—the emaciated man in front of him, holding out his hand, could not be Guillermo. If he'd met him on the street, he would not have recognized him. The honey-colored full face was now shrunken and grey. The muscular frame was no more, and worst of all, Guillermo looked like an old man.

It was only when Mitch felt the firm handshake, and noticed the steely-eyed look, that he sensed his friend may not be as bad off as he looked. As long as he had some strength and a determined will, he knew that his friend would survive.

"Let's go out on the patio," Guillermo said, placing his hand on Mitch's shoulder and leading him down the hallway to the patio door. "Benita's in the Keys for the day, and has left us some fruit, mango juice, and unsweetened tea."

"No Cubano sandwiches, Bucanero beer, or Saint Louis Rey Havana Club cigars?" Mitch said, as he took a seat beneath a huge umbrella. "What a place you have here, my good friend. There is nothing like palm trees blowing in the breeze, luscious flowers basking in the sun, and a small pond filled with colorful fish."

Guillermo joined Mitch at the table. "I can do without the sandwiches and the beer, but I must admit I miss my cigars. I've been smoking them since I was twelve years old. I've made an agreement with my new doctor that I can start smoking them again on my ninetieth birthday. That's my goal—to live long enough to light a good hand-rolled Cuban cigar. I still keep a box around, and take a whiff every now and then. But I never torch one up. They'll still be good thirty years from now, when I reach ninety."

"I have no doubt that you'll make it. You're like Kid Gavilan, a real warrior."

"I know I look like death warmed over, Mitch, but now I'm finally on my way back. The damn doctors who were first treating me were starving me, and wouldn't let me do a damn thing.

All they wanted me to do was shuffle along the sidewalk for a few minutes, then rest, and then do it one more time. After that, I was to pick up a three-pound barbell, curl it five times, and go to bed.

"Well I finally got tired of my treatment, and fired the whole lot of them. A friend of mine told me about Dr. Fernandez, a new doctor from Havana, who just opened his practice in Little Havana. He's only been treating me for a month or so, and I'm already feeling better. Next week I start working out with him at the gym, and I've been walking several times a day for short distances. Although there has been some damage to my heart, he believes that with a good diet, regular exercise, and, of course, no cigars, I will eventually be able to live a normal life."

"What about stress, Guillermo? What does he say about that?"

"He doesn't say much. He knows me well enough to know that stress is not much of an issue with me. I've always been able to deal with issues or jobs that would be stressful for most people, but not for me. I learned as a young kid in Cuba to let things roll off my back, and not let things get me up upset. You've worked with me. You know damn well that I can handle any stress this world can throw at me."

"I sure do. Although there have times I've wondered if you're really as calm on the inside as you are on the outside."

"The answer to that is yes. There's no difference. Stress played no factor in my heart issues. They have no idea what caused it. I've been told that it may have been a strange virus, but my doctor now tells me he doesn't know. He also said it's not a big issue, and writes it off as something that sometimes happens to people. Nonetheless, I'm no longer interested in a big job, with a lot of hours and challenges, mainly because it would cause Benita to worry about me. I can't do that to her. I've enough stashed away so I don't have to work. If I do work again, it will be for shorter hours. There's a good chance I'll spend my working days fishing off a skiff in the Keys, or the islands or, just maybe, with a little luck, in Cuba."

"I suppose it all boils down to this—you can do what the hell you want to, as long as long as you watch your diet and don't smoke Cuban cigars."

"You got it, my friend."

"Let me put you to work right now," Mitch said, bringing things to a head. "My gut tells me that things are coming to an end at Sycamore. Now is the time to give you the final report."

Guillermo nodded and reached for a tablet and a pencil on the table.

"Sycamore is in much better shape now than before you took it over," Mitch began. "That's all due to your leadership. Because you conscripted Captain Laggins, he took me under his wing, and together we able to improve the patient care on the wards. There is no patient abuse of any kind at the institution. I can attest to that."

"Good. I knew that Laggins was the key. We had to have him on our side to do anything. He's a remarkable human being, much more humane than his Marine exterior would suggest," Guillermo commented, scribbling some notes on the tablet.

"He sure as hell is. Do you know that he drinks depth charges at the Ding Dong Tavern after shift?"

Guillermo looked up from tablet, a puzzled look on his face. "A depth charge? What in the hell is that?"

"You dump a shot of whiskey, glass and all, in a mug of beer and swill it down.

Guillermo smiled and shook his head. "I guess you could say that's a two-fisted drink for two-fisted man."

"Or better yet, a powerful drink for a powerful man," Mitch added.

"Have it your way."

"I couldn't do a damn thing with the social-work staff, as far as therapy was concerned," Mitch said, eager to get back on task. "They were an eager group, young and green, but were too bogged down in paper work to do any therapy. So I had them streamline their paper work, with Ms. Bascom's guidance. They soon caught up, and were able to ensure that the inmates who were being warehoused could get to court, and on their way."

"That's great, Mitch. I always felt that those inmates were more like political prisoners. Many of them were being held because they were ignored by the court, and some didn't belong there in the first place. They were just being warehoused."

"Morale is much improved, and entire system operates more efficiently," Mitch continued. "However, I wanted to develop some new programs, but I knew we had little time, so I decided to bring two successful ones to the hospital."

Guillermo nodded approval and put down his pencil.

"With Graciela's help, we brought in a blind mobility program. They're using the catacombs to teach mobility travel."

"Just like the blind program that used the tunnels under the VA in Cleveland?"

""Right on," Mitch said, with a grin. "We also brought Abbot Arthur and his Trappist monks to start a vineyard in the vacant fields. Both groups are thriving, and are accepted by staff with open arms."

"Well I'll be damned! Providence has spoken. The monks have returned to their home. You know Sycamore Hospital was originally built as an abbey with catacombs and all the rest. If I wasn't so ill, I'd light a Cuban cigar. This is great, Mitch, just great."

"That's why we brought the monks to the hospital. My last act will be to publicize the hell out of it, get some television and newspaper coverage. Kenzie will put on a concert. I want to go out with a bang because I know the sale will be coming soon."

The doorbell rang.

"Mitch, would you answer the door? I have a cramp in my leg."

When Mitch opened the door, he stiffened, pulled back, nearly losing his balance. "Graciela," he stammered.

Graciela gave Mitch a broad smile, and brushed past him. She turned back and said, "I take it you and Guillermo have been on the patio."

"Yes." Mitch caught up to her before they reached the patio door. When he went to open the door, he caught a whiff of the red rose she was wearing in her hair.

Guillermo was standing by the table, camera in hand. "Let me take a picture of my two best interns. It would be good if you stood by the pond. That would make the best picture. The light is just perfect."

"Here, you better take these, before I change my mind," Graciela said handing Guillermo a box of cigars. "I shouldn't be giving you cigars. Whatever you do, don't tell Benita that I gave them to you. She would never forgive me!"

Guillermo smiled, but refused to accept the cigars. "They're not for me. They're for Mitch. Give them to him."

When Graciela handed him cigars, he looked at her. Her sparkling eyes with their long lashes pulled him toward her. He felt an urge to reach out and touch her smooth olive-colored cheek. He knew that she was still on his mind, and that made him shiver. "Thank you. Are these your father's cigars?"

"Yes they are. He just rolled them yesterday."

"Give him my thanks." Mitch took a cigar from the box and held it under his nose. "Nothing beats the smell of hand-rolled Cuban cigars. I will savor them."

"I hope that's all you do—enjoy their fragrance," Graciela commented, with a slight smile. "To smoke them is imprudent."

"Your words, not mine," Mitch countered. "At those rare times when one desires an hour of complete relaxation, devoid of all stimuli—a return to the womb one might say—nothing beats a hand-rolled Cuban cigar."

"Well put," Guillermo blared. "Now, let's take the picture."

Guillermo put the camera back on the table, and remained standing while Mitch and Graciela sat down. After a few moments, he began to speak. "After I had the heart issue, I resigned myself to the fact that we were not going to be successful at Sycamore.

"But," he said, raising both his voice and his index finger, "that's not what happened. "You both have made our efforts a success. I always knew they were going to close the hospital. The best we could do was to humanize it, and leave it better than we found it. But you two went way beyond that.

"I recognized early on that powers that be who hired me wanted my name only, and not the reforms they pretended to want. Bringing the blind and the monks to Sycamore was simply brilliant. When you publicize that, the community will see Sycamore in a different light. They'll see there have been positive changes. I can't thank you enough." Guillermo sat down.

Mitch and Graciela looked at each other, but said nothing. Mitch turned to Guillermo and said, "Graciela's the one who made it all happen. Had she not intervened, your prophecy would have come true, and we would have failed. And what's worse, she paid a price for it. The way she was treated, by even by the governor, was scandalous." He reached under the table and took Graciela's hand.

"I know. I feel terrible about that," Guillermo said sadly.

"Stop it," Graciela declared. "I wasn't treated any differently after I started helping Mitch than when I first joined the agency. All they wanted a female face, with good credentials, for window dressing. They didn't really mistreat me; they just ignored me.

"Helping Mitch was the first constructive thing I did after going to work there. It made me aware of what I was missing, and how I had to get out of that job."

Suddenly, Guillermo stood up. "I'm afraid we'll have to end this. I'm very tired and need to rest."

Mitch and Graciela got up, hugged their mentor, and started to leave. When they reached the front door, Mitch told Guillermo, "When this is all over, I'll contact you, and we can get together. I know Kenzie wants to see you before we leave for her next tour."

"That will be good, Mitch," Guillermo said, as he ambled down the hallway to his bedroom.

When Mitch closed the front door, he remembered he'd forgotten to call a cab. But the door was locked. "I need to call a cab," he explained to Graciela.

When he reached for the door bell, Graciela grabbed his hand. "Don't disturb Guillermo. He needs his rest. You don't need to call cab. I'll give you a ride."

Mitch opened the Corvette's door and slid into the passenger seat. "This is the first time I've been in a Corvette. It will be quite a treat."

Graciela slipped on her racing gloves and settled in the driver's seat. She gave Mitch a broad smile and put the car into gear. The Corvette lurched forward with such acceleration that Mitch was pushed back against his seat.

"Where to, kind sir?"

"Apparently the Indy 500," Mitch replied, fascinated by Graciela's skill at weaving the Corvette in and out of traffic. "A pit stop at the Fontainebleau Hotel would be in order."

"Good choice. The opulence there is beyond description."

"Kenzie made the reservation, not me. I would have preferred to stay in a much cheaper and less ritzy hotel. But I'm glad she did, because I've enjoyed being pampered in one of the finest hotels in the country. Everyone should have that experience, at least one time in their life."

"I'll bet you've had that experience many times in your travels, when she's on tour."

"Oh yes, many times over. It's one of the best perks of being married to an elite classical musician. You stay in the best hotels, eat in the best restaurants, and are generally catered to by all who are involved in the music world. But that does not mean much to Kenzie. She accepts it as something that she has to do. For her it's all music—the music, the performance, and even the long hours of practice and study."

Mitch paused and began to laugh. "I learned early on, in the second grade when the teacher jerked the tambourine from my hands, that I was not made to make music. But I certainly enjoy the benefits from one who knows how. If you really want to know the best part, I'll tell you. It's when Kenzie plays a classical piece, and then finishes with my two favorite songs—"The Rose" and "A Whiter Shade of Pale"—for my ears only."

"That would make a great romantic scene in a movie. I could see Raquel Welch playing the cello, and Paul Newman sitting by the fire place, taking it all in."

"That's enough about me," Mitch said, playfully shaking his index finger at Graciela. "Tell about your life in Miami. Are you happy?"

"I don't think in terms of happiness, so I can't say," Graciela replied. "I can say it feels good to be back in my old neighborhood, with my family, old friends, and the church that I was raised in."

"Are you working?"

"I'll be joining Esteban Fernandez, a physician from Cuba, who has just opened his practice in Little Havana."

"Is he the doctor who is treating Guillermo?"

"Yes, in fact, it was Guillermo who got me the job. I'm looking forward to doing some clinical work with patients again. I've had enough administration and politics; it's time to get back to some real work."

"Good for you, Graciela. You're an excellent clinician, on a par with Guillermo. It would be a shame if you didn't use those skills," Mitch said warmly.

"Oh, no," Graciela exclaimed, giving Mitch a hard look. "Don't imply I'm on par with Guillermo. No one is, least of all me. He's one of a kind, and you, of all people, know that."

Mitch chuckled. "Have it your way, Missy, but if you're not on par with him, you're so close, there's only a cigarette-paper's difference between the two of you."

"I suppose your cigarette-paper analogy is a reflection of the mining camp vernacular of your youth."

"Touché," Mitch grinned. When Graciela put her hand on the gear shift, he placed his hand on top of hers. "I'm really going to miss you."

"Here's your hotel," Graciela said, her voice quivering.

When the car came to a stop in front of the hotel, they sat there, looking at each other without speaking. After a few moments, Mitch finally spoke, in a voice not much louder than a whisper, "I want you to come in. We can have dinner, and spend some time together. I don't want you to leave."

Tears streamed down Graciela's cheeks as she took hold of Mitch's hands. "You would regret it," she sobbed, "and I could not stand that. You're attached to Kenzie and there's nothing I can do about that. And neither can you. Goodbye, my love."

Mitch opened the door and stumbled onto the sidewalk. As he watched the Corvette speed away and disappear in the traffic, he told himself that "sometimes life is too complicated."

CHAPTER 22

Mitch watched the luggage go around the baggage carousel, searching for his leather travel bag. When he leaned over to snatch it, he felt a hand on his shoulder.

"I'm so glad you're back. I know you haven't been gone that long, but I've really missed you."

Mitch dropped his bag, took Kenzie in his arms, and kissed her deeply. "We're not used to being apart," he said, smiling. "It's hard to remember the last time we were. It seems like it's been years. We've been together all the time since you began touring."

"I don't know if it's that so much," Kenzie said, taking Mitch's arm as they walked to the exit. "I think it has to do with the circumstances of this particular trip. I was worried about you, and really did not want you to go. I knew you had to see Guillermo in person to deliver what I'm sure was not good news."

"I did what I had to. Your setting up the meeting was the key. You always come through for me when I most need it. It wasn't the bad news about the hospital sale that bothered me. It was breaking my vow not to contact Guillermo during his covalence. He would not have taken it kindly if I had called him and set up the meeting."

"Do you think he really would have reacted that way if you contacted him, and not me?"

"Absolutely," Mitch replied, taking Kenzie's hand and squeezing it tightly. "Loyalty and honesty rule with Guillermo. You don't do go back on your word with him. It's one of the things I admire about him. You know what he stands for."

"How's his health?"

"That's hard to say. I was shocked when I first saw him. He looked like a man who is almost on his last leg."

"I'm sorry to hear that," Kenzie said, nestling her head in Mitch's shoulder.

"Looks can be deceiving. His grip and voice are strong, and, as you know, Guillermo is iron-willed. He was not happy with the treatment he received from his first doctors. They restricted his activities and diet too much. Now he's seeing a new doctor, a fellow Cuban, who he has great confidence in. The doctor told him that he had slight damage to his heart, and with regular exercise, a healthy diet—and no Cuban cigars—he could live a normal life.

"Right after Guillermo told about no more cigars, the doorbell rang. It was Graciela. She brought Guillermo a box of her father's prized hand-rolled cigars. He refused them, and told her to give them to me."

"So you met with Graciela!" Kenzie blurted out.

"Maybe she just came over to deliver the cigars, or maybe Guillermo invited her to met with us, since she was an important part if our work at Sycamore. If he did invite her, he didn't say anything to me. But I was glad to see her, because she was a real help to me."

"Yes, I'm well aware she was a real help to you," Kenzie said.

Kenzie's sarcasm stunned him and Mitch fumbled for words. Finally he said, "Kenzie, you're not thinking there is something going on between me and Graciela."

"It's not just a thought, Mitch. I know there's something between you two. I just don't know what it is."

Mitch knew that she was right. There were deep feelings between him and Graciela. He would've acted on those feelings, had Graciela not applied the brakes. Thank God she did, he told himself.

Deciding there was no need to hold anything back, he said, "When Graciela appeared, Guillermo took over, and began addressing us like he did when we were his students. He motioned us to take seats on the sofa, while he stood by a large oil painting of a bare-chested Earnest Hemingway, hauling a marlin onto the deck of the Pilar. He then delivered what could best be described as a dazzling lecture.

"He began by saying that he had resigned himself to failure, and ended by declaring, that thanks to us, our tenure—including his at Sycamore—had been a success. We did make positive changes, and have left the hospital in a far better place than it was before we came. As soon as he finished, Guillermo announced that he was tired and needed to rest.

"When we left the house, I remembered I forgot to call a cab. The front door locked when I closed it, and I could not get back in the house. I was going to ring the doorbell, but Graciela insisted that I not disturb him. She offered to give me a ride to my hotel."

Kenzie bit her lip and stared at Mitch.

"It was a short drive to the hotel, so we didn't have much time to talk. She told me how she was glad to back in her old neighborhood, with her family, old friends, and the church. I told her about being on tour with you, and how much I liked it when you would play music for me only.

"When we got to hotel," Mitch said, then paused. After a few moments, he said, "I asked her if I could take her to dinner at the hotel."

"Yes, go on," Kenzie said, her voice icy.

"She said no, because she knew that I was bonded to you. Then she said goodbye and left."

"Well at least I've learned one thing about Graciela. She has good sense."

Three weeks had passed since Mitch and Kenzie had the conversation about his visit with Guillermo. Mitch knew there nothing more to do at Sycamore, except remain at the facility until the final word came down to leave.

Not one to be sitting around twiddling his fingers, Mitch wanted to stage an event, officially welcoming the mobility program and the monks. The public would be invited. Tours of the vineyards, and perhaps, of the catacombs would be given. He envisioned a picnic-like atmosphere on the grounds, with refreshments, and even balloons for the children. Each participant would receive a graphic T-shirt commemorating the event.

Mitch reached out to the local media for exposure. Although he was promised coverage, he did not sense a strong interest in the event. The responses he received when he contacted community agencies were lukewarm at best.

Mitch was not totally surprised because he was well aware that Sycamore's public image was negative, and many in the community thought the place should be ignored. He recognized that the event would likely be a failure, unless he could come up with something to attract more interest.

There was only one thing that would stimulate the community enough to attract a huge crowd, and bring the attention that Mitch desperately sought. Would Kenzie perform at the event? Because of her position at the university, she had become a huge celebrity—written up in the newspapers and interviewed by local radio and television personalities.

Kenzie's performance would put the event over the top. But Mitch sensed that was no longer a certainty. When he'd first told her about the mobility program, she said she would be willing to perform to help publicize their program. Unfortunately, since his visit with Guillermo, each time he brought up the topic of her performing, she brushed him off and changed the topic.

Mitch decided he would soon bring things to a head. The opportunity came after they had enjoyed a delicious meal at Bloomington's finest Italian restaurant, and were lying in bed, reading. Since they made it a rule not to talk during reading time, Mitch reached over and gently placed his hand on the top of *The Mayor of Casterbridge*, Hardy's book that Kenzie was re-reading. Kenzie put the book aside, and looked at Mitch, her eyes flashing.

"I need to talk to you about something."

"It's about time."

Kenzie's curt response threw Mitch off balance. He stumbled with his words. "I want to know why you won't talk to me about performing at the event I'm planning. You know it's very important to me."

"That I do know, just as you know exactly why I've not talked to you about performing."

Mitch scratched his neck, and looked up at the ceiling. "I suppose it has something to do with Graciela."

"Your words, not mine."

"I told you the truth."

"I know that," conceded Kenzie, "but I have little taste for the abbreviated version."

"Well if that's what you want, I'll give it to you verbatim, or as close as I can," Mitch said a little shamefaced. "When she dropped me at the hotel, I asked her to come in. I said we could have dinner, and spend some time together. I remember saying that I did not want her to leave."

"She began to cry," Mitch said, his voice shaking. "She took my hand and told me that I would regret it, and she could not stand that. She said that I was attached to you and there was nothing she could do it, and neither could I. Then she said, 'goodbye, my love,' got in her car, and left."

"I don't love the woman, nor did I ever tell her, or hint that I did," Mitch said, a forlorn look on his face.

"That I know for sure. You were just intrigued," Kenzie said, kissing her husband. "You can now rest easy. My students and I have composed, and will perform, a special piece of music for the event. I'll do a couple of solos, and close with 'Back Home Again in Indiana.'

"Now let's get back to our reading."

CHAPTER 23

Mitch sat on a bench just outside the main entrance to Sycamore. He reached in his sport-coat pocket for his cigar case and butane lighter. After selecting a Cuban cigar, he held it beneath his nose and breathed deeply. Then he took his antique cigar cutter from his pants pocket and clipped one end.

Doing exactly what Guillermo had taught him, he held the other end directly above the flame and rotated it so the cigar would toast evenly. He was careful not to let the end touch the flame. When a small black ring of ash appeared and began to smolder, he placed the cigar in his mouth, and gently inhaled three times.

Satisfied that the cigar was burning evenly, he got up from the bench, and headed for the grassy field where the event would be held next week. He immediately spotted Kenzie, dressed in a tank top and denim shorts. She was leading several students and a group of monks carrying lumber up a small knoll to where they were building a stage.

Mitch stopped at one of the picnic tables the monks built for the event and sat down. He took a deep drag of his cigar, swirled the smoke around in his mouth, threw his head back, and blew a smoke ring in the air. As he watched it disappear in the blue sky, he reminded himself how fortunate he was that Kenzie was participating.

In fact, she had thrown herself head first into the project, allowing him to step aside. Take over she did. She met with the media, did radio and television interviews, as well as speaking to community groups. Her efforts had paid dividends, as the big event at Sycamore Hospital was now the talk of the town.

Mitch was amazed how efficiently Kenzie swung a hammer. As soon as the monks put a board in place on the frame, she would immediately nail it in. Catching her eye when she raised the hammer high about her head, he immediately let out a war whoop, began to clap, and did a little dance, prompting her to shake her head at him as she struck the nail.

His cigar went out and when he reached for his lighter, he glanced at his watch. To his surprise, it was after closing time so he put cigar in his case to finish later. Captain Laggins would be at the Ding Dong Tavern. Mitch wanted to catch him there, to discuss final plans for the big event.

When Mitch walked into the Ding Dong, he saw Donaldo Perriman next to Captain Laggins. This was a problem because he wanted to speak to Laggins by himself. Now any conversation would have to involve Perriman. He decided that did not matter because the two had become thicker than thieves. Laggins was now teaching mobility travel to the blind, and Perriman was giving lectures on blindness awareness to the correctional officers and inmates.

"Bring these two gentlemen another depth charge and a glass of cranberry juice for me," Mitch called out to the bartender. He slapped Perriman on the shoulder, and took a stool next to him.

"I figured you'd turn up here tonight, boss, to discuss security for the big event," Laggins said, leaning over the bar to look directly at Mitch. "I asked Donaldo to be here so we could have his input, since his program is inside the institution."

"I'm glad you did. It's the security of his clients that concerns me the most. They will be the most vulnerable, if we have any issues," Mitch added.

Perriman turned toward Mitch, then sat his glass down hard on the bar, drawing the attention of those sitting around. In a loud voice, he said, "I think, Dr. Gainer, you will find that the visually impaired are no more vulnerable than anyone else at the hospital. Same as people with good vision, visually impaired people are perfectly capable of taking care of themselves in most situations. In this environment, thanks to the teaching of Captain Laggins, our people are able to defend themselves, if the need arises."

"That's right," said the bartender, who'd come over when he heard the clank of the glass. "Why just last week, one of Donaldo's boys was in here and pinned the best arm wrestler in nothing flat."

"Holy shit," Mitch exclaimed, his arms behind his head. "I stand corrected, Mr. Perriman. Apparently the visually impaired are no more vulnerable than anyone else. Nonetheless, I still want extra efforts made to guarantee their safety during this event, when our campus will be swarming with visitors. Just remember, if something happens and they're harmed in any way, the blame will fall on me, and I'll likely be keelhauled.

"Keelhauled?" the bartender asked "What's that?"

"In the old days, they used to punish sailors at sea by dragging them beneath the keel of the ship," Captain Laggins replied.

"Well, that doesn't sound very good. Thank God there's no ships around here," the bartender said, reaching for the tap to pour another beer.

This brought a round of laughter from those at the bar. When the laughter died down, Perriman picked up his glass, pointed it at Mitch, and said, "What you say is true. It is also true that it would not only land on you. It will splash on me and Captain Laggins as well.

"None of this really matters. What does matters is that you had the courage to bring our program to the most unlikely place—the catacombs in a maximum-security prison. Granted there is some danger to our people here, but no more, I can assure you, than when they are crossing the crowded streets of downtown Indianapolis, during rush-hour on a Friday evening, or a Monday morning." With that, Perriman drained his drink and gently sat his glass on the bar.

"Now that you have put things in proper perspective, I feel much better," Mitch remarked. "There's one more thing I want to discuss with you. Since we've decided the program will be in operation during the event, do you think it would be all right if we allow a few selected people to visit the catacombs and observe the training?"

"Absolutely not," exclaimed Perriman, in a voice suggesting he was feeling the effects of his second, or maybe third, depth charge. "All the people attending who want to observe the program should be permitted to do so, not just a select few."

"OK, Mr. Perriman, we should not discriminate. All people can observe, if they wish." Addressing Captain Laggins, Mitch asked, "Would this present too much of a security risk?"

Captain Laggins twirled his glass, watching the full shot of whiskey spin around in the beer at the bottom. He looked at Mitch and replied, "It would up the ante a bit, but nothing we could not easily handle. There will be as much security on the grounds of Sycamore as there would be if we had a presidential visit. Every officer on our payroll, whether they're on duty or not, will be on the grounds, in uniform or in plain clothes.

"As you know, Dr. Gainer, our staff is well trained. Although I would not tell them this, they're as good as, maybe even better, than the ones I served with in the Marine Corps."

"That's high praise," Mitch said. "I won't fret about this anymore. I know you'll have the situation well in hand."

"Oh yes, we will, Dr. Gainer," the captain said, smiling. "You can set your clock on that."

"You fret because you care so much. That's a good thing." Perriman chimed in, patting Mitch on the arm.

"This meeting is now over with, gentlemen," Mitch said as he got off his stool to leave. "See you around."

Mitch rested his forehead on the wall beneath the shower head, closed his eyes, and turned the water on full blast. The nearly scalding water pummeled the back of his head, his neck, and shoulders. The surge of water brought with it a slight pain, replacing the obsessive thoughts that were flooding his mind. *Did I make a mistake letting the people go into the catacombs? Am I putting the blind people in danger? Should I call Captain Laggins and tell him that it's off?*

After toweling his beet-red body, Mitch jumped in bed, and reached for his Franz Kafka stories lying on the night stand. He had just adjusted his pillows when the telephone rang. Mitch knew immediately it would be Kenzie, who'd made arrangements to spend the night at the university with her students, so they could work on the final details of their performance tomorrow.

"Hi, honey. I'm sitting here, stuffing myself with pizza, while we put the final touches on our concert. I hope we do as well with that as we did with the stage. You'll be pleased."

"How did things go for you today? Did you get everything done that you wanted to?"

"Sure did. There's nothing left for me to do except to twiddle my fingers and watch the big event," Mitch answered in a flat voice.

"That does sound so convincing. What did you decide about allowing people in the catacombs to visit the mobility program?"

There was a long pause before Mitch responded. "As you know I was originally against it, because of security issues. After speaking with Captain Laggins and Perriman, I decided that it would be OK if a few select visit. When I suggested that, Perriman threw a fit, and demanded no one be excluded. So, all who want observe will be allowed to do so."

"What did Captain Laggins say?"

"He agreed, saying it would not be a problem because every officer, including those who were not on duty, would be on the grounds in uniform and plainclothes. In fact, he said there would be as much security as if we had a presidential visit."

"Well I suppose you went along with it, and have been obsessing about whether or not that was the right thing to do. You're probably in bed reading, after scalding yourself in a hot shower."

Mitch began to laugh, "You're right, Miss Smarty Pants. Is there anything about me you don't know?"

"Not much. You're pretty easy to figure out. Besides I've chosen to share my life with you. I have to know you. As I've told you many times, I don't understand this scalding hot shower business. One of these days you're going to seriously burn yourself. You say it's healing, and helps clear your mind when you're conflicted. I see it as a form of self-punishment, for reasons I just don't understand."

"You may be right, but it doesn't matter. It works for me. And besides, I'm not an idiot. I don't burn myself and I'm not going to. It helps clear my mind and settle me down when I'm feeling very stressed, and my mind is racing with thoughts."

"I know, Mitch. It does work for you. It's just I hate to see you put yourself through all that. You need to find a better way to settled yourself down, like meditation."

"That's not for me. I guess I'm like a junkie who needs a fix. All I know is I don't like the feeling when I get all wound up and my mind is racing with thoughts I know aren't worth acting on. It doesn't happen often, but when it does, I don't let it get to the point where I'm panicky. A real hot shower does the trick. Then I know I've got things under control emotionally.

"I'd already made my decision to let people into the catacombs, although there's some risk in that. I know that's the right decision because my bread is buttered by Perriman and Laggins, so to speak. They're two of the best professionals I've worked with. I trust their judgment. It's important to them that people see what they've accomplished at Sycamore. I'm not going to deny them that, just because I don't like to take risks."

"You would never know that. You sure take a lot of them. Remember when you went to the burial of an old Indian, to assure that he was buried in his fine beadwork shirt, and came back beaten up, with a concussion."

"I sure do," Mitch said. "That was a great day for me. The old Indian had asked me if I would stand beside him, and guard his shirt when they lowered him in the ground, so he could take it to the other side. And I told him I would, and I did."

"You're lucky you didn't get killed."

"Well, I didn't, and I don't get burned when I take hot showers! Are you going to wear your trademark—your emerald-green concert dress tomorrow?"

"Certainly, this is an important performance, and I want to bring my best. The students have put together a remarkable composition. They'll have the opportunity to introduce it to a large audience and display their talents, which I believe are considerable. I've spoken with the music critic for the Indianapolis Star. He told me he'll write a review so the students will get a lot of exposure. And this will no doubt surprise you. Abbot Arthur offered the choir of St. Aloysius Abbey to be part of the performance."

"I'll be damned."

"I've auditioned them, and believe me, they're outstanding. I did have to agree that they could sing 'The Roses of Picardy' for the abbot's mother. She's celebrating her 100th birthday and will be there."

"That's just great. I've always liked that song. It was one of my grandfather Angus's favorites."

"They'll also sing 'Amazing Grace,' 'The Battle Hymn of the Republic.' and end the concert with "Back Home Again in Indiana.'"

"Let ask you one thing, Superstar. Do you worry that the monks will upstage you?"

"That would be welcomed! See you tomorrow about noon. We'll meet at the house, so we can freshen up for the concert.

"Till then, my love. Sleep well."

CHAPTER 24

Mitch gasped when he walked out on the stage to check out the audience. Before him was a sea of people, packed together like sardines, sitting on picnic tables, benches, blankets, lawn chairs, and the ground. There was not a visible patch of grass on the field.

He looked behind the stage and saw the same thing. There were people, people, and more people. He could see the line of cars in front of hospital, waiting to get in the parking lot to deliver even more people. The crowd rivaled the crowd Kenzie drew in an outdoor concert in Baden-Baden, Germany.

At Kenzie's insistence, and because he was master of ceremonies, Mitch wore a suit. He choose his three-piece brown-herringbone tweed, so he could wear his Grandfather Angus's Waltham pocket watch with its 24-carat gold hunter's case, and a watch fob with three elk's teeth. It was Angus's most-prized possession, purchased in Halifax at the turn of the century.

Mitch took the watch out of his vest pocket, opened the case, checked the time, and ambled over to the microphone.

"Ladies and gentleman! Welcome to the first concert ever held at this historic hospital, built in 1915. Today we celebrate our two new additions to the hospital: the Mobility Program for the

Visually Impaired, and the new vineyards managed by the monks from St. Aloysius Abbey. Our program will open with the Indiana University Student String Quartet, playing their original composition, 'Moonlight Echoes.'

"Kenzie Fairfax Gainer, artist-in-residence at Indiana University's Jacobs School of Music, will then play Bach's 'Cello Suite No. 1, in G major.' "

A roar of approval burst from the crowd. When the crowd quieted, Mitch continued. "The St. Aloysius Abbey choir will perform the 'Roses of Picardy.' in honor of Abbot Arthur's mother Maeve's 100th birthday. They'll perform 'Danny Boy,' and conclude with 'Back Home Again in Indiana.' At the end of the performance, the audience is welcome to visit the vineyards, and the mobility program, located in the catacombs of the hospital."

While the string quartet was winding their way through "Moonlight Echoes," two inmates slipped out of the laundry room, tiptoed down the hall, and ducked into a broom closet.

One of the men, lean and muscular with a round face, a buzz cut, and a dark complexion, handed the other man a small bundle for clothes. "Here, Kid, take these. They're that asshole guard Curley's pants and shirt. He's about your size so they should fit you."

"Oh no, Guido, why did you have to get Curley's clothes? He's a horrible man. I don't want to touch his clothes, let alone wear them," the small emaciated man with shaggy hair remarked, in a high-pitched whiny voice.

"Shut the fuck up and put the clothes on, or I'll bitch slap you! We're lucky the guards were dumb enough to believe we were doing them a favor, washing their street clothes with our prison rags. Little did they know they were contributing big time to our escape."

Kid quickly changed clothes. Holding his prison clothes in front of Guido's face, he asked, "What do I do with these?"

Guido seethed, and slapped the clothes away. "Don't wave those dirty rags in front of me, you dumb fuck, you stupid bastard. Mix them in with the garbage in that fucking can next to the brooms!"

Kid quickly placed the clothes in the garbage can and stood before Guido, shivering. Guido patted Kid on the head and said softly, "It's OK, Kid. Settle down. You'll be just fine. Listen closely. Once we get into the vent, we have to be quiet. That means no talking.

"Here's exactly what we'll do. I'll take the cover off and pull myself up in the vent. Then I'll reach down and pull you up. I'll move forward when you get in. You put the cover back on, and be sure it's secure. The duct will be level for a short distance. Then it'll suddenly drop down to the next level, so be very careful when we're crawling downhill.

"Once we get to the catacombs, we stop and wait until we hear the door open and the people come in. You stay still and I'll crawl to the end of the duct, open that vent cover, and go outside. You wait until I motion you to come. Don't get in a hurry to crawl out. Take your time, and above all be quiet! Remember, no talking! No talking!

"Once you're outside, put the cover back, and walk side by side with me. We'll talk quietly about how good the concert was and other bullshit. Don't panic if you see a guard. They won't recognize us. Once I spot our man from the outfit, we'll slowly weave our way through the crowd until we're behind him. We'll follow him to the parking lot, and then, Kid, he'll drive us to the airport. We'll take a private plane to Mexico, and we'll soon be on the beach, drinking piña coladas.

"Have you got it, Kid?"

Still shivering slightly, Kid nodded yes.

"Good! Remember—be quiet, be cool, and no talking." With that, Guido pulled himself into the vent and crawled inside.

While Guido and Kid were crawling into the vent, Mitch was standing, arms folded over his chest, next to the stage, observing the audience. This was his habit when Kenzie was on stage performing. She had just begun the Bach Cello Suite.

He could tell that the audience was already intently involved with her music. Some were moving their heads in sync with Kenzie's pulling the bow across the strings. Others were staring straight ahead. No one was talking; there were no other distractions. It was as if the entire audience was one with Kenzie and the music she was making.

Satisfied with what he saw, Mitch closed his eyes and took in the music. He saw her now, just as she's been when he first watched her walking down the aisle, bow in hand, in St. John's Anglican Church in Halifax. Little did he know when he became intimate with Kenzie that it was not just her, but her music as well. As time went on, he began to see that they were one and the same. He was glad they were.

At the same time that Kenzie finished playing the Bach Suite and announced she would play "The Swan," by Saint-Saëns, for an encore, Captain Laggins was taking a smoke break. He was sitting at a table, jotting down a few things that he wanted to say to those visiting the mobility program.

Suddenly there was a loud noise. Leaping up from his chair, the captain looked around. The noise was coming from the room's corner air vent. Grabbing his chair, he ran to the vent. He stood on the chair, and when he reached to touch the vent, it popped open. The two inmates toppled out, knocking him to the floor.

The two men flailed away at the captain, now lying motionless on his back, smashing him in his face and stomach.

Guido got to his feet, kicked Laggins in ribs, and screamed at Kid, who was still throwing punches. "The goddamn chair is broken. Get your ass over there and move the table underneath the vent, so I can stand on it, and get back in. We've got to get the hell out of here before everybody comes!"

Pushing the table to the vent made a loud screeching sound, alerting Donaldo Perryman, who was nearby in the tunnel. Perryman burst into the room. Guido jumped off the table, picked up a chair leg, and moved toward Perryman. Kid followed behind. Perryman let out a yell, placed his right forearm under his chin, lowered his head, and charged forward, thrusting upward at the last moment, before striking Guido flush on the chin with the top of his head, and in the neck, with his powerful forearm. Guido swung the chair leg, barely missing Perryman's head, landing it instead on his shoulder.

Blood and teeth flow out of Guido's mouth, spraying Kid's face as he jumped on Perryman's back. The three men crashed to floor, with Perryman still holding onto Guido's neck with his right arm and Kid's neck with his left. The two convicts were screaming, squirming, and kicking, trying to break free from Perryman's vise-like grip, to no avail. The powerful blind man gritted his teeth and applied even more pressure.

Kenzie signed the last autograph and hurried over to Mitch. He was in front of the stage, watching the stream of people flow down the grassy slope to the parking lot below. Throwing her arms around him, she planted a kiss on his cheek, and whispered in his ear, "Thanks, honey, for letting me perform here. I don't think I've ever played better, nor had more enjoyment than I did today."

Mitch held her close, and kissed the top of her head. He took her face in his hands and said, in a voice loud enough for the students standing nearby to hear, "You're right, my love. You set the standard today, and your students were part of it. I'm damn glad it happened here."

Kenzie was slightly flushed. She was a private person who seldom, if ever, displayed emotion in public. "I'm going to the house to change. Then, I'm taking the students out for a meal, so we can critique our performance."

"Sounds good. I'll see you later." He gestured to the students and took a money clip out of his pocket. "This is for services rendered in a magnificent performance," he said, handing each student a crisp one-hundred dollar bill. As he walked away, he turned around and handed the first violinist two one-hundred dollar bills. "This is for the meal. Ms. Gainer seldom carries money, and does not use credit cards."

Mitch stood there, watching Kenzie and her students disappear into the throng of people leaving the concert. Although he knew that it was right for Kenzie to celebrate this peak performance with her students—since they were the ones who made it happen—he could not help feeling abandoned.

Suddenly the air was filled with the shrill sound of sirens. Mitch immediately took off full speed toward the sound, and was shocked when he saw a police car and two ambulances pull up at the main entrance of the hospital. Weaving his way through the crowd, he spotted a correctional officer he knew, standing by the ambulance.

"Winston, what in the hell is going on?"

"Two inmates were trying to escape and got into the catacombs through the air vents and ducts. They took down Captain Laggins."

"Oh, no!" Mitch's lips were trembling as he tried to speak. His arms hung loosely by his side and his fists were clenched.

"Don't worry, Doc," the officer said, patting Mitch on the back. "The captain's been ruffed up a bit, but he's OK. Those bastards apparently jumped him. That's the only way they could have taken him down. But they sure as hell got theirs. That blind guy caught them, and boy did he work them over good. They're coming out on stretchers. That blind guy must be one tough son of a bitch. And just think, he can't even see!"

The hospital door burst open. Captain Laggins, his head wrapped in a huge bandage, appeared in a wheelchair, being pushed by a stoic police officer. Alongside was Donaldo Perryman, a bloody white towel wrapped around his head, marching in military step with his walking stick tucked under his arm like a swagger stick.

The bystanders, including reporters, newscasters, and other community dignitaries, applauded as the two men approached the ambulance. Mitch hurried to Laggin's side and reached down to help him stand. The captain immediately pushed his hand aside and declared, "I can get to my feet by myself." Mitch watched Laggins place his hands on the arms of the wheelchair, strain, push himself to his feet, and shuffle into the ambulance, taking a seat on a bench. Perryman followed close behind, taking a seat on a bench across from the captain. The ambulance doors closed, the sirens blared, and the vehicle sped toward the nearest hospital.

The crowd slowly began to disperse. Mitch wandered aimlessly until he spotted his car out of the corner of his right eye. He snapped to attention, and began pushing his way through the mass of people. He had to get back to the house on the hospital grounds as soon as he could and figure out a way to contact Kenzie who was probably out to dinner with her students.

When Mitch opened the front door, he was surprised to see Kenzie, in her pajamas, curled up in an afghan on the sofa. As soon as she saw him, she threw her arms around his neck.

"Oh Mitch, I'm so sorry, so sorry. The prison escape is just terrible," she muttered in his ear. "I heard about it on the car radio when I left the concert."

"It wasn't an escape," Mitch said sharply. "It was an attempted escape, thanks to Donaldo Perryman. He caught the two of them and pinned them on floor until help came."

"I heard on the radio that he and Captain Laggins were injured."

"They're bloody, that's for sure. The ambulance took them to the hospital. The bottom line is they'll be OK. Thank God both of them are tough as nails."

Kenzie sobbed and buried her face in Mitch's shoulder.

"Let's not talk about it now, "Mitch whispered. "Let's go to bed. We can sort things out in the morning."

CHAPTER 25

At first light, Mitch threw back the covers, waking Kenzie from a sound sleep.

"Oh, I'm sorry, dear. I didn't mean to wake you," he whispered. He leaned over and kissed her on the cheek. "I'm going to the hospital to check on Laggins and Perryman. I'll be back as soon as I can."

Kenzie groaned and turned over, burying her face in the pillow.

Mitch decided to make a quick stop at his office before visiting the hospital. When he pulled into his parking space, he saw that his name had been removed. His stomach tightened. This was not a good sign.

He hurried to the front door, but when he reached to open it, he found it was locked. Then the door opened. Captain Laggins appeared in the doorway.

"What are you doing here?" Mitch stepped back, a shocked look on his face.

"They let me out at daybreak. Hell, they only kept me overnight for observation. I have a few stitches on the back of my head. They think I have a slight concussion, but they're not sure. My ribs are black and blue. I'm a little sore, but that's it." The captain placed his hand on Mitch's back and guided him to a nearby bench.

"What about Perryman? How's he doing?"

"He's fine. Right now he's back in the catacombs, working with the clients. He has a few stitches in his forehead from head butting. Unfortunately, his collar bone was broken when that rotten bastard hit him with a chair leg."

The captain paused, clenched his fist, and smacked the palm of his hand. "I'll tell you Dr. Gainer, he saved my life. There's no doubt they would have beaten me to death if it wasn't for him. Perryman is one tough son of a bitch."

"That he is." Mitch paused, rubbing his chin. "Tell me what happened."

"I fucked up is what happened! I knew the air vents to the heating ducts were the only way, other than the door, that a person could get into the catacombs. I just didn't think there was any reason for anyone, particularly an inmate, to want to do that.

"In fact that's not what they were trying to do. They were going to follow the ducts to the outside grate, and escape during the crowd. Apparently the duct dropped straight down from the floor above, and they could not hold themselves back. They crashed in into the vent with such force, it broke loose. That Guido is big boy, strong as a bull. If he crashed into the vent with full force, it would definitely come apart.

"The bottom line is I did a stupid thing. I reached up to touch the vent, and when I did, the goddamn thing came open. They fell on top of me. I know better than that. I put myself in a vulnerable position when I reached up. I fucked up, but you're getting blame!"

"That why the hospital door is locked. I have orders not to let you on the grounds. The sale is going through soon, and they want you out of here pronto."

"That figures," Mitch said, leaning back on the bench, clasping his hands over his stomach, and twirling his fingers. "What

I don't like or even want to hear, is that you fucked up. You did nothing wrong. It's me that fucked up. I put you, Perryman, and the blind people in harm's way. I have to be responsible."

"But you didn't want people in the catacombs. Perryman and I talked you into it," Laggins insisted. "If we had listened to you, we wouldn't have been in the catacombs. They were not trying to escape through the catacombs. The duct above the catacombs leads to the outside. They intended to go through the duct, to the next vent, and get lost in the huge crowd. There was probably someone outside to help them get away. Guido has deep mob ties. But, they fucked up, and tumbled out like two monkeys."

"Get this straight, Captain Laggins," Mitch said, loudly and clearly. "Neither you nor Donaldo Perryman talked me into anything. I listened to you both, considered my options, and made what I thought was the best decision. Obviously it wasn't. You and Perryman were badly beaten and needed stitches in your heads.

Laggins hung his head before saying, "I can't even let you in to clean out your office. I'll see your possessions are shipped by Federal Express. I hate to say this, Dr. Gainer, but I must ask you for your key."

Mitch dropped his key in the captain's hand. He walked away, then suddenly turned around. "Send my belongings to me at Chinook's Lodge and Casino, Nugget Valley, Idaho. If there is anything left that belongs to Guillermo, ship it to him. You have his address. Say good-bye to Mrs. Bascom from me, and tell her that I have nothing but high esteem and affection for her."

"I will if I can. Like you, she's been barred."

"Well, I guess they have to clean out all the vipers," Mitch chuckled. "Good-bye, Captain Laggins. I have a feeling that our paths will cross again. I hope so. You're one of the best I've been around."

When Mitch opened the door, Kenzie was standing in the doorway. She threw her arms around his neck and held him tight. They remained in the doorway for a few moments, arms wrapped tightly around each other, swaying back and forth, until finally collapsing on the sofa. Kenzie cradled his head and whispered in his ear, "I'm sorry, Mitch. So sorry."

Mitch got up. "I think I'll have a beer. Do you want one?"

"I'll have a glass of wine." As she watched him leave the room, she thought how difficult it was to comfort him in times like this. She'd learned he had to find comfort within himself.

When Mitch returned with the drinks, he handed Kenzie a glass of wine, and flopped in a seat in a chair across the room. He took a drink, then set the bottle on the end table. "I suppose you know what happened?"

"Yes. Captain Laggins called and told me they locked you out. That was not called for. To lock you out and not even let you clear your office is deplorable. You don't deserve that."

"Oh hell, that's nothing. It was going to end like that anyway. What disturbs me, and bothers me the most, is that my stupidity resulted in two men being severely injured, your finest performance being ruined, and the final legacy of Sycamore being one of violence and bloodshed. Now, how's that for an exit?"

"You're being too hard on yourself, and you're also wrong. You brought dignity and civility to a brutal environment. You brought the monks and blind people to the campus. People liked and respected that. They won't forget. They won't blame you for the attempted breakout. That's not your fault."

"The hell it isn't. I made a bad decision, allowing people in the catacombs after the concert. If I would not have done that, no one would have been injured. Remember when we talked about it, before I made the decision? You did not think it was a good idea. You even said you would not do it because there was risk involved."

"You're right. I would not have made that decision," Kenzie acknowledged. "After all, Sycamore is a prison, and with that population, there would some risk that something could happen. But you know more than I do, and you did not make an impulsive and irrational decision. You considered all the factors, including input from Captain Laggins and Donaldo Perryman, and made an informed decision that you were comfortable with."

"Yes I did," Mitch said, forcefully. "If I had to do it over again, I would probable make the same decision. My big mistake was that I should have stopped—after Laggins and I settled things down and Sycamore was functioning at a better level than ever before. But, no, I wanted to make a bigger impact, and stretched it too far. That was bound to have a disastrous outcome, and it sure as hell did.

"But that's all past history. Let's get back to living. It's time we retire to the bedroom." Leading Kenzie, he caressed her backside and whispered, "You sure have a fine derriere, madam."

"Are you sure you're up it, fine sir?"

"I'll let you answer that. And, by the way, I'm sorry you missed out on your celebration with your students last night. I was damn glad you were here, waiting for me last night. I sure as hell needed you to weather the storm."

"I have something to tell you," Kenzie said, throwing back the bed cover. "I didn't want to tell you until the big event were over, and last night was not the time, because of all the commotion.

"The performance really was the end of my residence. After I tie up a few ends, I would like to go some place where I can relax, and rest up before the tour. How about if we kick back in Nugget Valley?"

An Abbey Returned

"You know, my love, I may make terrible decisions that cause people grave injuries. But I can say that I'm psychic, and make some good ones as well. I've already made arrangements to send my belongings to Nugget Valley."

CHAPTER 26

"I just got off the phone with Guillermo's housekeeper. She told me Guillermo and Benita are in Key West." Mitch joined Kenzie in the bedroom, where they were boxing their possessions to ship to Nugget Valley. "She said he knew I would be calling, and to tell me he was given a clean bill of health. He's now at full strength to do whatever he wants to. He'll contact me when he sorts things out."

"That's great news, Mitch! Do you think he's aware of what happened at Sycamore?"

"Certainly, he's aware," Mitch snapped. "And so is everyone else in the country that has access to a newspaper, television set, or a radio. Thank God most of the tattle is focused on the blind superman, Donaldo Perryman, who captured the two convicts and the pre-eminent performance of Bach's 'Cello Suite by you, my wife, Kenzie Fairfax Gainer."

Kenzie chuckled, and picked up her emerald green concert dress. She hugged it close to her chest, then carefully folded it, and gently laid it in the box.

"You'd think that dress was alive, the way you pamper it," Mitch said.

"It is alive! Alive in the same way your marbles are alive. You shudder if anyone goes near them. Who knows what you would do if any one touched them. You don't even like anyone looking at them."

"You don't see me touching your dress."

"Here, you can touch it," Kenzie said, holding the dress out in front of her."

"No way." Mitch pushed the box aside, took her in his arms and carried her to the bed. After giving her a lingering kiss, he held her by the chin and smiled. "We've done enough work; it's time for a break."

Later that evening, after they had finished packing, they were sitting at the kitchen table enjoying, cold cuts, cheese, and a bottle of Mateus Rose. "You know I've been thinking, and I believe the real reason Guillermo is in Key West is because he's planning a secret trip to Cuba."

"What! You know travel to Cuba is illegal. Besides, with all the political unrest, it would be too dangerous for him to go there."

"I know that, but I also know Guillermo. He absolutely despises Key West. I know that for sure, but I don't know why. My suspicion is that it has something to do with his fleeing Cuba and coming to the States.

"There's no way that Guillermo would go to Key West to sort things out, or for any reason, except for one. He could easily travel from there to Cuba by boat. It's only eighty-five nautical miles from Key West to Havana. That makes it a good place to leave from."

"But what about Benita? Would she go too? I can't imagine her going along with such a plan."

"I doubt she's involved. He'll probably tell her he's going fishing for marlin in the gulf for a few days."

"I don't know what to think, Mitch. It sounds a bit farfetched to me, but as you say you're psychic, so there may be something to it. Whatever it is, I just hope it turns out well. But now, I'm tired and we need to go to bed. Remember, we're leaving early tomorrow morning. I'll leave my Audi here with Abbot Arthur since we'll be taking yours."

"It's about a two to three day's drive to Glacier National Park where we can spend a few days and take in the sights. From there it's a day's drive to Nugget Valley."

"I'd think I'd like that. We might have to cut short our time in Nugget Valley. Remember we open in London in two months, and I'd like to spend time in Edinburgh to practice."

"Good. That's exactly what we'll do."

At the same time that Mitch and Kenzie were checking into the Stage Coach Inn in the Wisconsin Dells, a private plane with a huge black war horse painted on each side, touched down at the Weir Cook Airport.

Squire Young, dressed in an English-tweed hunting jacket, with a leather patch on the shoulder, matching trousers, and an extended-peak tweed country cap, led his executive assistant, Maurice, and two pilots down the airstair to a waiting limousine. The men were whisked away to the Omni Severin Hotel in downtown Indianapolis.

Young uncorked a bottle of Dom Perignon, chose a fat pear from the basket of fruit on the table, and stretched out on a lounge chair on the balcony of his penthouse suite.

"I hate to tell you, boss, but you won't be seeing Mitch Gainer," Maurice said, joining Young on the patio.

"What!

"His wife finished her residency and they left the day after the concert for Nugget Valley. They'll be at Chinook's Mother Lode until they leave for her tour in Europe."

Young took the last bite of pear, deposited the core in the wastebasket, and then thoroughly wiped his hands and mouth with a linen napkin. "That certainly changes things," he muttered scratching his ear. "I had no intentions of ever going back to Nugget Valley. You know, years ago, I left there under not the best of circumstances. Now I'm being drawn back. I have to speak face to face with Mitch Gainer, and I need to do it as soon as I can. I'll leave tomorrow, after we meet with the racing team. It'll be our last stop before going on to Nugget Valley.

"You stay here, Maurice, and keep an eye on things at the hospital," he said in an authoritative tone. "Above all, keep a low profile. That means keeping your mouth shut, and your eyes and ears open. If you can facilitate their moving things along quicker, do it. The sooner we get in there, the better.

"Hang out with monks and share your expertise in wine and wine making with them. Leave the blind program be, but give me your impressions of Donaldo Perryman and Captain Laggins."

"Got it, boss."

Each time Young was in Indianapolis, he made a point of checking in with his racing team. That meant that he would host a scrumptious luncheon, catered by one of the top chefs in the area. The luncheon was always held at the Indianapolis Motor Speedway, since Young referred to the speedway as the temple of motor racing, and he wanted his team to be exposed to the best.

When he hired personnel for the racing team—be it a driver, a pit man, a engineer, a publicist, a secretary, or even a janitor—he told them all the same thing. "There is only one expectation at War Horse—that you give your absolute best. Because you're the only one who knows your best is, I will stay out of your way, except to facilitate your progress in delivering your absolute best."

A position with War Horse was coveted by the entire racing community, because Young paid beyond top dollar and treated his staff well. Never in his years in the racing business did he have to let anyone go, or have anyone leave, except to retire.

The luncheon was a carbon copy of all Young's luncheons. The food was luscious; the conversation stimulating, and a good time was had by all. At the end of the meal, Young asked if there were any issues or concerns anyone wanted to raise. There was no response, except from one of the newer drivers, a young bright-eyed curly-headed kid from the mountains of East Tennessee.

He stood, and announced in a distinct southern twang, "It's been pretty dang quiet around these parts, boss, except for the gal who sneaks in here at night and spins her yella Corvette around the track. Well, she sure did spin it one night a few weeks ago when she turned circles all over the track, hit the wall, bounced off, and dug whopping ruts in the infield."

"That was Graciela Cevallos. I don't understand what happened. She's an excellent driver," a woman said, shaking her head.

"She sure as hell is," one of the drivers chipped in. "She's good enough to drive for us."

Squire Young stood up and rapped on his glass with a spoon. "Just who is this Graciela Cevallos?" he asked.

"She was the commissioner of mental health and was involved with Sycamore Hospital. The governor recently fired her and she left town. It's too bad because she was talented and a real asset to the community," the public relations director, a tall immaculately dress woman in a tailored business suit, added.

"Yes, I know who she is. She's the Cuban woman I see with Dr. Gainer at Inocencio's," a mechanic, who had a habit of bouncing his leg when he spoke, added.

"I take it that's Dr. Mitch Gainer," Young said, smiling.

The mechanic nodded yes.

An Abbey Returned

Squire Young shrugged and reached into the inner pocket of his coat, withdrawing a stack of 500-dollar-bills. He placed the bills on a plate, and passed it to the person next to him. "Each of you takes one, except the drivers, who can take two."

Young stood, raised his glass and said, "Ladies and gentleman, this is the end of our fortunate gathering. Until our next gathering, may good fortune smile on you. Remember my door is always open to you. Do not hesitate to use it, if the need arises." He then bowed and left the room, followed by Maurice.

CHAPTER 27

The early morning sun shone down on the crystal clear water of Swiftcurrent Lake, reflecting the towering snow-covered peaks that surrounded the body of water. Mitch and Kenzie were at Many Glacier Hotel in Glacier National Park, enjoying a room-service breakfast on the lakeside suite's balcony.

"You know, Kenzie, it was here at Swiftcurrent Lake that I did one of the more stupid things in my life," Mitch said looking up from a map he'd been studying.

"It was in the summer of my last year in high school and I came here partying with some miners I was working with. We joined up with some Canadian loggers. One of them said nobody swam in the lake because the water was too cold.

"I remember saying that I liked swimming in cold-water mountain lakes, and that I could swim across the lake, because it was not larger than the ones I swam across in Nugget Valley. Someone bet me fifty dollars that I couldn't do it. Without thinking, I just took the bet."

Kenzie looked up from her Eggs Benedict and rolled her eyes.

Mitch continued, "Just before I dove in, I heard some old geezer standing there, taking it all in, call out, 'Don't be a fool kid. That water is cold enough to freeze the balls off a brass monkey.'

"And boy, was he right. When I hit the water, it took the breath right out of me. I was in a state of shock. I just started stroking as hard as I could for the shore across the lake, kicking my feet as close to the surface as I could, because the water beneath was unbearably cold. My body was in pain, but for some reason I didn't understand, I just kept swimming for the distant shore.

"When I turned around for the first time, and looked back at the dock, I sensed that I was not too far from the middle of the lake. I realized there was no turning back. For just a moment, I felt panicky, and thought I might not make it to shore. So I closed my eyes, kept my head out of the water, and moved my arms and leg as fast as I could.

"When I finally reached the shallower water at the opposite shore, I stopped swimming and tried to force my legs to hit the bottom. But they were numb, and the deeper water was intolerable. So I started swimming again. Or should I say tried to swim again, because I could hardly move my arms and legs. As luck would have it, there was a small rowboat tied to the dock, with an exceptionally long rope. I was able to grab onto the boat and the rope and pull myself onto the dock.

"I was laying flat on my back when the guys I was with came running over with a blanket, and wrapped me up like a mummy. The man I made the bet with stood over me and said, 'I thought for a while you were going under, but by golly, you made it across.' He laid a fifty-dollar Canadian bill on my chest. I had it framed and put it in a safety deposit box in Nugget Valley. If you like, I'll show it to you."

"I think I'll pass," Kenzie said, with a smile. "What I want to know, did this debacle end your swimming in a freezing-water lake?"

"Hell no," Mitch roared. "The guy came back the next day and bet me a hundred dollars I could not swim across the lake again.

This time I side-stroked across, with not a whole lot of difficulty. I took his money, and won the admiration of the fine-looking blonde he had with him."

"Did you frame that bill, too?"

"No, unfortunately, I spent it on the blonde ... just kidding, of course."

"I bet," Kenzie said, getting up from the table to answer a knock on the door. When she returned, she was smiling from ear to ear. "I just received a telegram. It was the first one I've ever received. I thought they were a thing of the past."

"No, not too long ago Western Union phased out the couriers, but you can still send telegrams. When I was a kid, I thought it would be great to be Western Union messenger. I liked their uniforms and the little round hats they wore on an angle."

"It's from Abbot Arthur," Kenzie said, seemingly ignoring Mitch's comments. "It seems he's quite taken with my car that I left for him. He says he's driving it every day to ensure that it's in fine working order. The car will be washed at least once a week. He made a specific point that they would only use 100-percent-cod-oil-tanned sheepskin chamois cloths for drying. Lastly, he assured me that he and his brothers would see that the vehicle would remain in tip top condition for my return."

"What! I thought you gave him the car."

"I did. Abbot Arthur just does know it yet. I was afraid if I simply gave him my Audi, he might not accept it, thinking it too opulent. This way, he'll keep the car and use it.

"If we do return, and I'm sure someday we might, I'll just ask him to keep it for me."

"You're a clever lady, although a bit shady. You're right on one thing. Abbot Arthur would not have accepted the car if you just gave it to him. He's far too principled to do that."

Mitch checked his watch, and got up from the table. "We had better shake a stick if we're going to do the 2.6-mile nature trail around the lake, before heading out for Nugget Valley. I want to be diving into a big Porterhouse at Chinook's Mother Lode before the sun sets."

"Better to dive into a big slab of beef than diving into a frozen lake," Kenzie said, playfully slapping Mitch on his bottom when he walked by.

Mitch got his wish, and at sundown, he and Kenzie were seated at a table with a superb mountain view at Chinook's Mother Lode. Surgically cutting a piece of the fillet portion of a twenty-two-ounce Porterhouse steak, Mitch inspected it carefully before gobbling it down. "There's nothing like a USDA-prime Porterhouse steak," he said, smacking his lips together and shaking his head. "I'm glad to see they're carrying on the tradition of having the best steaks in Nugget Valley. That would have pleased the hell out of Chinook. He always told me when I was a kid that 'a Porterhouse steak three times a day for your board was as good as gets.' "

"Just what are you talking about?' Kenzie asked, looking up from a small bite of her six-ounce fillet.

"Oh, those are some of the words of Chinook's favorite country song, 'I'm Ragged But I'm Right.' He didn't have three Porterhouse steaks a day, but he always had one for breakfast. That's why to honor him, the twenty-two-ounce Porterhouse on the menu is called Chinook's Signature."

"All I can say is that your arteries would applaud your choosing a much smaller portion of less fatty beef."

"There's only one thing missing from the most perfect day I've had in a long time," Mitch commented.

Kenzie finished off her last asparagus spear, wiped her mouth with a napkin, and put her fork down. "And what's that?" she asked.

"It's my mother, sitting at the slot machines, breaking the house," Mitch said in a melancholy tone. "It's the image of her that I have carried with me since she died. I think it's because when she came to Chinook's Mother Lode to live, she found a peace and happiness that had eluded her all her days. It was never more evident than when she was at the slot machines, pulling the handles. It was very fortunate for me that she shared her newly found peace and happiness with me. It left a good taste in my mouth. I miss her," Mitch concluded, tears welling in his eyes.

Mitch dabbed his eyes, and got up from the table. "You know my love; it's good that there is one place in the world where I don't have to pay a check."

"You've paid the check many times over, Mitch," Kenzie said, taking his hand. "If it weren't for you, there would be no Chinook's Mother Lode. You've already bought and paid for it. Come on, it's time to go to our suite. I want to jump in bed and finish a good book."

"You go on ahead. I'll be up soon. I want to visit the Adam Grant room and check out the new painting."

Mitch turned on the small light hanging above the new Adam Grant painting he recently had purchased. After switching off the other lights, he took a seat on a bench directly across from the huge painting. He was immediately immersed in the three dimensional painting of a woman, a circus performer wearing a small copper-colored ornament on her head, looped earrings, and a cape. In her hand, she held a small hoop for juggling. She was standing with one foot on a small platform. Behind her hung a burgundy colored, rumpled canvas, held up with ropes. Next to the platform was a small ram's head poster with the word "mystic." Directly behind the poster was a larger faded portrait of an old bald-headed man with a white beard, holding a pole. Lying on the floor was a paper with the words "July 4th."

An Abbey Returned

The door opened and the lights came on. Mitch turned his eyes away from the painting, and there was Squire Young, wearing a plaid deerstalker hat, an English hunting jacket with a leather patch on the shoulder, and knickers.

"Squire Young? Is that really you?" Mitch leapt up from the bench and rushed over to shake his hand. "Your pockets are stuffed with shot gun shells, so you must have come to Nugget Valley to shoot some birds."

"Pheasants to be exact," Young explained. "But that's not why I came here. I came to see you." He suddenly paused, stared at the painting, then walked over to the bench, and sat down. "Cut the lights, if you will. I'd like to study this painting more. I don't remember it."

Mitch turned off the lights, and joined Young on the bench." You wouldn't remember it because it's a new painting. It's one of his Mystic Series paintings. A woman reporter from Toledo, Ohio, who'd edited Chinook's stories I found in an old trunk, gave it to me. She had to downsize and didn't have room for it. She knew that Chinook's Mother Lode would be a good home."

"She's certainly right on that account. This painting fits well with your collection. I've told you before, and I'll tell you again, this Adam Grant, this Holocaust survivor, is unsurpassed in painting the human figure."

"Yes, I remember you saying that. Adam's works seem to have profound effects on people. For example, one night I was stressed out and couldn't sleep, so I decided to visit Adam's paintings to relax. It was very late, and when I entered the room, the lights were off. When I turned the lights on, there was someone asleep on the bench. It was Andy Brogan. You remember him?"

"Sure do. He was the most efficient lounge and restaurant manager I've ever worked with, and a marvelous bloke," Young replied.

"Andy got up from the bench, clenched his fists, and charged me. I had to fend him off until he recognized me. He said he was having a bad dream and was back in the war, fighting the Japanese. I knew Andy suffered from shell shock and had sleep disturbances, nightmares, and flashbacks of the horrors of his wartime experience.

"When I ask him why he would come here to sleep, on these uncomfortable benches, I remember he waved his finger at the paintings and told me it wasn't comfort he was looking for. It was peace, and he found that among Adam's paintings. He went on to say that the paintings were about survival to him, because a man who survived the Holocaust, a far worse war then he'd experienced, had brought to life these strong and beautiful women.

"He would come to the Adam Grant room, a few hours before he started his early morning shift in the restaurant, so he could get some good sleep. I told him I would put a hide-a-bed or a good sofa in the room so he could sleep more comfortably. He said no, things were fine the way they were. As far as I know, he continued sleeping in the Adam Grant room until he left.

"What, you're telling me Andy Brogan no longer works here. That shocks me! I thought for sure he was a lifer," Young remarked.

"It shocked me, too, when he left, two or three years ago. He took up with a woman from the reservation and moved to Great Falls, Montana, so they could spend most of their time hiking and backpacking in the Bob Marshall Wilderness Area."

"I didn't sleep here like Andy," Young said, getting up from the bench. "But I certainly spent my share of time with Adam Grant's paintings. I was in and out of this room for short periods virtually every day when I needed to clear my head. Duty on the bridge meant that I had to be 100 percent focused at all times.

When I felt myself losing my concentration, I would pop into the Adam Grant room to refresh myself."

"Yes, I remember you, standing on the balcony, arms folded across your chest, watching everything that happened on the gaming floor below, like a sea captain standing on the bridge of a ship, watching the crew," Mitch chuckled. "You even called the balcony the bridge. That's how you ran the casino. You were only on the gaming floor to resolve a problem you spotted from the bridge.

"I remember when I first interviewed you, and asked you what your modus operandi was. You took me to the balcony, and simply said, 'You can see it all from here. The trick is to know what to look for. And I do.'

"That's when I knew you were the right man for the job. And, as they say, the rest is history. You developed one of the most successful casinos in the country. What's even better, you trained Dalton Snipe to replace you on the bridge when you left."

Young frowned, turned his head away for a moment before revealing, "My leaving Chinook's Mother Lode was the lowest point of my life. Having to slip away like a thief in the night because I got involved with the wife of a trusted friend. That was not my finest moment. And worst of all, I betrayed you as my boss, and you did not deserve that."

"That's enough, Squire," Mitch said, placing his hand on Young's shoulder. "You didn't betray me, and you certainly did not slip away like a thief in the night. You drove away with your horses, and left your horse farm to the tribe.

"In fact, your leaving turned out to be a good thing. It put things completely in the hands of the tribe, which had always been my goal. Dalton Snipe has continued, and the casino has not skipped a beat since you left. Now will you tell me why you traveled to all the way to Nugget Valley to see me?"

"It's not just you I came to see. It's Kenzie as well. I suggest we discuss this over a gourmet meal and a good bottle of wine tomorrow evening."

CHAPTER 28

"I've bribed the chef and he's agreed to prepare lobster-stuffed beef tenderloin with béarnaise sauce. It's the specialty he learned in his culinary training in Paris," Squire Young said. Mitch and Kenzie took their seats at the table. "I've reserved this V.I.P. room so we can discuss our business and enjoy a fine meal in privacy."

"This will be a real treat," Mitch said, smacking his lips together. "I remember Chef Vinnie. Andy Brogan hired him to work around the bar and restaurant when he was just a kid. The kid was so good in the kitchen that we sent him to culinary school in Paris after he graduated from high school. If memory serves me, after finishing culinary school, Vinnie was a top chef in Cannes for a few years, before coming back to the reservation.

"Have you ever eaten lobster-stuffed beef tenderloin?" Mitch asked Kenzie, sitting at the table across from him.

"Yes, one time in Paris. It was scrumptious. You'll love it," Kenzie replied.

Squire Young got up from his seat at the head of the table, wheeled over a liquor cart, and poured three glasses of champagne. "Here's to the beauty of friendship," he said, raising his glass. Mitch and Kenzie stood, joining him in the toast.

An Abbey Returned

They sat down in silence for several moments, before Squire Young folded his hands on the table and announced, "Let's get our business over with, so we can move on to the delicious meal that awaits us. First, I'll explain how I came to purchase Sycamore Hospital. As you know, when I left Nugget Valley, I moved to California, to be closer to Hollywood and the movie business. My Friesian horses were in constant demand for movies. I made a bundle of money which I immediately invested in an auto racing team."

"I didn't know you had an interest in auto racing. I was surprised when I read in Indianapolis Star that you were the owner of War Horse Racing Team," Mitch interjected.

"It didn't surprise me. I knew that Squire was interested in driving fast cars, from our romps around the dusty roads on the reservation in his Bentley," Kenzie added.

"Driving Bentleys is one thing, but driving racing cars another," Squire said, raising his finger at Kenzie. "I simply wanted to own a racing team and be involved in the sport. My interest in race cars was cultivated during my summers in Le Mans, France, when I was young. In fact, I attended a Le Mans race each year I lived in Europe.

"My racing team brought me to Indianapolis because, to many, it's the auto-racing capital of the world. I liked the area immensely, far better than California, and wanted to purchase some property to develop. I was approached by a conglomerate to join them and head up their project to purchase some land to develop a casino. They were politically connected and had inside information that gambling would soon be legalized in Indiana."

"Yes, you certainly made quite a splash around here," Mitch said, flippantly. "I remember Graciela Cevallos, the mental health director I was working with at Sycamore, telling me about this

Englishman named Squire Young who had developed casinos in England and Nugget Valley, and was now going to turn Sycamore into a casino. She was dumbfounded when I informed her that I'd hired you to develop the casino at Chinook's Mother Lode, and that you were just the man for the job."

Mitch paused and cleared his throat. "What didn't make sense to me was your being involved in a business venture. I could not see you purchasing property to build a casino, based on inside information that the gambling laws were going to be changed. After all, this is conservative Indiana. To change the law to allow gambling is a long shot at best."

Young laughed aloud, and poured everyone a fresh glass of champagne. He pointed his glass at Mitch and said, "Touché to you, my insightful friend. I quickly shed those chaps.

"There was no way gambling would be coming to Indiana, any time soon, if ever. This is the conservative Midwest, which I have no need to disrupt. Besides the mob would never allow Las Vegas-style gambling. As you well know, when it comes to games of chance, they rule more often than not."

"Tell me, Squire, then what are your plans for Sycamore?" Mitch asked.

Young lowered his eyes, unfolded his hands, and began tapping on the table as if he were going to type his words. "Although I was only given a tour of the grounds, I immediately fell in love with the property. What amazed me was that it housed a maximum security prison hospital. It seemed to me that the place was designed for something finer than that."

"It was," Mitch chimed in; recounting the story of the original abbey and the state's turning the property into the hospital.

"I didn't know that," Young said. "Maybe that's why they had so much misfortune with hospital. It simply was not a good fit."

"You can say that again," Kenzie added.

"Well, anyway to continue my story ... I did nothing to dispel the chatter that legalized gambling was coming to Indiana, and that we were going to develop a Las Vegas-style casino. It was a good bargaining tool, and the main reason I was able to negotiate such a good buy. Simply put, the powers that be wanted a casino, and thought I was just the man to deliver it.

"Since I had no interest whatsoever in using the property for a casino, I toyed with several ideas. The first was developing a complex for my racing team. I even considered building a NASCAR Speedway and bringing the tour close to the hallowed grounds of the Indianapolis 500. That would be a real coup, if I could pull it off. In the end, I decided it would be too much time, work, and energy, and the likely reward would be one large headache.

"I also considered a tour-level golf course, a Wimbledon-style tennis court, some rodeo grounds, a horse track—but nothing stuck in my mind. All I knew for sure was that I wanted Sycamore to be home for me and my War Horses.

"I recognized that the purchase was going to be difficult because the property was in high demand. There were many potential buyers with the money to pull the sale off. To gain an edge, I was able to move the negotiations to my turf in California."

Mitch broke out laughing. "I'll bet you flew them to L.A. in your private plane, and put them up in a suite at the Beverley Hills Hotel!"

Young uncorked another bottle of champagne and refilled their glasses. Turning to Kenzie, he said, "Your husband is correct, I did fly them to L.A. for the meetings, but I did not put them up at the Beverley Hills Hotel. You and Mitch are the only two people I would do that for. They were flown back to Indianapolis immediately after the meetings.

"This kicker for the deal is that I was able to offer them a cash deal, which made them salivate. They insisted that the sale be done in complete secrecy, which is the reason I did not contact you and Mitch when I learned Kenzie was doing a residency at Indiana University. When I am working a deal, I go into hibernation."

"Did you know I was working at Sycamore?" Mitch asked.

"Yes, I sure did! It was a real shocker when I read in the Indianapolis Star that you had taken over the hospital, after the superintendent had a health issue. I thought you were tucked away as Kenzie's manager."

"He was, until his mentor came knocking with a challenge Mitch could not resist," Kenzie blurted out, her eyes flashing.

"What Kenzie said is basically true, but there is more to it than that, Squire," Mitch added. "Do you remember Guillermo Gerona? I think you met him one time at Chinook's Mother Lode, just before you took over the casino."

"Yes, I sure do. He's the Cuban chap you were working with in Cleveland."

"He was also my mentor at the VA when I was in graduate school. The state did a national search and selected him as superintendent to reform the hospital, with the caveat that if he could not achieve this goal, the hospital would be sold. He knew that I was in the area with Kenzie, so he contacted me, and asked if I would help him."

"So he's the superintendent you replaced."

Mitch nodded yes. "The first thing he told me was that he had just learned that the state only pretended to be interested in reforming the hospital and keeping it open. Their real intent was to close the hospital and sell it."

"Bureaucrats are a deceitful lot more often than not. You're far better off to pay little attention to what they say, and instead, watch closely to what they do."

"Well put, Squire," Kenzie said, broad smile on her face.

"When I think back on this, I'm amazed at Guillermo's reaction to this sham," Mitch remarked, shaking his head. "All he said was 'I was hired to reform Sycamore Hospital and that's what I'm going to do.' Even though I felt like I was buying a ticket on the Titanic, I told him I'd jump on board and help him.

"Guillermo is an incredible leader, leading by example mostly. It was not his style to direct things from his office, as other superintendents did. When he was at the hospital, he was out and about, interacting with anyone who was a part of the hospital, be they inmates or staff. He humanized the place—that's what he did. Then he got sick and had to leave," Mitch said sadly.

"And you stepped up and took over," Squire remarked. "Good for you, Mitch."

"There was nothing good about it.' Mitch snapped. Kenzie reached over and took hold of his hand. He gave her a warm smile, and then continued, "I wanted to hold things together and build on the foundation that Guillermo had established, if I could. As to exactly what I could do, I wasn't sure, because by that time, the hospital was providing excellent custodial care for the inmates. This had therapeutic value as well, and was about all that could be expected, due to a population that was, in my opinion, being warehoused there.

"There were patients whose behavior was judged to be too severe for the prisons and state mental hospitals. There were people who were referred by the court to be evaluated and treated for mental illness, so they could later be brought to trial."

"The problem was that those who were sent there tended to remain there in limbo. And the criminal-justice system did not give credit for years served at Sycamore.

"I remember one poor fellow who had been there for five years but never brought to trial. His offense was barroom fighting. The police had a difficult time arresting him, and took him to a state mental hospital. He punched one of the attendants, knocking him down some stairs, and causing spinal damage. The hospital would not admit him, so he was taken to Sycamore. I raised a ruckus with the attorney general's office to get him finally brought to court."

"What do you think will happen to him?" Kenzie asked.

"I suspect he'll be tried for assault for the barroom fight, and probably felonious assault for injuring the attendant, and sentenced accordingly. The point is he has already been incarcerated at Sycamore for five years, but he'll receive no credit for that time. He should have been returned to the court for trial years ago. There is little doubt that had I not intervened on his behalf, he would still be at Sycamore today. He is just one of many prisoners who were trapped there."

"How did you feel about the sale?" Squire asked.

"One word—ambivalent," Mitch replied, with a smile. "There's a lot more to it than that. A part of me believed the hospital should be closed, and what the state did with property was no concern of mine. But because of their dishonesty with Guillermo, another part of me wanted to sabotage the sale, or at the very least, make it difficult."

"Tell him the whole story, Mitch," Kenzie chimed in. "You thought one of the reasons the hospital was a failure was because it was built as an abbey, and should have never been a prison hospital to begin with."

"Yes, I know the history," Squire said, "dismal as it was. My attorneys assured me that there were no illegalities, and that the state had a clear title to the property."

"I realized that," Mitch concluded. "I shifted my focus to adding new programs to Sycamore before it was closed."

"So it was you who brought the blind mobility program to Sycamore Hospital," Squire declared, a broad grin on this face. "Where did you get that idea?"

"When I was interning at the VA in Cleveland, a blind agency was using the tunnels in the basement to teach mobility training. It was an excellent program, and the VA received recognition for hosting it," Mitch replied. "Since Sycamore had unused catacombs, I thought the same thing could happen there. And it did."

Squire nodded his agreement. "What about the monks? I suppose you recruited them as well."

"Yes, with the help of Graciela Cevallos. She was the one who'd recruited Guillermo, and was very supportive of our work at the hospital," Mitch replied.

"I learned that St. Aloysius Abbey, well-known for fine wine in Amish country, was looking for land to expand their vineyards. Our unused land would be more than suitable. I wanted to bring the group to the hospital to grow grapes and make wine."

"Yes, I'm well aware of the wine made by the monks of St. Aloysius Abbey," Squire, cheerfully interjected. "They make finely textured wine that's highly enjoyable for all settings."

"The land has been put under cultivation and will eventually be a source of income for Sycamore. But more importantly, the monks are a perfect fit in a place that should have remained an abbey," Mitch declared, puffing his chest a bit.

"Excuse me, gentlemen," Kenzie said, getting up from her chair. "I have to powder my nose."

Squire Young reached for his briefcase on the floor next to him. He placed it on the table, opened it, and took out two documents.

After returning the briefcase to the floor, he began thumbing through one of the documents.

As Mitch watched Squire scan through the documents, he realized it was fate that had reunited him with this cunning Englishman whom he admired. That pleased him.

Kenzie slipped back in the room with barely a sound. When she took her seat, she looked directly at Squire, and said, "When Guillermo, and then Mitch, came to Sycamore, it was known as a Chamber of Horrors. It was shunned by the community, who saw it as sinister prison where people were being abused, rather than a hospital where people received treatment.

"That's what Guillermo and Mitch inherited, and yet in a relatively short period of time, they changed the image of the hospital to a more positive one. I think this new image can be used to your advantage in any endeavors you undertake. You've made a very wise purchase, Squire."

Squire smiled, and gave Kenzie the thumbs up. "As they say in L.A., it's now show time," he announced, handing them the documents. "This is the charter of the War Horse Center of Spiritual Pursuits."

Mitch and Kenzie, both speed readers, devoured the document in no time. "This is stupendous, Squire," Mitch said. "It certainly is," Kenzie echoed. "Tell me, what inspired you to put together such a colossal enterprise?"

Squire uncorked another bottle of champagne, and poured each a fresh glass. "To the War Horse Center for Spiritual Pursuits," he bellowed, lifting his glass high in the air. Mitch and Kenzie raised their glasses and joined in the toast.

Leaning back in his chair, Squire closed his eyes, and remained silent for several moments, before saying softly, "It was at Kenzie's concert, when the monks' choir was singing 'The Roses of Picardy.' I experienced a spiritual awakening. At that exact moment, I knew what I would do with Sycamore Hospital.

"Rather than reinventing it, I would add to what was already there. The blind and the monks would remain as they are. I will add a place where people from all walks of life can come to study and experience spirituality.

"I'll fill you in on all the particulars over time. For now, I'll be focusing on ridding the hospital of the remnants of the prison before its conversion to a spiritual center. We'll be constructing an amphitheater for concerts and presentations, and most importantly finding the right man or woman to shepherd the spiritual center. Any suggestions or comments?"

"Only one," Mitch said. "Consider starting your spiritual director's search with Guillermo Gerona. I don't think you'll have to look further."

"It is my hope that you both will be formally involved with the center and will accept seats on the board of directors."

"I'd be honored," Mitch responded enthusiastically. "Me too," Kenzie echoed.

Turning to Kenzie, Squire said, "I need your expertise on the design and construction of the amphitheater, which will be completed by next year. Plans are being made for a yearly concert series. It would be wonderful if you would bring music to the spiritual center, and be the inaugural performing artist."

Kenzie blushed and stammered, "I'm much honored."

"Well, that settles our business. It's time for the feast," Squire announced. "Incidentally, the amphitheater will be named the Kenzie Fairfax Gainer Amphitheater."

CHAPTER 29

"Tell me, Missy, how does it feel to have an amphitheater named after you?" Mitch asked playfully. He and Kenzie had just left the restaurant, and were walking through the gaming floor in Chinook's Casino.

"To tell the truth, I don't know how I feel. This whole evening with Squire Young has been overwhelming, to say the least, with his stupendous presentation of the spiritual center, the delectable meal, and all the champagne. Ask me in the morning, after I've had a night's sleep to digest everything."

"Just think, Squire Young will build a state-of-the-arts arena for you," Mitch said. "It will rival any amphitheater in the country. It wouldn't surprise me, since it will be part of a spiritual center, that it will have a medieval design."

"You have a great imagination," Kenzie said, kissing Mitch on the neck.

"It's not my imagination, my love. I know Squire Young."

"I was surprised, and a little shocked, that you strongly suggested Squire contact Guillermo for the director's job. Don't you think that your mentor has had enough, considering what he has gone through at Sycamore?"

"Remember Kenzie, Squire said it was his intent to build on what was already there. Well, that didn't mean just the blind program and the monks. It meant you, me, and, I think, Guillermo as well.

"There is little doubt that Squire knows all about Guillermo and his ability. My guess is that he wants to hire him as director. That's why I suggested that his search should start and end with Guillermo. It's to let him know that I endorse him for the position."

"All the intrigue ceases to amaze me," Kenzie added, with a smile. "I remember that immediately after you told him to contact Guillermo, he announced he had to fly back to Indiana tonight. Do you think that has to do with his hiring Guillermo?"

"For the most part, I imagine. When Squire is on a project, he is 100-percent focused at all times, and moves like a ramrod. It comes naturally to him. Speaking of moving, I think it's time for us to turn our attention to your tour. Our work here is finished, and we need to move along to Europe. First, we should go to Baden-Baden, and rent a cottage in the Black Forest. We can take in the baths to rewind."

"Sounds good," Kenzie sighed.

"Let's visit Chinook and Mother one last time before we leave."

"Look, Mitch, the moonlight and sparkling stars have illuminated the trail. We won't need your trusty pocket flashlight tonight," Kenzie said, as they stepped outside, into the cool mountain air.

Mitch took Kenzie's hand and led her to the gently sloping trail that meandered through a grove of huge cedar trees to a small meadow. In silence, they followed the trail to the very end.

When they emerged from the trees, they came face to face with two large stone monuments, glowing in the bright moonlight.

Directly in front of the each was a bench. Mitch led Kenzie to the larger of the two monuments where they sat down.

"Each time I come here, I'm reminded how fortunate I was to have had Chinook in my life when I was young," Mitch said, reaching in his pocket for his flashlight. He shone the light on the reddish-colored granite monument, with the letters CHINOOK etched near the top. Below was Chinook's walking stick with the solid gold coyote head handle, embedded in the stone.

"He took me under his wing when I was young, and taught me about life. Most importantly, he was the one who had my back. I could always count on him. And even today, when I get in a pinch and don't know what to do, I turn to him. I think 'what would he do?' and that's where I find my answer."

Out of the corner of his eye, Mitch caught a glimpse of a figure emerging from the forest. Leaping up, he shined his flashlight on a man with shoulder-length hair, held together with a red bandana, wearing a beaded hide shirt, breechclout, leggings, and moccasins.

"Farrell," he exclaimed, moving toward his childhood and spiritual friend, his hand extended. "I knew you'd turn up. You always do." They shook hands. Mitch put his arm around Farrell's shoulder and led him over to Chinook's monument, where Kenzie was now standing.

"Kenzie," Farrell said, in a voice that was little more than a whisper, "Weeko says you play music for the spirit. She has your record and plays it all the time. I like it too."

Kenzie blushed, then smiled, and took his hand. "Thank you, that's very nice. Is she here? I'd like to see her again. I've missed her."

"No. Weeko stays with her people in the Black Hills. I stay there too, most of the time. I come here, because the Sun Dance starts tomorrow."

"When you get back home, you tell her that I'm honored that she likes my music. Also tell her I'll be doing another recording this year, and I'll send her a copy."

Mitch and Farrell walked up to the monument, each placing one hand on Chinook's walking stick. They stood there silently for several minutes, hands on the stick, before joining Kenzie on the bench.

"When I put my hand on Chinook's walking stick, I could feel his presence. For a moment, I could hear the sounds of cards being shuffled in the distance," Mitch muttered under his breath.

"Chinook's with the spirits, only here," Farrell said, as he got up from the bench, walked up to the monument, and placed both hands on the walking stick.

Mitch reached for Kenzie and drew her close. He held her tightly in his arms, and buried his tear-stained cheeks in her hair. After a few moments, they ambled over to the other monument.

"When Mother's time was short, I asked what her wishes were for her monument. She told me she wanted one just like Chinook's. And that's what she has," Mitch said, his voice cracking. His hand shook as he shined his flashlight on the name, LAURA GAINER, and the etching of a slot machine with the words, THE QUEEN OF THE SLOTS.

"Laura's with the spirits, Mitch," Farrell said, placing his hand on Mitch's shoulder. "She's smiling."

Kenzie placed her hand on Mitch's other shoulder. With the touch of two people he deeply loved, Mitch suddenly felt warmth radiating within. He turned to Kenzie, and said, "Farrell's right. My mother is smiling, and so am I." They headed back to the lodge.

The moonlight disappeared when they entered the thick forest. Mitch reached again for his flashlight.

"No need for light," Farrell said, putting his hand over the flashlight, blocking out the beam.

"That's much better," Kenzie remarked.

When they reached the end of trail, and stepped out in the bright lights of the parking lot, Farrell suddenly leapt in front of Mitch. "Mitch, you must come to the Sun Dance tomorrow at daybreak."

"What!" Mitch put his hands in his pocket. "I can't go to the Sun Dance. We're leaving tomorrow. Kenzie has to go back on tour."

"We can put that off for a few days," Kenzie chimed in. "You're always talking about the Sun Dance, and how important it is. Now's your chance to go with Farrell. I think it would be really good for you, Mitch."

"Spirits do not call white men often. They call Mitch, but he does not answer," Farrell added. "I think he may be afraid of the Sun Dance."

"I'm not afraid," Mitch declared. Turning to Kenzie, he asked, "Would you go with me?"

"I'd love to," Kenzie replied, taking Mitch's hand. "It's something I've been curious about since I first came to Nugget Valley."

Farrell pulled Kenzie aside, and whispered something in her ear.

"No, I've not passed through the menopause."

"I'm sorry, you can't go to Sun Dance," Farrell said sadly.

"He's right. Only post-menopausal woman are allowed to go the Sun Dance. That's because they now have their wisdom, and can be shamans or medicine women," Mitch explained.

"Well, I'll just have to wait a few years, boys," Kenzie said. "Rest assured, Mitch, I'll be there with my fiddle, watching you, for your three days and night in the sun. I'll even play 'A Whiter Shade of Pale' to pick you up when you're dragging."

"Will you bring your cello?" Farrell asked.

"That's good idea. I think I will," Kenzie replied.

"I need to set you straight on a couple of things," Mitch said to Kenzie as they watched Farrell disappear into the dark forest. "The reason I have avoided participating in the Sun Dance was not because I was fearful. It was because I did not feel that I had earned the right.

"Chinook told me that sometimes the Indians would ask a white man to join the dance. And, if they did, he should only accept if he knew that he had earned the right. If he joined the dance but had not earned the right, then he risked angering the spirits. That was not good."

"Earned the right—how do you do that?"

"He didn't give any specifics. He just said, 'you'll know if you have.' It's a spiritual thing."

"That leaves a lot unsaid."

"I know but that's what Chinook called the Indian Way. You don't have to understand it. You just follow it. That's what I did. Each time I was asked to join the Sun Dance, I did not feel I had earned the right, so I declined—even though that's not what I wanted to do. That's the way it's been, except for tonight. When I asked you if you would go to the dance with me, and you responded like you did, I felt, for the first time that I had earned the right."

"You certainly have earned it, many times over," Kenzie said. And she kissed him on the cheek.

ABOUT THE AUTHOR

Robert MacGuffie is a professor emeritus at Bowling Green State University, where he taught at the graduate level for more than twenty years. In addition, he has worked as a psychologist in private practice for over forty years and has published numerous articles, text materials and monographs on topics in the field of psychology.

MacGuffie is the author of a series of adventures starring protagonist Mitch Gainer and set in his home region of northern Idaho. *An Abbey Returned* is the fourth book in the series which includes *Chinook's Farewell*, *Chinook's Spirit* and *Chinook's Mother Lode*.

Made in the USA
Columbia, SC
06 June 2023